THE EIGHTH CIRC

To Green Dragon.

Best Wishes

Gary D...

The Eighth Circle of Hell

THAMES RIVER PRESS
An imprint of Wimbledon Publishing Company Limited (WPC)
Another imprint of WPC is Anthem Press (www.anthempress.com)

First published in the United Kingdom in 2012 by

THAMES RIVER PRESS
75-76 Blackfriars Road
London SE1 8HA

www.thamesriverpress.com

© Gary Dolman 2012

The moral rights of the author have been asserted in accordance
with the Copyright, Designs and Patents Act 1988.

All the characters and events described in this novel are imaginary
and any similarity with real people or events is purely coincidental.

A CIP record for this book is available from the British Library.

ISBN 978-0-85728-923-0

Cover design by Laura Carless

This title is also available as an eBook.

THE EIGHTH CIRCLE
OF HELL

Gary Dolman

22🦢 THAMES RIVER PRESS

CHAPTER 1

"In my experience, little girls who beg for mercy seldom deserve it."

Elizabeth sees his mouth moving, sees it framing the words — those words. She hears them inside her head, filling it, creeping through her body; through her arms, her legs, turning them to ice.

His hands lift and reach out towards her, overpowering, unstoppable. She wants to beg him for mercy, to beg him not to do it, but the undeserved words gag in her throat. She tries to turn, tries to push him away but her leaden limbs refuse to heed the shrieking, shrieking screams of her brain. Then two more people are there, with their smiling, laughing faces — a man and a woman. They catch her arms and hold her fast as he smiles the very smile of the Fiend, and reaches down for her.

"Elizabeth Wilson has lived in workhouses since she was a girl of fifteen, Mr and Mrs Fox."

The Master of the Knaresborough Union Workhouse smiled benignly as he pushed open the door to his private office.

"Which amounts to forty-five years in total, barring a few months she had as a pauper apprentice. She had, let me see, thirteen years at the Starbeck Workhouse before it closed and then the rest here, at the Knaresborough Union. But in all that time, I believe you are the first visitors she's ever had. Well perhaps not; I'm told there was one other but that was many years ago and it all came to naught.

Please, take a seat. I've asked that one of the better pauper girls brings us some tea and then I'll have Elizabeth fetched from the infirmary."

The warm, lilting Geordie accent tempered his otherwise austere appearance.

The Master's office was very much like the man himself; large and ascetic but softened here and there by a few more comfortable furnishings. One of these was a pair of plump, buttoned leather settees and Atticus and Lucie Fox sank obediently onto the nearest of them while the Master settled into its mirror twin, separated from them by a low and highly polished coffee table.

He regarded them inquisitively for a moment, like an angel at the Gates of Paradise, and smiled once again.

"Are you relatives of Elizabeth, do you mind me asking?"

Atticus shook his head.

"I don't mind at all, Mr Liddle and no, we aren't relatives; Mrs Fox and I are privately-commissioned investigators. We've been asked to trace the whereabouts of Miss Wilson on behalf of our principal who is a close relative of hers."

"I see. May I perhaps know the identity of your principal?"

"Certainly, he's Dr Michael Roberts of Harrogate. Miss Wilson was taken in as a child by her uncle, Alfred Roberts, who is Dr Roberts' grandfather."

"Alfred Roberts the great philanthropist?"

Atticus nodded: "The very same."

"Another of his great acts of kindness, no doubt," said Liddle.

He sighed reflectively.

"There's many a poor orphan or pauper child that Alfred Roberts sent on to a better life abroad or found a situation for in the houses of the gentry. I believe I read somewhere that he even had his own house built larger to take many of them in himself, until he could move them on."

"That is true; it was a large annexe he added to the rear of his house. He took Miss Wilson in shortly after he had it built. That was many years ago when the second of her own parents, her mother, passed away. Alfred Roberts was her mother's elder brother and her only living relative. Dr Roberts told us that she ran away around two years after his grandfather first took her in and, as we now know, eventually came to be here, in the union workhouse."

Liddle nodded genially.

"I've heard a great deal of Dr Roberts. He's recently become a firm acquaintance of Mr Manders, our Medical Officer here, and as I understand it, he's a psychiatric doctor of no little renown."

The leather of the settee creaked under him as he leaned forward, conspiratorially.

"We have, as you might imagine, quite a number of lunatics and imbeciles here. Dr Roberts freely gives us any help and advice he can. He's a philanthropist in the family tradition; there is no doubt of it. What you tell me is fascinating though. I knew that Elizabeth had come to be in the workhouse under rather... mysterious circumstances shall we say, but until now I knew very few of the details. She's obviously well educated and gentle-born, but Lizzie – Elizabeth, that is – never speaks of her life before she went to Starbeck. In fact, by all accounts, she rarely spoke at all for quite a number of years. Sister Lovell, the workhouse nurse, has known her the longest; in fact, it was she who finally got her to speak again."

He was interrupted by a timid knock on the door. It opened and a tall, gangly girl appeared, blushing heavily and carrying a handsome, silver tea tray as if it might suddenly turn on her at any moment and bite.

"Curtsey, Sally," the Master reminded her sharply.

"I'm sorry, Mr Liddle."

The girl paused to curtsy clumsily and then slowly, with infinite care, set the tray down on the coffee table.

Liddle watched each of her movements intently, almost hungrily, as a cat watches a bird.

Then he said: "Thank you, Sally. Is M... is Sister Lovell fetching Lizzie?"

"Begging your pardon, sir but Lizzie needed to be changed before she could be fetched. She's gone and wet herself again; made a right mess on the floor and no mistake."

"Is she resisting the nurses?"

"Yes, sir, it took three of them to change her: Matthew and Tom and Edith. Edith said that Lizzie would rather stink and be sore all day than be washed and have fresh clothes."

Liddle sighed and nodded wearily.

"Ah well, she keeps the women in the laundry house well employed I suppose. Please pass my compliments to Sister Lovell, Sally and ask that she be brisk."

The girl hesitated.

"Please, Mr Liddle, Miss Lovell asked me to say that she needs me to help her with her rounds tonight and that she's arranged for Edith to bring you your warming-pan and polish your tables. She said that you would understand."

The girl curtsied again and after a quick, nervous glance at Atticus and Lucie, she hurried, almost ran from the room.

Liddle frowned.

"I do declare that the last thing I need to see before I retire to bed is that old crone Edith in my bedroom. I shall be having nightmares tonight and that's a fact. If the Master of a workhouse can't choose a pretty pauper girl to bring him his night time bed warmer, what can he do?"

They had finished with her at last. Please let it be over now, please, Lord Jesus. She felt dirty, sullied and used, just as she always felt after he had finished and dressed her again. She was a wicked, sinful girl and she had deserved it — needed it even. She deserved everything he did to her, just as she had deserved for her mama to go away. Her mama was in Heaven with Jesus and his angels. How could she have stayed to love a sinful child such as her? Why would her mama have been bothered with such a wicked, wicked creature as she?

She would shut it away. She would hide this memory along with all the others, festering away in that farthest, most remote part of her mind she kept especially for them.

Except that they wouldn't lie still. Not these days. They wouldn't stay there, far away, where they couldn't hurt her. Every time she sensed that bitter, oily taste on her tongue, every time she saw eyes leering at her, hungering for her, every time she felt hands pulling at her clothes, the memories tried to come, tried to hurt her. She could hold them off by day, with busy and with the knife. But at night, when she could no longer be busy, they would come. They would spill into her dreams and turn them into nightmares. And it seemed that these days, there was no day and no night; that she had no knife and that her busy had gone.

She tasted once more the bitterness on her tongue and smelled it again in her nostrils. It was her medicine — her medicine for wicked girls. It helped. He always said that her mama would be pleased with her for taking it so well, with so little fuss. It helped her to be more... compliant to her punishments. Somehow, it seemed to make the punishments less real, almost as if they were happening to another little girl whose mama had gone away. And it helped her to hide away the memories when they had finished.

"Aha, Miss Lovell, I would like to introduce Mr and Mrs Atticus Fox to you. They are privately-commissioned investigators no less, who have been engaged by the grandson of Elizabeth's old guardian to trace her whereabouts. Have you fetched her?"

The shadow of what might have been panic flitted across the old, grim face of the nurse as rather stiffly, she wished them a good day, before turning again to the Master.

"I have, Mr Liddle; Lizzie is waiting outside in your vestibule. I've taken the liberty of giving her a small dose of chloral hydrate to settle her down a degree."

The Master nodded sagely.

"That was very sensible, Mary. That chloral hydrate of yours is a godsend and we don't want to distress her any more than we need. Now, please, sit down and pour the tea; Elizabeth may have some with us too, as a special treat for her. Mr and Mrs Fox have some questions they would like to put to you about her whilst I fetch her in from the vestibule."

He had come for her.

Oh, Mama, please come for me first. Please take me with you to be with Jesus, to be an angel like you. Don't let him take me. I don't mean to be wicked, I really don't. Please believe me. Please ask Jesus not to let him take me away to his gentleman friends.

A single memory: A ring of laughing, jeering faces, with strangely disembodied voices, and of hands touching her, feeling her, escaped from its secret place and seared across her mind. There again was the bitter, oily taste in her mouth and there again, the hurt, deep down in her belly.

CHAPTER 2

Seeing Elizabeth Wilson as she was shepherded gently into the Master's office was something of a shock for Atticus and Lucie Fox. They had been told by Dr Roberts, their principal, that by now she would be in her sixtieth year. But as Lucie remarked afterward, she looked at least twenty years older than that. She moved slowly and painfully, almost like an automaton, under her shapeless blue and grey workhouse dress, her skeletal hands clutched tightly before her as if in perpetual supplication. But the most striking, and by far the most distressing, thing about Elizabeth was her eyes. Clear blue and intense, they blazed out from her gaunt, lined face, hidden deep within the shadows of her shabby poke bonnet. As she stood cowering in the room, she seemed to stare right through them as if they were nothing more than unseen spectres between her and some far-distant horizon.

"There is no need to stand for a pauper woman, Mr Fox." Liddle chuckled good-naturedly at Atticus' faux-pas.

"On the contrary," Atticus replied, indignation stiffening his tone.

"'Who sees with equal eye, as God of all, A hero perish, or a sparrow fall.' Those are not my words, Mr Liddle; they are Alexander Pope's in, 'Essay on Man.'"

A charged silence stretched out between them.

"I'm no god, of course," Atticus continued, "But I strive hard to see with that same equal eye and I believe that manners and courtesy should too. Miss Wilson was born into a respectable family but even if she had not been, even if she was a sparrow and not a hero, she is still a woman, a woman of age, and I will still stand for her."

Without waiting for the Master's response he turned to Elizabeth.

"Good Afternoon, Miss Wilson, my name is Atticus Fox and this is my wife Mrs Fox. We are both delighted to make your acquaintance." His polite bow was followed by a heartbeat of silence as Lizzie's distant gaze slowly focussed onto him. It was transformed instantly into wretched terror. She began to cower and tremble like some tiny, whipped animal and her reply was husky and no more than a whisper.

"Please be merciful, sir," and then after a moment, "Jesus."

"There's no call for blasphemy, Wilson," Liddle rebuked her sharply. "You're safe, Lizzie; you're quite safe. You're with me; you're with Mary."

The nurse stood and took Elizabeth's arm from the Master. Cradling the tightly-clasped hands in her own, she murmured reassuringly until gradually, Elizabeth's gaze slackened and dropped back once more into the infinity.

"Miss Wilson seems terrified of us, Sister Lovell," Lucie whispered, "Or at least of my husband. That's in spite of your sedative... chloral hydrate, did you say it was?"

"Yes, ma'am."

Mary Lovell pursed her lips and gently steered Elizabeth to a high-backed chair that stood next to Mr Liddle's large, mahogany bureau. She folded her into it and said:

"Lizzie has a very nervous disposition. She's timid, extremely timid, whenever she is around gentlemen."

"So I see."

Lucie watched curiously as Elizabeth began to rock gently to-and-fro, quietly singing a lullaby to herself under her breath. Her hands, trembling slightly and still balled tightly together, slid along the polished desktop until they came to rest next to a small pile of unopened letters which were pressed down by a handsome, silver paper-knife.

"What is her condition? I am a nurse myself, although retired now from the profession."

The taut lines on Sister Lovell's face seemed to soften a little at that. She crossed the room to perch on the edge of the settee next to the Master.

"Well, Mrs Fox, Lizzie suffers from profound nervous anxiety as you can see. Also, since shortly after her mama died, which happened when she was just thirteen years of age, she has had long and very deep periods of melancholy. They've increased over the years and especially so over the eighteen-eighties. Now that she is old and senile, she seems depressive almost all of the time."

Her eyes were suddenly shining in the light streaming in through the sashes of the windows.

"And how was she between her melancholic episodes?" Lucie's voice was keen with professional interest.

"She was employed in the workhouse bakery."

"And excellent at it she was too," added the Master, "She did the work of two ordinary paupers and did it thoroughly. I think it was because of her time at the Starbeck Workhouse. Most of the old, parish workhouses used to believe they were there just to provide relief from destitution, but at Starbeck they were very progressive; they laid great store in discouraging idleness by insisting on austerity and good, honest, hard work.

But Lizzie was never idle. Behind that shell she casts around herself, she is — or rather she was — a very diligent, industrious woman. She's just an imbecile now of course."

"Manic-depressive psychosis, do you suppose it was?" Lucie asked, ignoring Liddle's final remark.

"The Medical Officer here thinks it might have been, but to speak plainly, I've made it my business to ask a proper psychiatrist about her and we don't think so. There is no history of it in her family and she has never — well, hardly ever — shown any degree of recklessness. It was always quite the opposite actually; she was very controlled in everything she did."

"Manic-depressive psychosis is a profound disorder of the mind," Lucie explained in response to her husband's quizzical look. "It causes the sufferer to be alternately depressed and manically euphoric, often, as Sister says, quite recklessly so. It appears to run in families."

"But we don't know her family history, do we, Sister Lovell?" Liddle interjected. "She never speaks of it; she never has."

"But don't forget that I knew her family, Mr Liddle, and I knew it well. Before I found the situation at the workhouse at Starbeck, I was employed for a while as Lizzie's governess. Her mama, Beatrice Wilson, was the dearest, kindest lady you could possibly imagine. After she died, I was kept on by Lizzie's uncle, Alfred Roberts, who had become her guardian, if you could call him that; he was no true guardian of hers."

"But how could that be, Sister Lovell?" Atticus asked, puzzled. "Alfred Roberts was well known as a benefactor and friend to orphans and homeless children. Surely he didn't neglect his own flesh and blood?"

The nurse glanced down, pressing her thin lips tightly together so that they almost seemed to disappear as she aligned the edge of the tea tray precisely with that of the table.

"No, Mr Fox, he didn't neglect her; he didn't neglect her at all. It was quite the opposite actually. Let me just say that I am very glad indeed that Alfred Roberts is now a feeble, frail old man."

"That is a very harsh opinion to have of an old gentleman and a philanthropist," Atticus exclaimed.

"He might well be old," the nurse replied coldly, "But he was no gentleman and never, ever a philanthropist."

"Do you know his grandson, Dr Michael Roberts?" Lucie asked, quickly moving the conversation on.

Sister Lovell hesitated for a moment.

"I resigned from the Roberts' employ many years before Dr Michael was born. His father John Roberts was only a boy of twelve when I left."

"And you were Miss Elizabeth's governess you say?"

"For most of my time there, yes I was. Lizzie was three years — just three years, mark you — older than John when she fled to the workhouse. I left very soon after her."

"Was she old enough to understand the principle that governs the workhouses, Sister Lovell?" Atticus asked. "I believe they call it the, 'Principle of Less Eligibility.' Conditions inside the workhouse should be much less comfortable than those outside, so that only the truly desperate would seek relief there."

"Elizabeth Wilson was truly desperate, Mr Fox."

Several seconds ticked by as they waited for someone to ask the inevitable question, and inevitably it was Atticus who asked it.

"What could possibly have made her so desperate that she would leave somewhere like Sessrum House to seek relief in a poor-law workhouse?"

Sister Lovell looked down and minutely shifted the tea tray once more.

"Lizzie despised the... punishments that Mr Roberts liked to mete out to the children in his so-called care."

"I see. Well Dr Michael is the head of the house now and he would very much like for her to go back and to live there once again. He views the fact that she fled Sessrum House for a workhouse as nothing less than a stain on his family's honour — an injustice in his words — that he very much wishes to repair. That's why he commissioned us to find her. He believes that Miss Elizabeth deserves to live out the rest of her days in comfort and in grace."

Sister Lovell threw a suddenly anxious look to the Master.

"I suppose it might be for the best, Mr Liddle, but she is so innocent, so very delicate."

"That is all the more reason for her to leave the rigours of the workhouse then. Come now, Mary, surely you haven't grown so attached to Elizabeth that you don't wish her to live out her remaining days in style? I realise that with her mind as it is, she won't fully appreciate the change in her circumstances, but surely living at Dr Roberts' mansion would still be infinitely preferable to her spending the rest of her life in a workhouse infirmary? It would almost be like paradise on Earth for her there. Anyway, I have made up my mind. She's an imbecile; she cannot work any longer and with this arrangement she'll no longer be a burden on the parochial finances. Heaven knows, they're stretched enough as it is. No, Mary, Lizzie shall leave for Harrogate today."

The nurse seemed to vacillate still.

"She would be living with Mr Alfred's grandson?" she demanded. "And he will take good care of her? Will you promise me that?"

"I'm certain Dr Michael will take care of her wonderfully, Sister Lovell," Lucie purred, her voice reassurance itself. "Alfred Roberts still lives at Sessrum to be sure, but in an annexe, quite separate to the main house."

The old nurse shivered.

"Mr Liddle, may I accompany Lizzie to her new home? I feel I ought to help her to settle in there and get her used to her new surroundings."

Liddle looked enquiringly at the Foxes.

"I have no objection whatsoever Mr Liddle, and neither would Dr Roberts I'm sure," Atticus confirmed. "In fact, he himself suggested that it would be a first-rate idea if someone were to come up with her to do exactly that."

The Master grunted his assent. "Then the matter is settled and the parochial union can be grateful they've one less pauper to pay for in their infirmary."

CHAPTER 3

"Are you sure we aren't to bring any more clothes from the workhouse for her, Mrs Fox?" Mary Lovell asked yet again as they walked down the steep, cobbled hill towards the Knaresborough Railway Station.

"She lost control of her, shall we say... bodily functions, months ago, and she generally needs to be changed several times a day. Strictly speaking, a pauper is supposed to leave the workhouse in the same clothes they came to it in. You have those in your parcel there. They were fine in their day, but that was nearly fifty years ago and the moths have been busy at them since."

"Mr Liddle will be in good humour," she added bitterly.

"He'll have his pick of the girls to fetch him his warming-pan while I'm not there. I'm sure that he could be persuaded to let us fetch another shift or two for her."

They formed an incongruous group: the tall, redheaded gentleman in a top hat and frockcoat carrying a thick, pewter-topped walking cane, and the frail, cowering pauper woman in her threadbare dress and poke bonnet, supported on one side by an elderly nurse and on the other by a pretty young woman carrying a brown paper parcel neatly bound with string.

"That really won't be necessary, Sister Lovell. Dr Roberts has engaged a seamstress to make her up a whole new wardrobe of clothes," Lucie replied patiently, "With fashionable, bright colours and lace."

Mary Lovell beamed as she leaned in close to her charge.

"Do you hear what Mrs Fox says, Lizzie? She says you are to have a set of new clothes, all for yourself, and all fancy with pretty colours and lace. You will look beautiful again."

Elizabeth kept her eyes fixed warily on the back of Atticus' frockcoat.

"No, Rachel, no, Rachel, you are," she exclaimed, suddenly and harshly.

Several people turned to stare at them.

"I'm Mary, Lizzie, not Rachel. Rachel died years ago. She was only ever old when you knew her and she was never beautiful. I'm Mary, Lizzie. Do you remember me? I'm the one who's making sure no one hurts you, that no one hurts you ever again."

"Where's my mama?" Elizabeth asked.

"Your mama is dead too. She's with Jesus and his angels and your papa. You'll be with them again one day soon, I promise."

"You mentioned in Mr Liddle's office that Elizabeth has senile dementia, Sister Lovell," Lucie said. "She's just called for her mother, even though her mother died nearly half a century ago. The dementia must be quite advanced?"

The nurse patted Elizabeth's wringing hands. She was singing something that sounded like 'one-and-eight-and-eight-and-one' again and again under her breath.

"Yes, I'm rather afraid that it is. As Mr Liddle said, Lizzie had always been a very hard and precise worker who rarely, if ever, made any mistakes. Then around two or three years ago, we noticed she was starting to make lots of silly errors; putting her dress on back-to-front in the morning for example, or missing ingredients from her baking, or getting dressed for church on the wrong day. She began to forget things that had happened only that week, or even just that day, yet she could remember vividly events that happened years and years before. As time went on and her condition deteriorated, she started to believe that she was living further and further back in the past; that she was at Starbeck Workhouse again for example, or even as she often seems to now, that she is back with Alfred Roberts. That might be why her anxiety attacks have grown so much worse recently. But you know the worst part, Mrs Fox, the very worst part of it all is that it's almost impossible to talk to her properly these days. I can't reach her, I can't reassure her. She can only understand odd words of what I say. I'm afraid that very often it seems as if I'm speaking to a very little girl and not an old woman at all."

They made their way slowly onto the station platform and into the shade of the verandah, to where the first class carriages would stop. The curious glances and bald stares they had begun to notice on the short walk from the Union Workhouse intensified and hardened into glares of outrage and indignation. As they stopped and Lucie took Atticus' arm, an elderly gentleman in a silk top hat and cape coat stepped forward and confronted Mary Lovell.

"What are you doing bringing your old crone to this end of the platform, woman?" he demanded. "Trying to beg with her, I'll be bound. Well, you'll get nothing from us. You can take her and you can throw her back into the poorhouse where she belongs; we've already more than paid for her idleness and her bread and water with our taxes."

He grabbed Elizabeth's chin in his leather-gloved hand and jerked it up, glowering into her face.

"And who the devil do you think you're staring at, you damned, impudent old witch?"

Elizabeth's gaze drifted into the man's glare. She started violently and began to whimper softly. And then his hand was gone, as a puce-faced Atticus smashed the man's arm away with the heavy end of his cane.

"These ladies – both of these ladies – are with us," he roared. "They both have first class railway tickets and they are both entitled to stand anywhere on this platform they choose. So you – you can mind your own damned business, sir."

Mary Lovell spoke over the top of the bonnet on Elizabeth's cowed, shivering head; the cold menace in her voice cutting through the atmosphere more venomously than anything Atticus had said.

"This lady has suffered horrors in her life such as you can only imagine. All of them, mark you, all of them suffered at the hands of supposedly respectable gentlemen like you; with your first class railway tickets and your silk top hats and your fancy clothes. You and your friends can all go to Hell."

The gentleman stared at her, aghast, his mouth framing words he could not seem to utter. Then, his spirit broke, and he turned and rejoined his companions, massaging his arm and muttering indignations under his breath.

Like a summer evening after a storm, the atmosphere on the platform lightened, and Miss Lovell, breathing heavily, began once more to sooth Elizabeth.

The station master's shrill whistle turned their heads towards the gaping, black mouth of the railway tunnel at the far end of the platform. Suddenly their train was there, disgorged and puffing slowly along the length of the platform where, in a cloud of steam and clattering of couplings, it hissed to a halt.

CHAPTER 4

The shrill whistle shrieked along the length of the train and dissolved into the warmth of the afternoon; dissolved everywhere, that is, except inside her head. There it compounded with the silent screams of her anguish and grew louder and louder and louder.

She concentrated with the whole of her being on the rhythmic clicking of the carriage wheels as they glided over the joints in the tracks. She closed her thoughts to everything except her urgings of the train to go faster, for the clicks to be louder, more staccato, to overwhelm her, to crowd out whatever it was they were taking turns to do to her body. She could feel the echoes of their hands; the rough scratch of their whiskers; the stench of tobacco on their breath.

'Please, Lord Jesus, please make the train get to where it is going; please make it stop so that they will stop, and I can begin, again, to hide away the memories.'

But she had a knife now, in her sleeve. She couldn't remember how or from where she had got it but it was there. 'Oh, thank you, Jesus; thank you, Mama.' She would be safe now. She wouldn't have to bear those unbearable thoughts again and again and again. With a practiced hand, she laid the stiletto point of the blade against the softness of her skin and pressed. Delicious pain swelled through her consciousness, filling it and blocking out everything else. She deserved the pain, she knew. She was a wicked, wicked girl, but oh, how it eased the torture of her mind; how it chased away those thoughts and those awful, awful memories.

"Miss Elizabeth seems much calmer now," Lucie observed as the fields and hedges outside the carriage window suddenly gave way to the long lines of houses that were the outskirts of Harrogate.

"For a time, especially as we were crossing over the viaduct, I thought she might have needed another dose of your chloral hydrate."

A smile loosened the taut lines of the nurse's face.

"She must have remembered how much she loved the railway when she was younger. Lizzie hasn't been on a train since she was a young girl, but she was always spellbound by them. She always used to watch out for them from the workhouse windows and on Sundays after church, she would sit on the embankment by the railway line and watch the trains going past for hours."

She looked across at her charge and the warmth of the smile deepened and spread.

"Alfred Roberts used to have a shooting lodge at a place called Budle in the north of Northumberland, very near to the coast. It was an old, fortified tower and she used to be taken up on occasion on the train. The railway only went as far as Newcastle in those days but they always had the devil's own job to get her out of the carriage and into a coach."

The smile died abruptly.

"At Budle, she would spend all day standing on the roof, gazing out over the bay and across the North Sea. She said it was a horrible, horrible place and that she couldn't wait to get back onto the train."

"Dr Roberts insisted that she came by train," Atticus said, steering the conversation back to the present.

"He said that under no circumstances was she to be fetched by cab, or even by omnibus."

He shrugged.

"But he wouldn't say why."

The nurse nodded and patted the coarse cloth hanging from Elizabeth's skeletal arm.

"It's the sound of the hooves, Mr Fox. She hates the sound of the horses' hooves and she hates being shut up in a horse carriage. They all did."

"Where's my mama?" Elizabeth exclaimed suddenly.

She was answered only by the shrill whistle of the locomotive, shrieking down the length of the train as it coasted the long, curving approach to the Harrogate Central Railway Station.

The faces of the waiting travellers slid slowly past the window, regularly punctuated by the cast-iron legs of the station canopy and the enormous floral platform displays. Finally the train slowed and bumped once more to a halt.

Atticus stood and pushed open the maroon carriage door into the faint shroud of steam that hung over the platform like the mists of Eden.

"You're in Harrogate, Lizzie." Sister Lovell spoke as she might do to a tiny girl. "Do you remember Harrogate, Lizzie, where you used to live with your mama? Harrogate, where all the fine ladies and gentlemen live and where all the ailing are cured?"

CHAPTER 5

Sessrum House, Dr Michael Roberts' large, imposing town house, commanded magnificent views over its part of the Harrogate Stray; two hundred acres of grassed parkland that served both to open out the very heart of the elegant spa town, and to connect the many mineral springs and wells that drew the 'Ailing' from every part of the Empire. They came to take the curious mix of hydrotherapy and light exercise known as 'The Cure.'

The noise and bustle of the town seemed to scare Elizabeth. She drew stares; compassionate, curious and mocking from the crowds that filled the streets, as she shuffled along, softly singing the words to her nursery rhyme. She was singing the same line over and over and over again.

"Rock a bye baby, on the treetop. Rock a bye baby, on the treetop. Rock a bye baby, on the treetop."

"When the wind blows, the cradle will rock," Atticus snapped irritably, and then instantly regretted it. But he need not have worried; Elizabeth never broke her rote, not once, save for when they tried to pass the narrow, rubbish-strewn entrance to a ginnel. There, she seemed cowed into blessed silence and stood still, staring in dread into the deep shadows, until Mary took her hands and gently drew her past it.

By the time the little group had threaded its way laboriously from the railway station to the broad, stone steps that underscored the grand portico entrance to Sessrum House, the late summer sun had already begun to cast its broad shadow over the Stray.

"Do you remember this house, Lizzie?" Sister Lovell asked softly, tentatively. Without waiting for an answer, she added: "I don't reckon for a minute you could forget it, could you?" She turned the old woman gently around to face her, and peered into her poke bonnet. "You won't be punished any more, Lizzie, I promise. A kind man lives here now."

"Lord Jesus," said Elizabeth, quite distinctly.

"Not the Lord Jesus, Lizzie; just a man, but a kind man who will help you to feel better before you go to see the real Jesus and your poor, dead mama and papa, and..."

She patted Elizabeth's fingers.

"Your mama is dead but she's watching over you; the Lord Jesus is watching over you, and I'll watch over you too."

Atticus turned to her.

"Are you ready?" he asked.

She's dead! Dear Lord, her dear, sweet mama is dead. And yes, it surely is true. She had seen her pall being lowered deep into the ground, lowered onto the peeling, grey, mud-smeared coffin of her dearest papa, whom she had never even known. The bell had rung, and now she had gone to be with Jesus and his angels in Heaven. Or had she? Dear Lord, had she? She hoped and hoped that the vicar was right; that her uncle was wrong, and that her mama was safe in Heaven. She prayed and prayed that she was an angel for Jesus, just like her dearest papa. But her mama had said that she would never leave her. She had said that she loved her more than anything else in the world. Everyone had said that her mama would get better; that she wouldn't die like her papa had died. Everyone had said that she would be cured. They had said that everyone is cured at Harrogate.

But her mama wasn't cured and she had died. She had left her. Her Uncle Alfie said that her mama must have been especially wicked and sinful to die so young at Harrogate. But how could someone who was so especially wicked go to be with Jesus and his angels? Jesus hates people who are wicked. Her Uncle Alfie had said that she, Elizabeth, must be wicked and sinful too; that she was a wicked little girl who must be punished and have a special kind of medicine. But why did he smile so when he said that? And why did his smile chill her to her very core?

Atticus' sharp rap on the big knocking-iron of the door was answered almost immediately by Petty, Dr Roberts' butler. His neutral expression hardened briefly into curious disdain as he caught sight of Elizabeth at the foot of the steps, dressed as she was, in her shabby, workhouse uniform. She was huddled against a nurse; a woman who also awakened memories he had kept carefully hidden for so, so long.

"Good evening, Mr and Mrs Fox," he said, dutiful nonetheless.

"Good evening to you, Mr Petty," Atticus replied.

The butler's eyebrows rose a little. Atticus had referred to him as 'Mister' on a previous occasion, but it was still a surprise, it was still rare above stairs even for a butler to be accorded such respect as a friendly tone and a title.

"I have Miss Elizabeth Wilson, and Miss Lovell, a nursing sister from the Union Workhouse in Knaresborough, to see Dr Roberts," Atticus continued.

Even though he had been expecting – dreading, even – their arrival, the butler's expression stiffened yet further at the mention of the names, and of the workhouse. His eyes flickered briefly towards the Stray for casual eavesdroppers, but the gods were smiling and there were none.

"You had better all come inside, Mr Fox, if you please," he said hurriedly, and waved them in.

She followed the gentleman as he led her up the great, stone steps of her aunt and uncle's house. Lizzie had visited the grand house many times before, but that was always with her mama. This time she was alone, except, of course, for Mary. Her mama was with Jesus now and the house seemed different; much larger and strangely forbidding, somehow.

Her arm stung and she remembered her Uncle Alfie. He always insisted that she call him Alfie and not Alfred, even though her mama had told her that it was awfully disrespectful. He said that he'd had a special new part of the house built recently. It was called an annexe. She was to sleep there – in the Annexe – where she wouldn't be disturbed by the noise of the servants and where it was private. There would be other children there too; her cousin John, and those her mama used to call the 'waifs and strays.' Those were the children her uncle had rescued; the ones who were to be sent on to better lives. Her arm stung and she remembered the waifs and strays.

She remembered her uncle unlocking the door next to the scullery. It was a big door, with leather padding on the back just like a cushion, and it led to a steep, spiral staircase. She remembered him taking her around and around, down and down the staircase, with its cast-iron treads that rang when you stepped on them. The waifs and strays were all down there. They were in a big, special room called a dormitory, and they were all little girls.

The waifs and strays had a narrow, iron bed each, and a man called Mr Otter to look especially after them. She thought Mr Otter a little discomforting to look at, with his ugly, scarred face and his eyes like a monster. He had his own room, right next to the row of beds, but she thought that she would have hated living down there; it was so gloomy and depressing.

She thought it was strange that the girls all seemed frightened. Some of them were even sobbing. But why were they frightened and why were they sobbing? Didn't they know Uncle Alfie was a great philanthropist? Didn't they realise that he had saved them, and that now they could each look forward to a much better life?

Everyone said her uncle was a philanthropist.

When she told Uncle Alfie that the dormitory was gloomy and depressing, he had laughed. He had told her not to worry; that she didn't have to sleep in the dormitory with the waifs and strays. She was to have her own bedroom, just as if she were a grown woman and not a little girl at all. It would be the bedroom right next to his own son John's, with a beautiful, carved fireplace and an enormous brass bedstead that was almost too big to be just for one little girl. He said it was because she was his now. He possessed her. And Uncle Alfie was to sleep in the new part too – in the Annexe – so he could see her whenever he wished and he could always make sure that she was being a good, little girl.

He said that she had always to be a good little girl, and that she had always to do everything exactly as he said. If she took care to do that, then one day she too could be an angel with Jesus and see her dear mama once again, in Heaven.

"Mr Fox – Atticus, old fellow, and the delightful Mrs Fox – how wonderful it is to see you both again so soon."

Dr Roberts' eyes sparkled as he burst into the library where the butler had shown them to wait. He stopped abruptly and stared.

"And you have some first rate news for me I see."

"We have indeed, Dr Roberts," Atticus replied, grinning broadly.

Then with a flourish: "I would like to present Miss Elizabeth Wilson, cousin of your late father and until this very afternoon, long-time inmate of the Knaresborough Union Workhouse. I also have Sister Mary Lovell, a nurse from the same worthy institution who, with your permission, is here to help Miss Elizabeth settle in."

"You're most welcome, Sister Lovell, you're most welcome indeed. Furthermore, I hope I can persuade the Master to allow you to remain here permanently. After all, even when she's settled, I will still need someone to look after my Aunt Elizabeth through her dotage."

Dr Roberts stooped and gazed directly at Elizabeth, his eyes drinking in every detail of her features. He made no attempt to wipe away a single, large tear as it ran down his cheek and disappeared into his rich, dark whiskers.

"My own dear Aunt Elizabeth," he whispered huskily; "Dear God, what have they done to you?"

It seemed to cost him a mammoth effort to eventually wrench his gaze from her face. He closed his eyes tightly shut until, it seemed, he had forced something deep inside to quell itself, and then he spoke again.

"Mr and Mrs Fox, I would be honoured if you would consent to stay for dinner this evening and help me celebrate being united with my dear long-lost aunt. Sister Lovell – Mary – if you would be so kind as to help Aunt Elizabeth to get changed into her new clothes, I would be delighted if you too would join us. If you can remember her old bedroom, it has been prepared for her return."

She gazed despairingly around her room at the enormous brass bed, and the two beautifully carved angels cavorting under the mantelshelf. They were cherubs and they seemed almost alive – almost. If only they were, maybe they could help. Maybe they could carry a message to her mama, far away in Heaven. They could tell her to come and watch over her at night, to be her own guardian angel. Bad things happened at night. Night was when her uncle came to tell her how naughty she had been, with his medicine for wicked girls and his eyes that froze the very blood in her veins; those ravenous, beastly eyes.

And then, as she stared at the angels – the two little cherubs – she remembered the two worst memories of all. She remembered how they waited to torment her as they festered away, deep in that farthest, most remote part of her mind that she kept especially for them and their foul and loathsome kin. Her fingers gripped again the warm, silver handle of the knife lying hidden in her sleeve and she sobbed as the pain, the delicious, soothing pain kept the two worst memories of all from slipping their bonds, and from coming to hurt her.

CHAPTER 6

"So we've not just one, but two nurses in the room with us. Good lord, Atticus, if you were planning on falling sick, now would be an excellent time to do so."

Dr Roberts chuckled at his own wit and beamed fondly at his guests seated around the large teak dining table. It had been waxed and polished until it reflected the rays of the evening sun streaming in through the tall windows as perfectly as any of the glass table vases with their bouquets of sweet briar.

"Two nurses, and a doctor," Lucie reminded him.

"Ah yes, Mrs Fox, I am a doctor but a head-doctor only I fear."

Dr Roberts' eyes twinkled as he held up a finger in mock admonishment.

"And I'm not sure that counts. You see, I am a psychiatrist, and psychiatry is easily the least precise of all the branches of medicine. It's more art perhaps than science. Indeed many would say it's just one step removed from black magic."

"So why become a psychiatrist at all if you believe it to be so – ineffectual?" Atticus asked, deeply puzzled.

"I don't, Atticus. On the contrary, I believe it can be effective, very effective indeed. What I'm trying to say is that too many people, including sadly many of my own fellow physicians, believe psychiatry to be little more than a dark art and just so much mumbo-jumbo. But I disagree. I profoundly disagree!"

He slapped the table with the flat of his hand and Elizabeth started.

"Make no mistake: Pain of the mind – pain of the very soul itself – can be every bit as insufferable as any other pain, and oftentimes, far more so. Psychiatry can help to relieve that pain certainly, but unfortunately the path to relief is all too often a very long and tortuous one. We may take many – often very many – trips into purgatory before we finally get to paradise.

Atticus, Mrs Fox, let me share with you something of my own experience. If you feel better or worse towards me as a consequence, well then, so be it; it can't be helped. When I was younger..."

"Are you sure that this is wise, Dr Roberts?" Mary Lovell interrupted, grasping Elizabeth's hand.

Roberts' smile was serenely reassuring.

"I believe so, Mary, yes. There is no cause for alarm."

He put his elbows on the tabletop and pressed his fingertips together as if in prayer.

"When I was younger, in my adolescence and early manhood, I was tormented by all manner of anxieties; by all kinds of unwelcome thoughts that kept plaguing, kept torturing my mind. Maybe I was one step from madness, or maybe I was quite mad. Who knows? Perhaps it was others who were mad.

Before he took his life, my father told me how he had once gone away on a grand tour of Europe for the sake of his own sanity. It had helped him greatly, he said, and he urged me to do the same. So I did. The distractions of the great cities of Europe, and the time away from Harrogate, and especially away from this house, helped me to regain much of my health. Then, when I was travelling through Germany, I began to learn of the great advances in the fields of psychiatry and psychology that were being realised there. I had an epiphany. Standing in the middle of a Berlin slum, I determined right there and then to put whatever wit and resource I possessed into the treatment of mental illness.

I enrolled at the Charité institute in Berlin and eventually, I became a psychiatrist. I believed that if I could prevent just one person, even for a moment, experiencing the torment I had gone through, then my life and all my pain and suffering wouldn't have been completely in vain. It might actually have all been worth it.

I'm happy, of course, to treat the well-to-do of Harrogate, and where necessary, to pander to their hysterics and their ridiculous theatrics. They pay handsomely for my affectations. But let me tell you this: I'm happier still to help the poor and the destitute, to help those with real pain, real anguish; those in our own slums, for example, or those, like my poor aunt, who rot away in the workhouse infirmaries."

"Bravo," Atticus said.

"Bravo indeed, Dr Roberts," Lucie echoed. "It's very clear that Miss Elizabeth is in capable hands here."

Roberts' face was still flushed from his jeremiad as he turned to her.

"She's in excellent hands, Mrs Fox, and all the more so as she still has her devoted nurse and companion with her, as she has since childhood."

He smiled fondly at Sister Lovell, and his eyes suddenly reflected the sun as much as ever the table did.

"Mary, while I think of it, may I ask that you take the bedroom adjacent to Aunt Elizabeth's? It's the one my father had as a child. If she were to cry out in the night, you know as well as I that we would never hear her from the main house."

Sister Lovell nodded once, without speaking.

"My grandfather still lives in the Annexe too," Roberts continued.

"If they were by chance to meet, it might well trigger rather unpleasant memories for her, and it would be for the best if you were on hand to reassure her."

Sister Lovell pursed her lips and nodded once again.

"But if that is the case, wouldn't it be better if she was simply lodged elsewhere in the house?" Lucie asked. "It is a very large house after all."

Roberts stared at his aunt for a moment as he considered Lucie's question.

"I don't know if you are aware, Mrs Fox, but Aunt Elizabeth suffers from something called senile dementia. As a nurse, you'll know all too well what that means: that her brain is gradually deteriorating, and as a result, she's slowly and inexorably losing both her memory and her powers of reason. It's been demonstrated at the Charité that a sudden change of environment, a move from the familiar to the unfamiliar, for example, can greatly accelerate the condition. I've decided therefore, that painful though it might be in some ways, it is far better to return her to her childhood room. She will likely still remember it and that recollection in itself may well stimulate her mind. A strange room would undoubtedly frighten and confuse her, and might ultimately even shorten her life. If Sister Lovell is on hand to help settle any of the more unpleasant associations she may have with the room, then that's the very best anyone can do for her.

My aunt ran away from this house to escape ill-use at my grandfather's hand. I believe that if she can meet him now, without him causing her any harm, then that too might help to reduce the fear – the very great fear – she must undoubtedly still have of him."

"Mr Alfred is not joining us for dinner?" Atticus asked.

"No!"

Roberts' retort was a whiplash. It seemed to surprise even him.

"I'm so sorry, Atticus; that sounded far harsher than I intended. The polite answer to your question is that no, my grandfather will not be joining us for dinner, today or any other day. He will spend all of his days in the Annexe. As his doctor as well as his grandson, I insist that he never leaves it. There's a lock on the door between the Annexe and the rest of the house, and the double carpets, thick walls and heavy drapes across all of the doors mean that nothing will disturb him there."

"It seems sad that he must be locked away like that," Lucie said. "Is he so very frail?"

An inexplicably discomforting silence followed her question; a silence that was mercifully broken by the appearance of a large lurcher dog that nudged open the door. It stopped abruptly as it spotted the strangers and gently sniffed at the air. Apparently satisfied, it walked timidly into the room, wagging its tail affectionately towards Dr Roberts. It had a distinct limp.

Roberts clicked his fingers and the dog trotted obediently up to him. It turned and sat down against his boots, gazing up at his face in adoration.

"Aunt Elizabeth, Mr and Mrs Fox, Miss Lovell; I have the pleasure of introducing you all to Gladstone."

The dog's ears twitched at the mention of its name.

"Gladstone is my eternal friend and faithful companion, and is named after our great Prime Minister, the 'Grand Old Man,' now sadly out of office."

"He's a lovely dog," Atticus said, "With an intriguing choice of name. What made you name him for Gladstone?"

Roberts gently scratched the top of the dog's head, and the steady thump of its tail beating against the leather of his boots measured out several seconds before he replied.

"It was because I greatly admire Mr Gladstone the man, Atticus. I especially admire his work with prostitutes... and the child prostitutes in London."

He suddenly grinned.

"And because Her Majesty our Queen once complained that he addressed her as if she was a public meeting, and that's exactly how Gladstone here regards me."

They all laughed, except Elizabeth, and the atmosphere in the room lightened and lifted once again.

Lucie asked: "What happened to his leg, Dr Roberts?"

Roberts' grin froze as he looked down at his dog.

"Gladstone is a dog I had cause to rescue," he replied. "You see, he was once owned by a notorious scoundrel who lived just outside of the town. He used him to course hares, I believe. One day, I was out riding near to the hovel where he lived, and I came across him thrashing the poor beast with a cudgel. I can still hear the cries and the yelps even now. He had broken its leg already and he was well on the way to beating it to death."

He looked up and his eyes erupted in fire.

"So I took that cudgel from him and I held him down, and I damn well smashed his own leg for him. It was perfect, natural justice do you see, Mrs Fox. I did unto him exactly as he had done unto this poor, defenceless hound: An eye for an eye, a tooth for a tooth, and a leg for a leg. Then I brought the dog back here to Sessrum and nursed him back to health, both physically, which was easy, and – dare I say it – psychologically, which, as always, was that much harder. Two or three years ago, Gladstone would have taken one glance at you, Atticus, and run to hide in the scullery for the rest of the day. Now, well you can see for yourself, apart from that limp he has and the tiniest bit of skittishness, he is a perfectly normal and happy dog."

"But what if the scoundrel had killed the dog?"

The flames in Roberts' eyes burned brighter still.

"I'm not sure what I would have done in truth, Mrs Fox. Killed him, perhaps?"

He shrugged.

"I might have done. Who knows? Righting injustice is what I must do, you see? That was my epiphany all those years ago in Berlin; I must rescue those less fortunate than myself and try to give them some semblance of a normal... of a just and normal life. Like Gladstone here, and like Aunt Elizabeth. We only have one life, and surely everyone deserves at the very least for it to be bearable. There would be much less mental anguish in the world and so much more happiness if everyone was allowed a normal life, with kindness and simple, natural justice."

"Then you are to be warmly commended for your humanity, Dr Roberts," said Lucie, "And in continuing in the family tradition of philanthropy."

"The problem with Aunt Elizabeth," Roberts continued, a little hurriedly, as if perhaps he might have been embarrassed or otherwise discomforted by her words.

"The problem with Aunt Elizabeth is that she lost everything at the age of thirteen; her happiness, her family, effectively her whole life. Now her senile dementia means that she has no chance of ever regaining it. Yes, we can feed her fine food and keep her in warm, comfortable surroundings, but her essence – her mind," he tapped his forefinger frantically against his temple, "What made her Elizabeth Beatrice Wilson has gone. She's regressing further and further back into childhood. Eventually the point will be reached when the dementia finally overwhelms her and she moves on to the next world. Please God it will be kinder to her than this sorry one has been."

"But life in the workhouses can't have been nearly as bad as you say," Lucie countered. "The principles governing them mean that they don't provide for a life of ease to be sure, far from it, but that can't be to say that she was never happy."

"Lizzie was never happy; is never happy."

Sister Lovell spoke for the second time at the table.

"She only ever worked. She worked until she could work no longer. But not because she revelled in the fruits of her labour, or because she enjoyed the reward of an honest day's toil. Lizzie worked, and worked frantically, only to keep herself from thinking; from remembering the awful things that had happened to her. And when she wasn't working, it was only because she was either exhausted or buried under depression in the workhouse infirmary. Now that she is old and frail, she can work no longer, and so those memories must haunt her night and day. It must truly be purgatory for her."

Dr Roberts leaned back in his chair, twisting his napkin between his fingers as if he was trying to wring the very dye from it. The fire was burning in his eyes once more.

"It seems the very cruellest of ironies that something that robs us of our memories should be the very thing that tortures us with them. Well, no-one can change the past, but I for one, and Mary for another, are going to do our damnedest to make certain the remainder of her days are the happiest she has had since she was a girl."

He threw the rope of napkin onto the table. It lay there for a moment, twitching and uncoiling, mesmerising them all as their silence paid respect to his words.

"Now, Mr and Mrs Fox, we get back to business. I have two further commissions for you. Firstly, when she died, Aunt Elizabeth's mother left a fortune of several thousand pounds in her will as well as Halcyon, her family home. Aunt Elizabeth is the sole beneficiary of that will. I would like you to pay a visit to the lawyers who administered the estate and advise them that you have found her safe and well."

"Didn't your grandfather get his clutches on it all?" Sister Lovell asked.

Roberts shook his head.

"He wasn't the slightest bit interested in any part of his sister's estate, Mary; except for the two hundred pounds worth of course."

The nurse reached over and patted Elizabeth's trembling hands.

"Yes, of course; the two hundred pounds," she spat, "The most precious part of all."

Dr Roberts stood suddenly and lifted his wine glass high.

"That is enough talk of the past. The past cannot be changed, but rest assured, it will be mended. We look to the future now, so please, a toast: To Elizabeth Wilson and to simple, natural justice."

CHAPTER 7

"Have you bathed, Lizzie? Have you put on the new silk nightgown I picked out for you?" Her uncle's disembodied voice is faint and muffled behind the thick panelled door of her bedroom, but faint and muffled though it is, there is a strange, disquieting catch to it that sends minatory shivers down her back. "Let me see you."

The shadows on the door cast by the gas lamp begin to slide to one side, and then, all at once, her uncle is there. The faint smile on his lips is eclipsed horribly by the cruel hunger in his eyes as they creep slowly down her body. She feels all at once exposed, almost as if she is still in her bath and hasn't put on her new silk nightgown at all.

"Might Aunt Agnes kiss me and wish me sweet dreams tonight, Uncle Alfie?" she asks. "I should like that very much. I should like Aunt Agnes to tuck me into bed tonight." She hopes that she hasn't offended him.

"My wife, your Aunt Agnes, is feeling ill again tonight, and so she has sent me. Lizzie. You have been a wicked, sinful, little girl tonight; did you know that? You have aroused me, and you need to be punished – for righteousness' sake, and for the sake of your immortal soul."

She looks directly into his eyes, those beastly, ravenous eyes, and it is as if she is looking into the eyes of Satan himself.

"Please have mercy, Uncle Alfie. I don't mean to be wicked and sinful, honest I don't. I never meant to arouse you. I don't even truly know what that means. Please don't punish me. Please have mercy."

He reaches behind to jerk the heavy drape across the shadows on the door. Then he turns back to her and speaks the words, those words: "In my experience, little girls who beg for mercy seldom deserve it."

She is picked up and hurled bodily back onto her bed. Her scream of shock, her shriek of terror, is smothered and now he's on her – on top of her – pinning her down with his suffocating weight and the great strength of his arms.

"Uncle, stop; please stop."

'Dear God, he's going to murder me.'

Her pleas are extinguished as his mouth clamps down hard onto hers. The stench of tobacco, the rake of his whiskers, and then something else.

'Mama, please help me!'

His tongue, wet and massive, forces its way between her lips, between her teeth, filling her mouth. She gags.

'He's choking me. He's choking me to death. He's killing me in my bed!'

His hands are everywhere, squeezing her, hurting her. She catches his arm. She tries desperately to push it away but it's too strong, too big. Her breath stops and she writhes frantically, impaled on his tongue like a fish on a spear. There is a sound like rending cloth. His hands, hot, rough and callused, scrape across her naked skin. Her brain shrieks for air and for her mama. But her mama is dead. A bell tolls in her mind.

'Mama, please: Uncle Alfie is killing me. He's choking me. Please, for the love of man make him stop!'

And then the tongue and the mouth are gone. She can breathe. She gasps at the air; at the pure, wonderful air. She gasps and fills her screaming lungs and thanks God and her mama that whatever it was, it's over.

She looks up. Uncle Alfie's eyes, those beastly, ravenous eyes, are waiting. They burn into her soul, laying her bare once again. She is aware of one massive hand with its fingers spread across her chest like some monstrous spider, pressing her down, pushing her hard into her bed. His belt lies open, its big, brass buckle jingling against his fingers as he scrabbles at his buttons.

"Beg me for mercy; beg me for mercy again you wicked little girl." *There it is again; the catch in his voice, the menace, the sudden breathlessness, almost as if he has just run all the way up the ghastly, creepy staircase that leads from the garden and into her bed.*

"Mercy, Uncle Alfred, please have mercy."

Her pleas are screams of terror. He's going to choke her again. He's going to kill her, make her dead, really dead, as dead as her poor, dear mama.

But instead he lets his breeches drop. The jingling of the buckle is the ringing of a bell: Her death bell.

"Deus misereatur: May God have mercy. But there will be no mercy for you this night, Lizzie."

He grasps her wrists, pulls them high over her head and his eyes, those wolfish eyes, those eyes of the Devil sear into her once more.

Her shriek of terror becomes a screaming cry of pain, of excruciating agony without and within. Her very soul is being rent in two. His great weight smashes against her again and again and again, and each time it does, the pain, the very agony of the damned, erupts and utterly consumes her.

And then he stops and it's over — truly over — at last. The pain slowly dies to a throbbing ache, deep down in her belly. It dies everywhere, that is, except within her soul. There it will live on forever and grow stronger and stronger and stronger.

She rolls over and becomes a baby again, whimpering as her body twists and she clutches at her knees. 'Please forgive me, Mama, for...for...'

"You're a slut; you're a wicked little temptress."

Her uncle's bitter, hateful voice penetrates her agony in the silence of the aftermath.

"That's what you wanted all along, isn't it? That's why you aroused me in your silk nightgown."

Lizzie tries to understand him. She tries to comprehend what the words mean. But she can't. They are beyond her.

"No, Uncle," she whispers.

'Please forgive me, Mama, for... for being a slut, and a wicked little temptress.'

"Here, let me get you dressed. Two of my gentlemen friends will be coming to see you shortly. Mrs Eire will need to sew you back up in the morning too. We need to get our full money's-worth out of you don't we, my girl?"

His laugh is short and harsh.

"Because yes, you are my girl now; I possess you."

She is dragged roughly to her knees and a fresh eruption of pain bursts inside her. Her new, silk nightgown, torn, spoiled and bloodied now, is forced down over her head. The hands release her and she falls back onto her bed. She feels dirty; she feels sullied and used somehow, guilty of something she knows not. But then her uncle had said she was a bad, wicked girl and that she deserved the punishment for the sake of her soul... just as she had deserved for her mama to go away, and she understands at last the gnawing, gnawing guilt.

The pain has gone; all except for a stinging on her arm where her knife has tried to stop her from remembering. She feels tired, so very tired, and so weary, almost as if she were an old woman and not a little girl at all.

She looks around. Everything is the same; the angels, the bed, the thick drape hanging by the door. She watches the door. She always watches the door at night. Night is when the shadows move. Night is when bad things happen.

And then bad things did happen.

'Oh, Lord Jesus, help me!'

The shadows on the door are moving, just as they always move at night, when the door to her bedroom opens and her uncle comes in.

'Oh, please, please be merciful!'

Then, those words slip once more from their hiding place and burn a fiery path through her mind: 'In my experience, little girls who beg for mercy, seldom deserve it.'

Why does he make her say it? Why does he make her beg for mercy if she doesn't deserve it, if he won't ever be merciful? She is a wicked, wicked girl and the door is opening. Bad things are going to happen. Her body is numb, except for the stinging lines on her arm where the knife has tried to keep her from remembering.

She looks up and she sees them; those eyes, those beastly, ravenous eyes; staring at her, coming closer.

'Please, little cherubs, fly to the Lord Jesus. Beg him to make Uncle Alfie be merciful.'

Her fingers close around the warm, comforting handle of the knife. She pushes it against her skin. But it fails her. Dear Lord, she is numb. She can't feel the delicious pain, and she can't shut out those eyes — those beastly, ravenous eyes — or stop his mouth. She senses his lips parting and she hears those words once more, echoing in her mind: "Beg me for mercy, Lizzie. Beg, beg, beg! In my experience..."

Then, a power that is not her own takes her hand. It does what she has not the strength to do. She looks. Behold! There beside her is a beneficent, bearded face. It is the face of the Lord Jesus Christ, the Messiah — her messiah. It has to be the Lord Jesus Christ, and standing with him is a woman; a smiling old woman with kind, weeping eyes. It is the old mother, dear Old Mother Shipton.

'Lord Jesus, thank you.'

So she wasn't a witch at all; she was with the Lord Jesus. The Lord Jesus has come, so the world must have ended at last.

CHAPTER 8

Early the following morning, Atticus Fox eased open the sash of his dining room window. He rested his elbows on the sill and gazed out across the verdant acres of the Stray, as they slid down to the gardens of the valley below. Inhaling deeply on the wonderful mix of scents, he allowed the rousing music of the Temperance Band playing in the bandstand opposite to mingle with his own warm feelings of satisfaction in a job well done.

"You know, Lucie?" he purred, "It is a truly wonderful thing to know that we have just helped to transform a poor old woman's life for the better. I can see now why Michael Roberts gets so much satisfaction in doing what he does. Will Elizabeth Wilson ever recover enough to enjoy her new life, do you suppose?"

His wife was silent for a moment as she allowed their breakfast tea to tinkle into the cups.

"No, I can't suppose she ever will, Atty."

"But this is Harrogate. What about treatment with some of the spa waters?" Atticus suggested. "Chalybeate water is very good for the mind."

Lucie smiled. Her husband insisted on drinking several large glasses of the sweet, iron-rich chalybeate water every day. He was convinced it kept his brain in first-rate condition.

"Senile dementia is a very serious condition, and it's completely irreversible Atticus. There are no waters and no medicines in the world that will change that. No matter what we might do, her mind will slowly perish and her brain will steadily lose its function, until she dies."

Atticus pushed the sash closed and the music died abruptly to a muted whisper. He turned back from the window.

"So Mary Lovell and Dr Roberts are right then? Elizabeth has lost everything – her entire life?"

Lucie nodded.

"I'm afraid so. She lost it first to depression and now finally, she's lost it to senility and dementia."

She shrugged.

"I agree with Sister Lovell that Elizabeth was never a manic-depressive though. I've seen eyes like hers before – in soldiers returning from war. I'm almost certain from what I've seen of her that Elizabeth Wilson has a form of battle-fatigue."

"Battle-fatigue: But she's spent her entire life around Harrogate. She hasn't been within a thousand miles of a battle."

"Perhaps not, but she has certainly suffered some form of severe trauma to her mind nonetheless; I'm convinced of it. It might be to do with her being orphaned. Her papa died when she was just a babe-in-arms, and her mama when she was thirteen."

"There are lots of orphans in this world, Lucie, but precious few of them suffer from battle-fatigue, especially ones who are taken in by philanthropists. Why should she..."

The heavy, insistent rapping at the front door killed Atticus' question stone dead. They exchanged suddenly anxious expressions and waited, hearts pounding, to see who it was calling at this early hour. Social calls were strictly for the afternoon, and something about the knock told them instantly, and with utter certainty, that something was terribly wrong.

They weren't kept in suspense for long. Soon the housekeeper led in a tall, handsome man in a footman's livery, whose sweating, gasping face was familiar.

"Sir, ma'am – this is James, Dr Roberts' footman. I beg your pardon for showing him straight in, but he tells me that his errand is very urgent."

"Very good, Mrs Morris, you did the correct thing. Please would you bring us some more tea? The poor man looks fit to drop, as if he has run all the way from Sessrum House."

"Begging your pardon, Mrs Fox, but I have. I've run right across town. Dr Roberts has asked that I fetch you directly. You see, last night, Miss Wilson murdered Dr Roberts' grandfather. She murdered him with a paper-knife."

The steady ticking of the clock in the hall beat against time that had frozen.

Atticus was the first to recover.

"Where is Miss Wilson now?"

"In the smoking room of the Annexe," James replied, "Being guarded by the nurse who came to look after her. A pretty job of looking after her she's made of it too, I do declare."

"Yes, yes," Atticus cut across him impatiently, "And where is Dr Roberts?"

"I left him waiting for you and Mrs Fox, sir. He sends his compliments and asks that you be as quick as you're able."

"Very well, very well, we will come directly; the tea will have to wait. Another murder for us, Lucie! And we thought it was just a search for a long-lost relative. Lead on James; *Quo Fata Vocant* – Whither the Fates call! There's no time to lose. You can tell us the rest as we walk."

CHAPTER 9

As the magnificent portico of Sessrum House came into view at last, they could see Michael Roberts anxiously pacing the broad steps that footed it, like a demented cerberean hound.

"Mr and Mrs Fox, thank the Lord you came so swiftly."

His face collapsed in relief as he caught sight of them.

"There has been a ghastly, ghastly accident. Please come inside, quickly."

"James has already told us that Miss Elizabeth stabbed your grandfather to death," Lucie explained, "And that she was found in her bed, singing a lullaby, covered in his blood."

But instead of climbing the steps towards the still-open front doorway to the house, Roberts led them away to the side, past some ancient hydrangea bushes whose swaying, mop-headed flowers seemed to be jostling for a better view of the unfolding drama. Then he turned down a little path that branched away around a dirty, slime-covered statue of some ancient, mythological figure.

"I'm afraid that what he told you is quite correct, Mrs Fox. Petty, my butler, found my grandfather stone dead on the floor of Aunt Elizabeth's bedroom whilst he was making his early morning rounds. He was covered in stab wounds, mainly to his face and chest."

He hesitated, looking suddenly revolted.

"One of the blows pierced his eye-socket and penetrated into his brain. Death, thankfully, was instantaneous then."

"Where are you taking us?" Atticus asked.

"There is a direct entrance to the Annexe," Roberts explained.

"It will be quicker and more discrete if we go in by that. It's just a little further."

He stopped. There, in front of them, set deep into the shadows of the rear of the house, was a large doorway. The door's original varnish was bleached and peeling, and a dark sheen of moss seemed to be creeping across it from its heavy, stone surround. There was something else about the door that struck them both as being odd in some way too, but what that was, neither Atticus nor Lucie could immediately place.

Across the broad stone lintel above them was carved an inscription: '*Omnes Relinquite Spes, O Vos Intrantes,*' and above that, a carved relief of the same mythological figure whose statue marked the beginning of the pathway.

"Abandon all hope, ye who enter here," Atticus instinctively translated the words.

Roberts shivered in the coolness of the shadows.

"Abandon hope indeed," he said.

"A curious choice of words for the entrance to a gentlemen's club," Lucie remarked.

Roberts nodded.

"My grandfather rather enjoyed the effect they had on his... guests."

"The relief is the Norse goddess Freya," Atticus said.

"Indeed it is, Atticus."

"And so was the statue at the start of the path."

"You are very observant."

"Thank you Doctor, but observation is a basic tool of our profession."

"There are no knobs or latches on the door," Lucie exclaimed suddenly, realising all at once what had seemed so odd about it. "There is only that door knocker in the shape of a cat's head."

"That is also correct, Mrs Fox," replied Roberts. "In its day, this was the private and very secret entrance to what my grandfather and his friends used to call their 'Friday Club.'

"Friday – Freya's day; I see the connection with the statuary now," Atticus exclaimed.

"Admittance was strictly by invitation only," Roberts went on, "And those invitations were extended only to a very small, shall we say, select group of gentlemen. They always had to knock before they were admitted. But I came out this way to wait for you, and so I left it unlocked for us."

He hesitated for a moment, and then, seeming to gather every last particle of his will, he pushed tentatively on the door. It creaked painfully as it slowly swung wide on its great, iron hinges, as if it was a door that was very seldom opened.

"Are the police here already?" Atticus asked.

Roberts hesitated once more.

"No Atticus, they're not."

"Ah, that's fortunate; we generally find it is far better to examine a crime scene before the police arrive. They do have a tendency to trample all over any evidence that isn't staring them directly in the face."

"I haven't sent for them at all if truth be told. I sent for you both instead. I am conscious – despite my grief – that this is a very delicate matter; a very delicate matter indeed."

"How so?" Atticus asked.

Roberts looked deliberately at each of them in turn. He licked his lips. "Well, you see; I commissioned you both to trace Aunt Elizabeth's whereabouts, and to bring her back to live here. I also arranged for her to sleep in the very same part of the house where her uncle still lives, or lived I should say, and from where she departed in rather, shall we call them, abrupt circumstances. People might surmise that it was foolhardy of me, and then they might delve further. My reputation – you'll understand I'm sure – might be compromised. That's why I called you first. I thought you both could carry out any investigation that might be needed and then hand it all over to the police in a more, shall we say, circumspect way."

Atticus was aghast.

"Dr Roberts, this is a criminal matter of the most serious nature. You haven't lost your dog; it is a murder. You really must inform the police directly. Mrs Fox and I will happily liaise with them on your behalf if you wish, but you must let them investigate your grandfather's death in the proper manner, circumspect or not. To do anything other would be to immediately arouse their suspicions and might ultimately land you in front of a jury yourself for perverting the course of justice."

It was Roberts' turn to look aghast.

"I'm so sorry, Atticus, I had no idea. We just thought it was for the best."

"So," Atticus continued, mollified now, even perhaps in truth, a little excited, "Show us this Annexe, and while you call for the police, we'll take the opportunity to examine the scene of the murder."

Roberts nodded wearily, as if succumbing to the inevitable, and then, steeling himself like an actor about to enter onto some grand stage, ushered them through the doorway.

They found themselves at the foot of a deep, wide stairwell. But this was nothing like the modern, comfortable surroundings of the rest of the house. This place was grim and austere, more akin to the tower of some medieval castle or dungeon than to a fashionable home. The walls towering above them were of raw, naked stone, and what appeared to be iron torch rings tracked the rude, uncarpeted stairway as it spiralled upwards. On the wall immediately opposite the door was a gigantic oil painting; a glorious depiction of a flame-haired maiden astride a racing chariot pulled by two enormous, snarling black cats. In the chariot's wake, a host of naked, dancing maidens snaked off into the far distance.

"You have already noticed my grandfather's particular penchant for the goddess Freya," Roberts growled in answer to Atticus' unspoken question.

Atticus nodded.

"The Norse goddess of love, beauty and fertility," he said.

Roberts turned sharply towards him. The briefest shade of accusation in his expression subsided quickly to a brooding thoughtfulness, before he turned away once more and led them in silence up the stairs.

The chill air at the foot of the well became all at once warm, almost oppressive, as they climbed the stairway. They reached the top and came to a second door. This was also very solidly made and peculiarly devoid of any furniture, barring a knocker that was again cast in the shape of a snarling cat's head. Above it, painted in black gothic script was a second legend, but this time in English.

Atticus read: "'Freya is the receiver of the slain. Lördag cleanses your body and your tongue.'"

He frowned in puzzlement.

"What does that mean?"

"It means that my grandfather was a very strange man, Atticus." Roberts' tone was grim.

"But what does it really mean?" Lucie persisted.

"It means that my grandfather and his Friday Club friends had a strange fascination with the Vikings, Mrs Fox. Lördag is the Viking name for Saturday."

"But it was a Friday Club," Lucie reminded him.

Roberts hesitated, his hand hovering against the door.

"Exactly so, and as I said to your husband, Mrs Fox, so I say again to you: My grandfather was a very strange man, a very strange man indeed."

He pushed at the door and it rolled wide, like a curtain parting on an opening night stage.

"This," he announced, "was my grandfather's Friday Club."

They looked. In front of them, a large, airy, high-ceilinged room was set about with around a dozen or so chaises longues. Like the stairwell, the walls were of brute, naked stone, but here they were softened by a large number of heavy, hanging tapestries; nude studies of Freya, and of other women and girls in various degrees of nakedness.

Atticus stepped forward into the cooler, fresher air of the room and he heard Lucie's voice speaking his own first impression.

"This carpet is very deep," she said.

"It's a double carpet," Roberts replied, "Intended to muffle the late-night noise from the club so that it wouldn't disturb the rest of the household."

"How very thoughtful of your grandfather," Lucie remarked.

"Oh, yes," Roberts said bitterly, "It was. It was very thoughtful indeed. This Annexe was laid out with a very great deal of thought: Double carpets, thick walls with those heavy tapestries covering them to deaden any sound, curtains over all the doors. Everything was meticulously planned down to the very last detail."

"Are they some of the members of your grandfather's club?" Lucie asked, pointing towards a large, grey photograph. It was mounted high on the wall above their heads. A group of obviously well-to-do men smirked back at them from within a handsome, brass picture frame. Curiously, a fine, wire mesh covered the face of the photograph, almost like the grill of a prison window.

"Those are the members in their entirety, Mrs Fox," Roberts replied without looking at them, "Plus a steward called Mr Otter my grandfather employed. He's the brutish-looking one on the left. There only ever were a dozen or so of them at its height. It's closed down now, of course. I use this room only occasionally as a smoking room or when I need to be alone to collect my thoughts. But I keep that photograph up there to continually remind my grandfather of his former associates."

"Happy memories," Atticus said, and Roberts frowned.

"Sister Lovell, Miss Elizabeth," Lucie exclaimed suddenly.

Atticus looked round. There, framed just inside another doorway directly opposite them were the slight figures of Elizabeth and her nurse.

"Mary," Roberts said gently, "Would you mind sitting with Aunt Elizabeth for a while in here while Mr and Mrs Fox examine the scene of the... the incident?"

He hesitated.

"I'm going to have to call the constabulary I'm afraid; Mr Fox insists on it."

Miss Lovell looked as if she had been struck. Her eyes, full of appeal, darted between Atticus and the doctor and finally settled onto Lucie.

"Must we, Mrs Fox?"

"You must," said Lucie gently, "My husband is right to insist."

Then she asked: "How is Miss Elizabeth?"

Miss Lovell regarded Elizabeth, and her expression softened to something between fondness and pity. She shrugged.

"Lizzie is just as Lizzie always is, Mrs Fox. I don't even believe she knows what... what she's done."

Friday, it must be Friday. Friday was when she and the waifs and strays were brought here, to this room with its bare stone walls, and its foul stenches of liquor and tobacco. Friday was the day he brought his gentlemen friends here too, to smoke and to drink, to play cards and to...

Often his gentleman friends brought other little girls who had been wicked and who needed to be punished too. Sometimes the little girls didn't even know that they were wicked. Some even thought they were to be taken as servants or maids into the gentlemen's houses. Instead, they were given their medicine for naughty girls and taken into the other rooms of the Annexe. They were taken away for their punishment. Sometimes the gentlemen would take them off in their carriages for the night; sometimes for days on end. Elizabeth had often been taken away in the gentlemen's carriages, and each time it happened, it had seemed as if those particular days would never end.

They had to beg for mercy. The gentlemen might be more merciful if they begged, if they pleaded with all their souls not to be punished. Sometimes the punishments would be over more quickly if they screamed and writhed and showed how much it hurt them. But always, they had been wicked. Always, they needed to be punished. And always, they screamed.

But Uncle Alfie would not punish her today. Today, Uncle Alfie's eyes had gone forever. Uncle Alfie had gone to be with Jesus in Heaven. Perhaps he might tell her mama that he and his gentleman friends had punished her enough, that she had done everything he had wanted her to and that now, now she was surely a good little girl. Now, at last, the world must have ended and her mama could come to fetch her to be an angel in Heaven too.

CHAPTER 10

To their disappointment and intense frustration, Dr Roberts had already had his grandfather's body moved from its place of discovery in Elizabeth's bedroom to a scrubbed-top table in what he called the 'Surgery,' a tiny room adjoining the Annexe's scullery.

As they entered this makeshift mortuary, Atticus kept his gaze determinedly focused on the little square, black and white tiles that made up the floor. The examination of corpses, and most particularly those that had died a violent or unnatural death, was thankfully a very rare part of their profession, but one he still left very much to his wife, who by contrast seemed to positively revel in it.

"Oh, upon my word," Lucie exclaimed, pulling up a large, involuntary wave of nausea from the pit of her husband's stomach.

"What is it? What do you see, Lucie?" Atticus took a deep gulp of air, holding it fast in his lungs for one, two, three seconds, as pinpricks of sweat began breaking out across his brow. There was also, he noted, an ominous tightening in his gut.

His wife glanced at him.

"Well, Alfred Roberts is certainly dead, and likely has been for several hours. There is an awful lot of blood present, and most of it has dried on his skin and his nightclothes, or at least has thickened. There are many – very many – deep puncture wounds to his upper chest and neck, and still more to his face. As Dr Roberts told us, one of the blows pierced his left eye-socket and quite took out the eyeball."

Here, even she paused.

"It was a violent, I would say an almost frenzied, attack. I also suspect that he was suddenly overwhelmed by his assailant, because there is no sign of blood or injury to his hands or forearms. There almost certainly would have been if he had tried to defend himself."

"He was suddenly overwhelmed?" Atticus repeated.

"That's how it seems. There's a heavily bloodstained knife lying next to the corpse too, one which could well be the murder weapon."

There was another, longer pause.

"Yes, the width of the blade appears at first glance to match the wound dimensions exactly. I can see fingerprints in blood on the handle too; small ones which would likely belong to a woman or a grown child. They are very clear; in fact, they are unusually clear. I can make out heavy scarring that would fit with the owner having spent their life in manual work – in a workhouse perhaps. Atticus, I will check of course, but I would wager our fees to a farthing that these are Elizabeth Wilson's bloody fingerprints on the knife."

"Let me see it, Lucie."

Atticus glanced up long enough to take the knife gingerly between his forefinger and thumb.

"It's an envelope knife; a very handsome one too. Yes, I see the fingertip prints you mentioned and I can see the scarring clearly. Let me see; there's an inscription on it too – on the blade. It's just about polished out but if I carefully smear just a little of the blood across it... yes, I can make out some of the words: 'Presented to Mr Thomas Liddle,' and: 'Union Workhouse, Eighteen Eighty Four.' The rest is illegible."

The inescapable weight of evidence crushed them into silence.

Then Lucie said: "The case is easy then, Atticus. It was Elizabeth. So we shouldn't be congratulating ourselves on helping to save a senile old woman from poverty at all. We should be trying to come to terms with the fact that we've unwittingly contributed to an old man's murder, and maybe to our senile old woman being hanged for it too."

Atticus nodded gravely.

"You're right, Lucie. Old Mr Roberts is dead and there's no changing that."

He sighed helplessly. "And what this is going to do to our professional reputation I shudder to think; just when we were beginning to build something of a name for ourselves too. There's no point in crying over spilt milk though; what's done is done, and we must be professional about it all. Come, Lucie, let's go and see exactly where Alfred Roberts met his death."

The door to Elizabeth's bedroom was still wide open, revealing an exquisitely carved fireplace on the chimney-breast opposite, complete with a pair of white, marble cherubs. But as they entered, slowly and tentatively, they could see that the cherubs must really be fallen angels, because the scene within was hellish.

The pillows and the counterpane of the bed were smeared and streaked in blood, which had mellowed with the passage of the hours into the colour of fine, burgundy wine. Several thick, glutinous reddish brown stains sat on the pile of the rug beside it. The room had been freshly and fashionably decorated in the new 'liberty' art style, with its flowing, natural lines and, as if in macabre homage to this, a curving, spattered serpentine of arterial blood swept low across the wall adjacent.

Lucie stared at it for a moment.

"Dear God, Atticus, but the devil has been at work in here! This is without a doubt where Alfred Roberts was killed. One of the blows must have severed an artery."

"Tell me," Atticus murmured, "How in God's name the frail old lady we met in the workhouse yesterday could have done this?"

CHAPTER 11

When a somewhat shaken Atticus and Lucie Fox re-entered the smoking room of the Annexe, they found Elizabeth sitting by her nurse on one of the chaises longues, gently rocking to-and-fro with her hands clasped tightly in her lap. She was singing her lullaby 'Hush-a-Bye, Baby' quietly to herself, seemingly oblivious both to the dark stains of her uncle's lifeblood, smeared starkly across the pure white silk of her new nightgown, and of the photograph opposite her, with the accusing leers of the man himself and of his gentlemen friends, gaping mockingly down at them, safe in their gilded cage high on the wall.

"Miss Wilson – Elizabeth – Lizzie," Lucie ventured gently, "Do you think we could ask you some questions about what happened last night?"

"It's one-and-eight-and-eight-and-one and one-and-eight-and-eight-and-one." Elizabeth's voice was harsh, like the call of a magpie or a buccaneer's parrot.

"She doesn't understand you, Mrs Fox."

Startled, Atticus and Lucie turned to see Dr Roberts standing suddenly behind them. He was looking visibly more relaxed now.

"I've sent James to run and inform the police, just as you asked, Atticus," he continued. "They should be here presently."

"Thank you," replied Atticus curtly. "Their job will not be difficult. The knife used to murder your grandfather was almost certainly taken from the Master's office at the Union Workhouse. It's covered in what must be Elizabeth's bloody fingertip prints, which I can assure you are entirely unique to her, and could have been left by no-one else. She's sitting there, drenched in his blood, and the murder was committed in her bedroom. No, the police will have an easy task in identifying who the murderer is. The difficult part will be in deciding what to do with her. If, as you say, she cannot even understand my wife's questions, then she surely won't be fit to stand trial."

His voice tailed away as Lucie walked slowly and purposefully up to Elizabeth. Kneeling, she gently took the old lady's right hand in her own and began to examine it closely. Elizabeth regarded her with mild curiosity as she gently rocked and sang her lullaby:

"And down will come Baby, cradle and all."

"There is a bloody palm print on the back of her hand," Lucie remarked softly.

"It's probably my grandfather's," Roberts muttered, "Or it might have been Miss Lovell's, from when she brought my aunt in here from her bedroom."

He watched, fascinated, as Lucie took out her pocket handkerchief and pressed it firmly down over the print with her own hand.

"There was blood everywhere," he continued. "We left it though. We wanted to be careful not to disturb any evidence of what had happened ahead of your arrival."

"Yet you moved the biggest part of the evidence: your grandfather's body, to the Surgery."

The remnants of Atticus' earlier frustration cut a new edge to his tone.

Roberts shrugged.

Atticus stooped to examine the hand Lucie was holding and as he did so, Elizabeth's gaze settled onto him. She stopped singing and let out a soft moan. A stream of dark, yellow urine pattered onto the carpet between her skinny ankles.

"It's fine, Lizzie, you're safe; you're quite safe," the nurse murmured.

"I'm so sorry!" Atticus was utterly mortified. "I didn't mean to startle her."

"You weren't to realise, Atticus." Roberts squeezed his shoulder reassuringly as he sidled past. Then he too stooped in front of his aunt.

"You've had a little misfortune," he said patiently, soothingly. "You need to go with Mary, Aunt Lizzie. You need to go with her now. She will get you washed and changed into a fresh, clean dress. Go with her now."

Elizabeth said "Yes, John," and began to rock once more.

'Go with her now... Go with her.'

The words pierced her soul like a dagger, spilling memory after memory from their secret places, and sending them skittering through her mind.

Uncle Alfie was looking down at her now, with his face full of contempt.
"Go with the lady now, Lizzie. Be a good girl for your dead mama and do as I say. I shall need my full two hundred pounds worth if I'm to feed you and clothe you all the while 'til you're grown."

The woman's — that woman's — loathsome face was there with her cruel, hard eyes and her thin lips.

"You paid two hundred pounds for her, Mr Roberts? I thought you said you'd inherited her from your late sister."

"I did, Mrs Eire, but what I meant was that she would have cost me at least two hundred pounds if I'd bought her on the open market."

The woman's eyes turned on her, appraising her from head to foot.

"She's pretty enough I dare say with nice manners and fine, blonde hair but I could have bought you half a score of girls just like her from Leeds or Bradford for two hundred pounds. They're all the same below stairs if you take my meaning. Anyways, like you say, she came to you for free so there's nothing lost I suppose, and nothing to fret about. Let's get her into the surgery and I'll patch her up and make her nice and fresh for you again."

"Thank you, Mrs Eire. But let me tell you first that the value in a fallen girl is not just in what's below stairs, as you so eloquently put it; it's in just how far you can make 'em fall. I've promised her to Mr Price next week so do a good job on her and there'll be an extra guinea in it for your efforts."

She felt again the woman's bony fingers biting into the soft flesh of her arm. She felt herself being dragged into the surgery, being pushed down onto her back, onto the hard table there. The woman's cruel eyes were boring into hers and the thin lips beneath them were moving.

"Here, drink this, you little two hundred pound whore. This is going to hurt and I don't want you wriggling about and spoiling my needlework, and costing me my extra guinea."

She felt oily liquid on her tongue, felt it falling into her throat and tasted its bitter, acrid tang. It was medicine for naughty girls, she knew. One of Uncle Alfie's gentleman friends had made her drink some so that she wouldn't remember him properly. But she did remember; she remembered he was a vicar and that he had come to punish her for the sake of her soul. Then she realised with a sudden wave of panic that she was going to be punished again, here, by this woman. But how could a woman punish her? She could still feel the stinging and still feel the hurt deep in her belly, where first Uncle Alfie

---

and then his two gentlemen friends had punished her already. How could a woman do that?

Mrs Eire was holding up a tiny sewing needle. Her thin lips were moving as she tried to thread it, but now she couldn't hear the words she was saying. The room was beginning to float and she was only vaguely aware of her dress being pushed up, of her knees being pulled roughly apart and of the sudden, sharp pains; pains that pierced her even through the fog of the medicine, stabbing and stabbing and stabbing.

Lucie Fox waited until she heard the door of the Annexe's bathroom click shut behind the nurse and her shambling charge.

Then she asked: "Dr Roberts, what could have caused Elizabeth to commit such a violent act? She's senile, but she's not mad as such, is she?"

"No, Mrs Fox, Elizabeth is certainly not mad, not in the true and proper sense of the word anyway, nor is she really an imbecile as the Master of the Union Workhouse would have us believe. She simply presents the classic symptoms of senile dementia; the loss of the memory of recent events, an inability to perform even simple tasks, a loss of continence, and so on."

His eyes darted along the hall towards the sudden sound of running water behind the locked bathroom door.

"Sometimes, it can also cause sufferers to be unmannerly, hostile and even downright violent, although until last night, we'd never observed anything like that in my aunt. I can tell you both in confidence that Aunt Elizabeth didn't have a happy childhood with my grandfather. Although he carefully cultivated this reputation he had of being a good, benevolent old fellow and a great philanthropist, he was impossibly cruel to her, and that, coupled with the death of her father when she was very young, and then that of her mother as well, has left her with deep emotional scars. I can see clearly now that my judgement was flawed. Those scars must have been ripped open again by the sight of her childhood tormentor, and I'm afraid that her emotions must simply have overwhelmed her. She already had a knife in her hand, which as you say, she had taken from the workhouse, and I suppose that the result was... inevitable."

Lucie frowned.

"But if she has senile dementia, she couldn't possibly have planned the attack with malice aforethought, so why did she steal a knife?"

"Have you seen Aunt Elizabeth's arms by any chance, Mrs Fox?" Roberts sounded suddenly weary.

Lucie shook her head, puzzled.

"Well, if you had, you would have seen that she barely has a patch of skin left on them that isn't covered in cicatrices – in old scars – and in new scars for that matter. Mary tells me that she has a fresh set of wounds that must have been made only yesterday, probably as you were talking in Liddle's office or even as you were bringing her across here. She cuts herself on her arms and on her breasts; she cuts herself with knives, scissors, broken glass, anything she can get her hands on, so that the pain of the wounds can shut out the pain of her memories. Mary tells me that she could never really be trusted with a knife for fear of her taking it away to cut herself. It's the memories, you see; it's her awful, awful memories."

"My wife remarked only this morning that Miss Elizabeth seemed to be suffering from a form of battle fatigue." Atticus said.

"Battle fatigue!"

Roberts' expression changed in an instant from weariness, to thoughtfulness, to downright exultation.

"You said that, Mrs Fox: that she suffers from battle fatigue? Ye gods, that's brilliant! I never thought to describe it that way. You're quite correct, of course; Aunt Elizabeth's experiences, traumatic experiences all of them, reinforced by a lifetime in the workhouse, have indeed caused her to suffer a kind of battle fatigue. I'll tell the police exactly that. Mrs Fox, you must tell them that too, and be sure to tell them that you are a nurse, a trained nurse... Battle fatigue, yes, of course."

The silence that followed was interrupted by a gentle knock on the open door. It was Petty, the butler.

"Excuse me sir, but I have two policemen from the West Yorkshire Constabulary here to see you; a Detective Inspector Douglas, and Detective Sergeant Hainsworth."

"Indeed you have, Dr Roberts, and with respect, sir, we should have been called for hours ago," said a disembodied voice from the corridor beyond Petty.

Then, without waiting to be shown in, two large and stocky men pushed past the butler and strutted into the room. Their entrance mirrored the inflection in their greeting, which was aggressive, disdainful and sneering.

The first's eyes darted around the room, appraising everything. They lingered for a second or two on Lucie, and then finally came to rest on Atticus and Dr Roberts.

"I am Detective Inspector Douglas; which of you gentlemen is Dr Michael Roberts?" he asked of the space somewhere between them.

The doctor made as if to rise from his chair but Douglas ignored him, fixing his glare instead on Atticus.

"And you are?"

"Fox, Atticus Fox, of A & L Fox, commissioned investigators," Atticus said, completing the sentence for him. "And this lady is my wife."

"Upon my soul," Douglas exclaimed, the sneer in his tone rank and unmistakable. "Detective Sergeant, it would seem that we're in the esteemed company of none other than the noted A and L Fox; Harrogate's very own commissioned investigators."

"Are we indeed?" the sergeant replied, taking up the game enthusiastically. "Now that's a treat, and no mistake."

"Isn't it?" Douglas agreed. "So that would explain why Dr Roberts took so long to send for us. Upon my honour, Sergeant, I wonder why he bothered to send for us at all. No doubt Mr and Mrs Fox will have the whole case sewn up already, with the murderer on the gallows, prayers said, and all ready to drop."

The detective inspector chuckled mirthlessly at his own wit, and then stopped laughing and said: "So why are you here, Mr Atticus Fox, commissioned investigator?"

Atticus, his heckles up, met Douglas' stare directly.

"We are here on Dr Roberts' express invitation," he growled. "There was a murder in this house last night, Detective Inspector. The likely perpetrator, a relation of the family as it happens, was traced, contacted and brought here by my wife and me only yesterday. That was our commission, not the investigation of the murder."

Douglas stared intently at Atticus for several, long, highly charged seconds, as if sifting his story for flaws. He found none.

"I am very pleased to hear it, Mr Fox. Reuniting missing relatives is what you people should be used for, and nothing more."

He held Atticus in a silent battle of wills for a few moments longer before turning his attention to Roberts.

"Now, Doctor, perhaps you can tell us exactly what happened here last night."

As he and the sergeant settled themselves comfortably side-by-side on one of the nearby chaises longues, Roberts licked his lips and darted a pleading glance to Atticus.

"May I?" Atticus began.

"No, you most certainly may not, Mr Fox. You brought this 'relation of the family' here, and so your task is complete. I asked the good doctor here what happened, and with all due respect to him, I expect him to answer me."

Douglas' eyes remained fixed on Roberts'.

"Very well, Inspector, here goes: The relation of the family Mr Fox previously described as the likely killer of my grandfather is my Aunt, Elizabeth Wilson. She used to live here many years ago with my grandfather, who was also her uncle."

"Your grandfather being Mr Alfred Roberts, the deceased," Hainsworth interrupted.

"Yes, Detective Sergeant. My aunt left the house when she was still just a girl and we decided that it would..."

"'We decided'? Dr Roberts... whom do you mean by 'we'?" Douglas demanded.

"I beg your pardon, Inspector Douglas, I meant 'I'. I decided that it would be for the best if she were to return here to Sessrum House to live out her dotage with me."

Douglas regarded him thoughtfully.

"And precisely why did 'you' decide that would that be for the best, Doctor?"

"It was because my aunt suffers from senile dementia."

Roberts' voice seemed suddenly stronger, more confident. He was on his home ground.

"She's quite elderly and her condition is deteriorating rapidly. I decided as a psychiatric doctor that it would be better if she lived here, under my direct care. I also brought in a nurse to attend to her daily needs."

"Very noble of you, I'm sure. And this happened only yesterday, as Mr Fox has so kindly told us already. But then tell me, why would you need, let me see, commissioned investigators, of Mr and Mrs Fox' esteemed reputation, just to fetch your elderly aunt to come and live with you? Surely any common cabriolet driver could have fetched her for a couple of shillings?"

Roberts hesitated and threw a second pleading glance at Atticus.

"Miss Wilson spent many years at addresses in Starbeck and Knaresborough, Inspector," Atticus replied for him. "Dr Roberts was not yet born at the time that she left this house, and the family had long since lost all contact. We needed to trace her whereabouts before we could bring her back."

Douglas' gaze shifted between Atticus and Roberts, and then fell on Lucie.

He said: "I have been a serving policeman for well over five-and-twenty years now, Mrs Fox. During that time, I have not been idle. No ma'am. I have developed many, very useful skills. One of those skills is the uncanny ability to know when someone is not being entirely straightforward with me, and I am getting that distinct impression now, with your husband and with your client."

Lucie smiled disarmingly.

"Very well, Inspector: What my husband and our principal have not yet had chance to tell you is that Miss Wilson has been living in workhouses since she left Sessrum House. Those were the addresses in Starbeck and Knaresborough my husband was referring to. She didn't care at all for her uncle who by all accounts was very unkind to her, and she fled to the poor-law when she was just fifteen years old."

"Ah, at last... Finally we make progress. Thank you, Mrs Fox. That wasn't too difficult now, was it? Don't be shy of telling us the family secrets. We're quite used to them. I always say, don't I, Hainsworth, that there's many a dark secret to be found lurking behind the prettily-painted doors of the well-to-do."

He leaned back into the chaise longue and rested his hands comfortably behind his head.

"Do go on with your tale, Doctor. It's becoming quite intriguing." Roberts licked his lips.

"Very well, Inspector: Sister Lovell, the nurse who came with Aunt Elizabeth from... well, from the Union Workhouse at Knaresborough, put her to her bed last night and then retired to her own room, which is just adjacent to it. I sat in here for a while and had a glass or two of brandy before going to my own room in the main house."

"Your own room in the main house?"

Douglas' raised eyebrows and accusing tone turned the statement into a stinging question.

"Yes, Detective Inspector. My aunt's, and Sister Lovell's, and indeed my grandfather's rooms, are all in this newer part of the house: It was built by my grandfather many years ago, and he called it the Annexe. Aunt Elizabeth was accommodated here after her mama died and she came to live with him. She occupies the very same room now."

"Why, wasn't the house big enough to accommodate her already?"

"It was quite big enough to house one little girl, Inspector, yes. But my grandfather was well known for taking in other children off the street. He also liked to entertain certain friends of his here, and he had the Annexe especially built to accommodate it all."

"Indeed, and it's a fascinating tale to be sure, but are you going to tell me what happened last night or not?"

Roberts' exhaled sharply, as if in grateful relief.

"Of course, Inspector, I'm sorry. This morning, I was awoken just after dawn by Petty, my butler. He had been doing his usual early morning inspection round of the house when he discovered my grandfather's body lying on the floor of my Aunt Elizabeth's bedroom, covered in blood. He had been stabbed to death."

Douglas was no longer looking comfortable or relaxed; now he was sitting bolt upright, watching Roberts as a terrier might watch a rat.

"And where was your aunt then?" he asked.

"She was sitting on her bed, still covered in my grandfather's blood, singing a lullaby. And she was smiling, Inspector. For the first time that anyone can recall, she was actually smiling."

"Smiling and lullabies be damned," growled Douglas, "Where is this Elizabeth Wilson now?"

"She is being washed and changed by her nurse. She will be back presently."

"But you would swear to the fact that she was heavily bloodstained when your butler found her?"

Roberts nodded.

"I would of course, Detective Inspector. You may have her night-dress as proof of it if you wish, and the knife she used to do it too. She still had it in her hand when we found her."

"And we can vouch for the fact that Dr Roberts' account is true and accurate, Detective Inspector," Atticus added. "The knife had evidently been taken from the Union Workhouse, from where Mrs Fox and I fetched her. There are also a number of bloody fingertip prints left on the handle, which my wife could easily link to the murderer."

"Fingerprint evidence, Mrs Fox? Very impressive; you shame humble policemen like us with your science."

"The technique is simple and open to all to use, and I know that several constabularies are already looking into it," Lucie replied patiently.

"So it seems clear that we can charge this Elizabeth Wilson with the murder of your grandfather," said Douglas, turning back to Roberts and ignoring Lucie's remark. "But I do have one vexing question remaining in my mind, however."

"Indeed, Inspector?"

The colour drained instantly and completely from Roberts' face.

"Indeed, Dr Roberts. What I am wondering is whether or not we should charge you too."

The doctor slumped forward, his eyes pressed tightly shut.

"Charge me, Detective Inspector? But why should you need to charge me, or anyone else for that matter?" he whispered.

Douglas hesitated before he answered, watching with relish the effect that his words were having.

Then he said: "You have already said that it was your decision, and your decision alone, to bring your aunt to live with you here."

Roberts nodded.

"So I assume it again was you who chose to move her into this... Annexe, near to your grandfather's room?"

"That is correct, Detective Inspector."

"Then surely it was your own blatant disregard for the fact that she had hated him since she was a child that contributed to his murder. It seems to me that you are as much involved in your grandfather's death as Wilson herself."

He waited again for the impact of his words to roll deliciously over Roberts before he added: "What do you reckon, Detective Sergeant Hainsworth; should we charge the doctor with Alfred Roberts' murder too?"

"I think we should, sir," Hainsworth said, taking up the game once more, "Although I suppose we might have a tricky task in proving malice aforethought."

"We might, Sergeant, that's very true, but it doesn't mean that he didn't possess it though. Dr Roberts, tell me: Did you have malice aforethought in bringing Elizabeth Wilson here?"

A vicious half smile curled his lip.

"Detective Inspector, with God as my judge, I thought only of making things right for my aunt."

Roberts' reply was husky, and as he spoke the colour rushed back into his face.

"Very well then, Wilson shall bear the weight of the charge alone. If what you say turns out to be correct, she should be hanged and rendering an account of herself before God by the time the month is out."

"Surely not, Inspector Douglas," Lucie cried, "Are you mad? She can't be hanged for it!"

The detective inspector regarded her coldly.

"No, Mrs Fox, I am far from being mad. If Elizabeth Wilson is a murderess, then the law is very clear: she will be tried and she will hang for it. May God, as they say, have mercy."

"But her mind is gone."

Lucie's expression was of pure outrage now.

"She had no idea what she was doing when she killed Alfred Roberts. How can she defend herself in a court of law? She has senile dementia, Detective Inspector, do you not understand? She has battle fatigue and she has senile dementia."

"Battle fatigue, Mrs Fox, battle fatigue; what nonsense is this?" Douglas stood now and he towered over Lucie.

She stood to meet him.

"I say that in my professional opinion, as a nurse who has worked in several military hospitals including Netley, Elizabeth Wilson has a form of battle fatigue. She is mentally incapable of standing trial for murder, or for anything else for that matter."

"And in my professional opinion as a psychiatrist, I endorse Mrs Fox' view entirely."

Roberts was as adamant as he was defiant.

Douglas stared from one to the other, for a moment, speechless.

"Don't you want justice for your grandfather, Doctor? Don't you want his killer to be tried and hanged for it, beloved old aunt or not?"

"That's just the thing, Inspector. It wouldn't be justice – natural justice – for my Aunt Elizabeth to hang."

"Then what would you have me do with her?"

Roberts gnawed on his bottom lip.

"Give me an Order of Guardianship. Have her discharged into my care and keeping. This Annexe is perfectly secure. There are locks on all of the doors and there are bars on the windows. Sister Lovell can both guard her and tend to her needs. She will pose no further threat to anyone. Let her live out her few remaining years, imprisoned if you like to call it that, here. It's the perfect solution."

In the hush that followed his words, Atticus glanced more closely at the windows. Roberts was perfectly correct. In front of each of the thick, wooden glazing bars there was another set of bars, much thinner for sure, but wrought in iron and painted white so as not to be immediately apparent.

"It is not my place to make that decision," Douglas said at last, his tone more reasonable now. "There are proper rules – the McNaughton Rules – to determine whether criminals are really insane or not, and it would only be the magistrate who could agree to her being kept here. Until then, Wilson will have to make do with a prison cell at the police station, and a sergeant for a nurse. There should be a police wagon at your front door by now, and as soon as Wilson is washed and dressed, that's where she'll be bound."

CHAPTER 12

Just as the inspector had predicted, a police wagon was already waiting by the steps of the grand portico of the house. It looked expectant, with its large rear door gaping as wide as the gates of Purgatory, ready to receive its next victim. The heavy horse between the shafts was dozing, head drooping, one great hind foot resting on an iron-shod toe.

Sister Lovell touched the side of Elizabeth's bewildered, panic-stricken face as she was guided up a set of awkwardly tiny steps by Hainsworth.

"You can come back, Lizzie," she said softly, urgently, "You can come back. I promise. It'll be for the best. It'll be as if nothing has happened, and Dr Roberts and I will look after you always."

"I wouldn't wager on it," Hainsworth chuckled.

He twisted Elizabeth's fingers from the frame of the waiting door and pushed her through it. A constable's arm reached out from the depths and slammed the door shut and Hainsworth rattled home a bolt.

"You can come back, Lizzie. It'll be for the best. You can have the baby and then, when you're strong again, you can come back here. It'll be as if nothing has happened. No-one need ever know. I won't tell, upon my honour I won't. The orphanage can bring the baby up and teach it its letters and you shall be married and have another one that isn't a bastard."

Mary's face swam in front of her own, somehow different but somehow the same, her lips strangely out of synch with the words.

She felt strong fingers prising her grip from the frame of the carriage door, felt strong arms pulling her inside.

A voice hissed in her ear. "Stop struggling, you little whore. It's you that's having the little bastard, so it's you that has to go to Brimston."

GARY DOLMAN

She was pushed down hard onto the seat and Mrs Eire's hard, pinched features replaced Mary's kindly ones. The woman's face broke into a sneer.
"Will it die do you think, Lizzie, when it's born? Or will it grow big enough to take your place in your uncle's club each Friday? Will it be enjoying the gentlemen's attentions when you're all wizened and old and not worth a tramps farthing, never mind two hundred pounds?"

Dr Roberts put his hand on Mary Lovell's craggy shoulders and they watched the wagon roll out sedately between the big gateposts. Then he felt them begin to shake as finally, she succumbed to her grief.

"She won't understand a bit what's happening to her, Doctor. That's the unbearable part of it all. I wish you'd let me sedate her before they took her away. She'll be so frightened in there."

"I'm so sorry," Roberts said softly, his own eyes shining bright, "But it's the only way. We need them to be sure that it's because of her mental condition that she can't answer any of their questions, and not because of anything we might have given her. She needs to pass those McNaughton rules, Mary – or she'll hang."

Mary nodded.

"I know. But she hasn't been able to stand the sight or sound of carriages since she went to Mrs Eire's old place at Brimston. Will she think the police wagon is Eire's carriage, do you suppose?"

A moment of agony flitted across Roberts' face.

"I can't bring myself to say that woman's name, Mary, but pray God, she does not."

The worst – the very worst – memory of all began to fulminate and stir in the black, secret places of her mind. She knew it would come. As hard as she tried to stop it, as hard as she begged the Lord Jesus to make it stay away, to leave her in peace, the more she knew it would come. It would surely come to hurt her again.
'Please let me have a knife to make it go away. Please, Mama, please come. I beg you. Please come now to take me to be an angel in Heaven, before it comes to hurt me again. Please let me be with you and Papa, and please let me be with Baby Albert.'
The worst memory of all came to hurt her.

"They go in a bloody sight easier than they come out, don't they, my little hussy?"

Mrs Eire's face smirked across at her from between her white, naked knees.

"Still, that's what you get if you play them kind of games with gentlemen."

She held up a little vial of liquid next to her face and shook it gently. The clear liquid filled with a froth of bubbles.

"Your governess, Mary Lovell, sent this for you all those weeks ago when you first came to Brimston. It's called chloral hydrate and it's not long been discovered. Even the Harrogate hospitals don't know of it yet but it's wonderful for taking away pain.

Mary Lovell said it might make it easier for you with it being your first and all. Of course I don't agree with giving it to you, not quite yet anyways. I believe that a mother should always experience every last particle of the blessing of childbirth; it's how God intended it. So I'll keep this for now if you please, and watch you count your blessings while you push the little bastard out. Then we'll see if it's a boy or a girl. Then we'll see if it's worth two hundred pounds or just an old newspaper. Then, maybe, we'll see if you can keep it."

And then, just an instant later, she could see it. It was a baby, a tiny, precious baby, streaked and smeared in blood, but beautiful and perfect in every way. She sobbed with joy and relief and reached out with her hands to take it, to give it a mother's love.

"It's a boy."

Mrs Eire jerked it out of her reach.

"You've had a boy, you stupid little witch. If it had been a girl, I'd have got nearly three shillings a week to raise it until it was old enough for the Friday Club, or until we could have sold it on. As it is, your uncle will just have the expense of paying for a baby farmer to take it away with nothing in return. That's a pretty way for you to repay his kindnesses to you, I must say."

"No, Missus, please no. Please let me keep him. I'll bring him up myself. I'll call him Albert after my dear papa. Uncle Alfie won't mind a bit; truly he won't. Or I can live here, at Brimston, with the other fallen women and bring him up here. The fallen women will help me. They won't mind either; I'm sure they won't mind at all."

The shadow of a terrible, terrible smile flitted across Mrs Eire's face.

"A boy is neither of use nor ornament to anyone here. Mr James is the only one interested in boys, and your uncle lets him use your cousin or gets

him other boys, already grown for him. Anyways, there are always plenty of boys going a-begging in the workhouses. No, little Miss Two Hundred Pounds, Mr Alfred wants you back in the Annexe and entertaining his friends. Little Albert here is going to the baby farmers. It's all settled."

She stepped forward and her bony fingers closed over Elizabeth's face, pressing it down, pushing her head back hard into the thin flock mattress. They forced their way between her lips, between her teeth, filling her mouth, choking her. She could feel liquid trickling into her mouth, down her tongue, into her throat, and she tasted the bitter, oily tang of her medicine. The room started to blur and spin and she watched, helpless, as Mrs Eire drifted through the door and away with her tiny, perfect baby. Her baby, Baby Albert, was being taken away from her, and her leaden limbs refused to heed the shrieking, shrieking screams of her brain.

And the worst memory of all refused to hear her brain as it shrieked and screamed and writhed again. The worst memory of all refused to be merciful to a little girl whose mama had gone away. It refused to go back to its hiding place to fester again, deep in that farthest, most remote part of her mind she kept especially for it and for its foul and stinking kin. The worst memory of all stayed until it had hurt her the most.

"Lizzie, dear Lizzie, I have some awful, awful news for you."

Mary's face was stricken, as white as the marble cherubs as she knelt before her.

"I don't know how to tell you this, Lizzie, but little Baby Albert... little Baby Albert has died. He lived only a few weeks with Mrs Eire's friend, and now Jesus has taken him to be with your mama and papa in Heaven. He's an angel now; a little cherub for Jesus."

Time stopped, as time always seemed to stop at this moment in her Purgatory.

"Died – little Albert has died? No – he can't have, Mary; he can't be dead. He's perfect. He's my perfect little baby; he's my precious."

"Oh, dear Lizzie, he is truly dead, but I'm sure that he never suffered. Think how he's safe now. He doesn't have to be hurt and punished; he doesn't have to have his mama die, or his papa. He's safe now and he's happy; he's with Jesus and his grandmama, resting on a fluffy white cloud in Heaven."

"But Mary, he never even got to know his mama. How can he be happy? I never got to hug him and kiss him and sing lullabies to him. I never got to love him. And now I never will."

"There's no use in crying now, Wilson."

The constable's expression was stern, but not unkind, as he sat next to her, swaying slightly with the movement of the wagon.

"What's done is done; it can't be undone, and now you've got to face the beak for it. I'll speak plain: I expect you to be hanged, but they say it doesn't hurt at all; just one drop and it's all over. Here, let me wipe your tears away with your sleeve."

He reached over and pulled at the loose fabric hanging from the bones of her wrist.

"Come now, Wilson, stop resisting me, I'm not going to hurt you. And stop staring so, it's very off putting. Oh, and that's just fine; now you've gone and pissed yourself. You silly old witch! You can bloody well clean that up yourself before we get to the station."

As she cowered in terror, Lizzie's huge, round eyes darted over his police uniform as if she was noticing it for the very first time and there was another sudden, loud spattering on the wooden planks of the wagon floor.

"Miss Lizzie, you must go and stay in your room. Mr Roberts only wants me to fetch Master John."

Mr Petty, the handsome young footman smiled fondly down at them both as they played on the floor rug of John's bedroom.

"Is it to go with Mr James?" John asked.

His sudden look of terror was an almost comical contrast to the grin on the face of the jack-in-the-box clown that he held on his lap.

"Mr James? Upon my word no... Why would Mr James want to see you? I hope you haven't been a-stealing from his cherry trees? No, it's a policeman – the paid policeman – who's come, and he wishes to speak with you directly, in the library. Your father says you must take care to remember everything he told you."

And then, after they had exchanged shocked and frightened glances, and once an ashen-faced John had disappeared through the door to the main house with Mr Petty, she jumped up and ran through the Annexe's smoking room to the stairwell beyond. Round and round, down and down the spiral stairs she ran, as fast as her legs and the hurt deep in her belly would let her. She heaved open the heavy door at the bottom and ran out into the sunshine.

Holding her breath, shielding her face, she skirted past the statue, the terrifying statue of Freya, whose blank eyes seemed to be following her even in her dreams, and ran, stooping, to the big hydrangea bushes under the library window. There, she crouched down and picked her way slowly and carefully under their branches, careful not to disturb the large pink blooms at their ends that would sway and tell tales and signal her presence through the library window.

Lifting her head tentatively above the mossy stone of the sill, she peeped through the little glass panes into the room beyond. The sound of her heart thumping in her ears almost drowned out the muffled voices within as they carried faintly through the glass. There was Uncle Alfie, and there was John, sitting stiffly by him on a settee, his face red and flushed. Seated directly across from them was a policeman, a real policeman, in uniform and everything, cradling his tall top hat on his knees.

Lizzie stilled her breath and listened. A deep, gruff voice she didn't recognise was speaking. It was the constable.

"So you can vouch for the fact that young Peter Lovegood never arrived that day and that he never accompanied your father and his acquaintances to Northumberland?"

There was a few seconds of silence and then John, his voice sounding high-pitched and strange even through the glass said, "Yes, sir."

"It's just that the Matron of the workhouse told us that she packed him off early that morning in the belief that he was coming directly here, to this house, in order to meet you, Mr Roberts. She understood you were to catch the early morning train north to Newcastle, and that Peter was to become an apprentice gamekeeper at your hunting lodge. Very excited about it all too he was by all accounts."

"Then all of those accounts are quite incorrect, Constable." Alfred Roberts' voice was a low growl, bristling with menace. "You have heard my testimony and now you have heard my son's. They agree on every point. The boy never arrived here and we went without him. It is quite as simple as that."

"I beg your pardon, Mr Roberts; I mean you no offence of course. It's just that a young boy in the care and keeping of the parish overseers has gone missing and his dead body was found floating off the Northumberland coast by a herring fisherman. He pulled it out of the water just south of the Holy Island and I'm being hard pushed to find out exactly what happened to him."

"How do you know that it was the same boy? There must be tens of thousands of young boys between here and the Holy Island."

"No doubt there are, sir, but you see Mrs Dixon, the Matron of the workhouse, was worried that little Peter might not be able to find his way all the way to your house. So she tied a label with his name and the workhouse address on it around his neck. It was still just about legible when he was fished out of the sea."

'Oh, Lord Jesus, please don't let little Peter Lovegood be dead after all!'

Lizzie slid down the wall until she was sitting on the damp, cool earth under the window. Her mind was a maelstrom of confusion.

But he did go with us that day, he did. He did catch the early-morning train with us to Newcastle.

Uncle Alfie and John were telling lies to the policeman. But should she go in and tell him the truth? A sudden vision of Uncle Alfie's ravenous eyes staring at her as he punished her as hard and as cruelly as he was able swelled into her consciousness.

No, she dare not. Perhaps it was a different Peter Lovegood the policeman was talking about? Yes, that must be it. Uncle Alfie was right; there had to be lots of little boys called Peter Lovegood between Harrogate and the Holy Island, because no one was allowed to tell lies to a policeman. That would be wicked. Yes, it must have been a different little boy called Peter Lovegood.

But the address! Oh, my dear Lord Jesus, the policeman had said there was an address.

Another image replaced that of Uncle Alfie in her mind. It was of Uncle Alfie's gentleman friend Mr James punishing her cousin John. She had seen him once, as she had staggered, bruised and bleeding, into her bedroom after she had been a very, very wicked little girl indeed. It had taken her uncle and four of his friends from the Friday Club to punish her that week, one after the other. Mr James had screamed for her to get out but it was too late; the image was burned forever into her memory. She had seen what he had been doing to John as he lay, face down on her bed, trembling and softly whimpering. It seemed abominable, but it answered all at once a question that had been niggling at her thoughts ever since she had known she was so wicked: How could boys be punished as she was, and as all the other little girls Mr Otter kept in the big room downstairs were punished? She had assumed, correctly it seemed, that boys were the same as her uncle and the other gentlemen without their trousers on, and now that she knew, she realised just how wicked little boys could be.

But if John could be so wicked, he might be telling lies now after all. There had been an address tied around the boy's neck. So it might just have been the same little Peter Lovegood – the boy who had gone with them that day across the sands but had never returned. And if John was telling lies to the policeman, Uncle Alfie must be telling lies to the policeman too. What if Uncle Alfie was wicked? The vision of Mr James, naked from the waist down rushed back into her mind but this time, instead of a naked, whimpering cousin John lying face down on her bed, there, in his stead, fat and as white as cook's fresh bread dough, was Uncle Alfie.

She shuddered and the image dissolved and was replaced by yet another. But this one was a real memory and so she shuddered again. This was one of those awful, awful memories she tried to keep hidden so far away, hidden in that most foul and secret part of her mind, and it had surely come to torment her.

A little boy of around ten years old was giggling and chattering incessantly in anticipation of the game of Viking Marauders he had been promised. He, along with John, Lizzie, and a pretty little, waif-and-stray girl called Sarah were to enjoy the game as part of a grand adventure at the seaside with her uncle and two of his gentlemen friends. They were even going to be allowed to stay up and play for most of the night before they moved on to Uncle Alfie's hunting lodge the following morning. And yes, she remembered now; the boy was going to be settled as a pauper apprentice to the gamekeeper.

Accordingly, they had travelled up to the county of Northumberland by express train and private coach, and then crossed on foot over to Lindisfarne, the Holy Island, along what her uncle had called the Pilgrim's Causeway.

The Pilgrim's Causeway, Uncle Alfie told them as they trudged out onto the broad, white sands and mud flats, was a path across the very bed of the sea itself. It was marked by a long line of ancient weather-beaten timbers driven deep into the sands, which had guided pilgrims to the Holy Island for centuries. The way, he said, was completely dry twice each day when the tide was low, but when the tide rushed back in, and it rushed back in faster than any child could run, it was quickly submerged under many, many feet of the cold, black waters of the North Sea.

Uncle Alfie had warned them that they must always be good little children; that they must take care to do everything, exactly as he said. Although the sands of the causeway looked pristine, he explained, even benign, and although they carried a saintly name, they concealed deadly channels and moving quicksands that could easily trap the unwary and the disobedient.

Dusk was just rolling in as they finally reached the sanctuary of the island. The great ruined castle of Bamburgh stood sentinel, stark and black against the crimson skies over the mainland just a few miles to the south. Below that, their own island was guarded by its smaller twin, a brutally rugged stone fortress crouched on a rocky mound. It was silhouetted against the lights and chimney smoke of a cluster of tiny fishing cottages. John had told her that his father owned one of the cottages there that he occasionally used during his visits to the island.

But Uncle Alfie hadn't taken them to the village. Instead he had quickly shepherded them the other way, out towards to the empty, desolate horizon to the north. That was where, he said, the very best adventures of all were to be had.

Peter, the little boy, had come from the workhouse at Starbeck. He had never seen the sea outside of a picture book before, and he was utterly mesmerised by the sight and the sound of the surf gently clawing at the sand and pebbles of the shore. He was enchanted as they followed it round, bustled along by Uncle Alfie, Mr James and Mr Price in a great, wide circle, to the far side of the island where there were no houses, to a tiny secluded inlet, nestled deep among the dark, whinstone rocks.

Uncle Alfie rested a large carpet bag he had brought with him on the top of one of these rocks and lifted out four neatly folded rolls of clothing.

"Come here, children," he said, "I've brought some dressing up clothes for our game. Put them on and then you can play awhile on the beach until we come back for you and begin our game in earnest."

She remembered the catch in his voice as he spoke – that horrible catch that always meant that she had been a wicked little girl and that she needed to be punished. She remembered the chilling smile he exchanged with Mr James and Mr Price; a hollow smile, that never quite reached his eyes. But no, surely she must have been mistaken. He must be breathless from their walk; that was it. Didn't he tell them, didn't he promise them, that this was going to be a game?

"We are going to re-enact the very first Viking raid on British soil," Uncle Alfie continued, "Which took place on this very island – the Holy Island of Lindisfarne – in the year of our Lord, Seven Hundred and Ninety Three. You four children are to be the Anglo-Saxon nuns and monks of the monastery here, and Mr James, Mr Price and I are going to be the Viking invaders."

So, giggling with excitement and anticipation, they ran to the rock to take their very own bundle of dressing up clothes from Uncle Alfie's trembling hands.

69

"Lizzie and I are dressing up as nuns," Sarah called excitedly across to the other side of the inlet to where the boys were changing *"What are you?"*

"We are monks," John shouted back. *"I think that when the Vikings attacked, they generally raided the monasteries first because they knew that they would find lots of gold and silver and other treasure stored there."*

"We had better keep a sharp lookout for them in that case."

Lizzie was excited, happy almost, for the first time since her mama had died, and since Baby Albert was born and then had had to go and be an angel for Jesus. Instinctively, she reached for the tiny silver cross hanging from its fine chain around her neck. Her papa had given it to her when she was born, and she pressed the warm metal to her lips. It tasted of salt.

"Please watch over us, Lord Jesus," she whispered, *"Especially here on your holy island, and please watch over the immortal souls of Mama and Papa and dear little Baby Albert."*

An image of a baby, a perfect, tiny baby seared a burning trail through her mind like the fiery path of a sky dragon.

"They're coming; the Vikings are coming," came a breathless cry from the darkness, *"A furore normannorum libera nos domine."*

"What did you say?" Sarah shouted back.

"It's a prayer the Anglo-Saxon monks used to say," John replied earnestly. *"It's Latin and it means: 'From the fury of the Northmen deliver us, O Lord!'"*

She wiped her eyes and smiled through the tears of the worst memory of all. Trust John to know all of that. Then she looked out across the sea and saw that John was right. Beyond the blackness of the rocks, beyond the lapping waves, there was a shape, darker than the night around it, and the gentle splash of what might have been oars.

Then she heard her uncle's voice over the whisper of the sea, strident and clear in the still night air: *"From the fury of the Northmen, God deliver you!"*

Even though he had said, even though he had promised it was just a game, and in spite of the muggy warmth of the Northumbrian evening, Lizzie shivered.

Then the boat was there, caught on the sand in a slough. The men, great, horned helmets on their heads and black cloaks billowing behind them jumped heavily onto the beach, scattering sand and pebbles as they began to run.

Sarah squealed, her cry a cry of excitement and delight.

"Nuns, virgins, monks, there on the beach!" bellowed Uncle Alfie. *"There's enough for every man. In Freya's holy name, capture them!"*

There was the sound of fast-crunching pebbles and as if in slow motion, Uncle Alfie and Mr Price pounded towards them. Their faces under their helmets were lit by the moon and twisted grotesquely into vicious masks of cruelty and lust. Lizzie knew that expression well and her legs turned to lead.

"Run, Sarah," she hissed, "Run as fast as you can. They want to hurt us; they want to really hurt us. It isn't a game."

Sarah screamed.

And then in their fury, they were on them. Mr Price ran bodily into her and bore her brutally to the ground. Pebbles pressed viciously into her back as she fought to push his suffocating, crushing weight off her. She felt his sharp teeth biting into her neck like needles, felt his hands pulling at her, pawing her. This was no game. He was too big, too strong. Mr Price was going to punish her. He was going to hurt her, here, now, on this beach, in front of Sarah, in front of her mama looking down from Heaven.

Sarah screamed. But, oh, thank you, Lord Jesus, it was a scream of terror and not of pain. Lizzie opened her eyes. Across the sand, she saw Uncle Alfie pinning the little girl to the beach. Both of her tiny hands were gripped in one of his impossibly large ones and his other hand was clutching her face. His mouth was inches from hers, framing the words, those words, the words she feared above all others: "In my experience, little girls who beg for mercy..."

"Stop there! Come back here, you little bugger."

It was the disembodied cry of Mr James coming from everywhere in the blackness.

"Roberts, Price, help me here, the little beggar's getting away!"

And then the great weight was off her and instead there was only a light, warm breeze playing around her naked thighs as she lay, panting in shock. She dared to open her eyes, dared to look up.

'Oh, thank you, Lord Jesus, thank you, Mama, thank you, Papa.'

There were her Uncle Alfie and Mr Price running away across the inlet towards the direction of the cry.

Sarah was crying.

"I don't care for this game," she sobbed, "I hate the Holy Island and I hate Vikings."

They huddled together on the lonely beach for what seemed like hours in the blackness of the night, silent except for the comforting murmur of the waves as they stroked and calmed the beach, and the sobbing of little Sarah. John appeared by them and one look into his pained, stricken eyes told her that he too had been wicked, and that Mr James had been intent on cruelly punishing him.

Then, at last, a faint rhythmic crunching of the pebbles disturbed the hush of the waves. It grew louder and louder and louder and the three huddled close, bracing themselves against whatever horror the new sound might bring.

They heard Uncle Alfie's voice before they could see him, and it was angry.

"You three there, fetch your clothes and come with us. Quickly now, you need to help us find that infernal little wretch Lovegood. He's run away from Mr James and we have to find him before anyone else on this accursed island does."

Mr Price saw it first: a miniature monk's cassock lying by the side of the track, roughly turned inside-out as if it had been thrown off in haste. And then Mr James shouted, and they all looked and there, atop one of the grassy dunes, was the silhouette of what might have been a small boy. He was naked and his skin was ghostly white in the bright moonlight. At the sound of the cry, the boy turned and fled away towards the flat sands of the causeway. They could hear him splashing noisily in the shallow waters as he ran.

"No, come back here, Lovegood, damn you."

Uncle Alfie rushed forward, and there was panic in his eyes. But by the time they had crossed the marshy hollow in front of them and stumbled up the steep dune beyond, Peter Lovegood had gone, and all they could see in front of them were the empty, black waters of the North Sea slipping silently past.

"There can be no doubt he would have made it across the causeway to the mainland," Uncle Alfie had said again and again as they waited for the waters to recede. "The water is quite shallow at that point."

Mr James and Mr Price had agreed enthusiastically with him.

"But," Uncle Alfie had said as he looked murderously at each of the children in turn, "You must still take care to hold your tongues. I do not want one, single word of this night's work breathed to anyone. Do you hear me? If you do, I swear I will have Mr Otter strip and flay you all alive. Then he will fetch you back here and he will throw each and every one of you, bound and gagged, into the North Sea for the fish and for the sea monsters to eat."

Sarah had screamed at that. On the long coach journey up the spectacular Northumberland coast, John had scared them all with tales of the Shoney, a fearsome sea dragon that inhabited those very waters. They had chattered and laughed about it then, and about the great game they were to play. But now, as they made their return in the very same coach, as they stole glances across the very same seas that sparkled now with silver and blue, they were all silent as the grave.

And then she was back in Master John's bedroom, the one adjoining her own, peering into the gloom under his bed. She knew he would be there, safe and cocooned in his own safe and special place.

"You told lies to the policeman, John."

She remembered hearing the tone of accusation in her voice.

A stark, white face turned towards her.

"Shut up and go away, Lizzie."

"Will you tell that to the Angel of Death when he comes to take you down to Hell? Will you tell him to shut up and go away, John?"

"Shut up; please, Lizzie, just shut up."

"The Devil punishes you for all eternity in Hell — in the Inferno. I don't want you to be punished, John."

She paused.

"Mr James is like the devil. He punishes you. I've seen him do it."

Even in the gloom of his safe and special place, Lizzie could see the colour flushing into John's face.

"He's punished me like that too," she admitted, feeling the colour tingling in her own cheeks. "It hurts ever so much."

"What, he's sodomised you too, Lizzie?"

John sounded incredulous.

"I didn't know that was what it was called, but yes, he's punished me like that, like he does to you. He's sodomised me and so has Uncle Alfie and so have some gentleman at Brimston."

"It's called sodomy because that's what the people used to do to each other in Sodom and Gomorrah. Those were cities in the Bible before God destroyed them and turned the people into pillars of salt. Its other name is buggery and it's against the law."

It wasn't until several days later that it struck her as being very odd: If God had turned the people of Sodom and Gomorrah into pillars of salt for being wicked, how could her uncle, in doing to her exactly what they did to each other — sodomising her — help her to be a good little girl? Perhaps, she thought, she needed to pay much more attention at Sunday school.

CHAPTER 13

"I've got Inspector Douglas' prisoner for you, Sergeant; the murderess from Sessrum House. She's an old girl, not what I expected at all. Her name is Elizabeth Beatrice Wilson."

The constable pulled a trembling Elizabeth alongside him and turned her to face the front desk at Harrogate Police Station.

"She doesn't look capable of murdering a currant bun," the desk-sergeant observed, laying a thick sheaf of papers onto the blotting pad in front of him.

"Maybe not, but she did for old Alfred Roberts at his house last night – brutally too, judging by the state that his body was in. And she killed him in her bedroom."

The constable gave a significant nod and tapped the side of his nose.

"She's a queer one, though; she pissed all over the floor of the wagon on the way here and refuses to clear it up. She doesn't speak, she doesn't answer me, she doesn't do anything except for to stare like that and hum that bloody nursery song 'Hush-a-Bye, Baby' over and over again. I swear, if she doesn't stop, I'll throttle her myself."

"Is she mad or an imbecile or something do you know?"

"She's reckoned to be an imbecile. Detective Sergeant Hainsworth told me that the man who owns the house – Alfred Roberts' grandson – is a doctor, and both he and two nurses there said that her mind was quite gone. I'm not so sure though… She seemed to understand a lot of what I was saying on the journey here."

The desk-sergeant shook his head in despairing outrage.

"Why don't they lock 'em up in proper asylums where they belong? But no, they insist on letting them go and live with their families and then what happens? They do someone a mischief. Then it's up to the likes of you and me to go and sort out the mess and lock them up here."

He sighed.

"What possessions has she got then, Constable?"

She watched his hand lift and reach out towards her. It was overpowering, unstoppable. She wanted to beg him for mercy, to beg him not to do it, not to touch her, not to hurt her, but the words she needed to say choked in her throat. She tried to turn; she wanted so much to push him away, but her leaden limbs refused to heed the shrieking, shrieking screams of her brain. Then his hand slipped into the folds of her dress, and she felt his fingers stretching, uncurling and reaching out for her.

The constable pulled his hand out from the pocket of Elizabeth's gown and held out an ancient looking matchbox, and a delicate silver chain with a tiny crucifix swinging from it.

"She has one child's silver necklace with a cross, and an old matchbox with... urgh, a dead moth and an old, shrivelled-up flower head in it."

He leaned over the desk and dropped the matchbox neatly into a waste paper basket.

"Well, one child's necklace, anyway."

The sergeant dutifully wrote it down.

"You'd better take her down to the cells, Constable, and be careful of her. You might want to put her in restraints as well, just to be safe. She's killed once and there's no telling what she might do next."

CHAPTER 14

"Please forgive me for deserting you like this."

Michael Roberts grimaced apologetically as he plucked an invisible speck of dust from the silk brim of his top hat and batted it away.

"But I really must go and see the magistrate as soon as I can. Aunt Elizabeth isn't strong enough to be held for any length of time in a police gaol, never mind stand trial for murder, and the longer it is before she's released into my custody, the more damage that will surely be done to her mind."

"Do you really think you can prevent her from being tried?" Lucie asked dubiously.

Roberts minutely adjusted the tilt of his hat in the large hallway mirror and squared his shoulders.

"If there's any justice in this world," he said to his reflection, "And if the McNaughton rules mean anything at all, then yes, my aunt will certainly not stand trial."

"But then if they don't try her, they'll surely just have her committed to a lunatic asylum?" Lucie persisted. "She has killed a man, after all."

Roberts turned from the mirror and looked squarely at her.

"You've seen the Annexe yourself, Mrs Fox. It's perfectly secure and all the facilities of an asylum are there, even so far as the presence of a doctor and a nurse. There would be no benefit, no benefit whatsoever, in committing her anywhere else."

CHAPTER 15

"Here you are, Wilson."

The constable stopped part-way along the cramped, narrow corridor and pushed open one of the heavy, black doors that repeated themselves endlessly along its starkly whitewashed length.

"Welcome to your new lodgings. Not as fine as you're used to I dare say, but cosy enough all the same."

He pushed her roughly into the cell and pressed her down onto a low brick bench that was covered by only the thinnest of straw mattresses. As she sat, a little cloud of dust blew up through the coarse hessian of the mattress cover and hung, twisting and turning, in the latticed stream of sunlight pouring in through a tiny grilled window.

"You heard the sergeant; I'm to put these restraints on you. There's no telling what a lunatic like you might do."

A heavy chain dangled from an iron ring set into the bricks above the bed. It was drawn tight by thick, iron manacles lying open and ready at each of its ends. The constable lifted each of Elizabeth's unresisting arms in turn and clamped the cold metal shut over her skeletal wrists.

"There, you're safe now."

He hooked a rusting metal pail from under the bench with the toe of his boot and bent down close to her face.

"If you need a piss, Wilson, be a good girl and piss in there will you, and not all over your mattress?"

She felt the cold metal snap shut against her wrists, felt the chain pull her arms hard against the heavy timber of the rack as it was rattled tight. She was pinned fast, she couldn't move, and a suddenly overwhelming, claustrophobic panic made her thrash and writhe to be free.

A pair of bony fingers caught her chin and held it fast.

"That's it, Lizzie; that's how they'll like it. They'll be queuing up to take their turn at you if you go on like that. I reckon you'll be a proper buttered bun by the time the day's through."

The fingers squeezed her face viciously and the long nails bit into her skin.

"If you're going to be here at Brimston for your confinement, my pretty, we might as well make an extra pound or two out of you while we're at it."

She laughed, a cold, humourless laugh.

"Two-hundred pounds to buy, but only two pounds a night by the hire."

The fingers were gone from her face but then she gasped in pain as she felt them clawing into the soft flesh of her naked breast.

"Five pounds when they can suckle some milk out of these."

She was at Brimston; Mrs Eire's 'Home for Fallen Women and Girls' nestled deep in the beautiful, rolling hills outside Harrogate. It was far enough away to prevent the good and upright ladies of the town from being corrupted by the moral diseases and easy virtue of the unfortunate inmates, but close enough to be a convenient journey for any of their men-folk who wished to visit, and perhaps to confirm for themselves just how easy that virtue was.

She remembered her first sight of the pretty, little farmhouse with the chickens scratching in the dust of the yard outside. She recalled the little stream tinkling past, sparkling in the sunlight, and she remembered her unbounded joy as she saw the two tiny girls playing contentedly by the road outside.

Sobbing, she had laid her hand on her own tiny bump and imagined the baby growing inside her and being born and playing alongside them in the fresh, vital air of the Yorkshire Dales. She remembered clearly that for the first time since her mama had gone away – and pray God that she had gone to Heaven – she no longer wanted to die.

Lizzie often recalled the other women and girls who lived at the farmhouse at Brimston. They had all either fallen, or perhaps been pushed, from the path of moral virtue. Whenever she remembered them, she always remembered her astonishment as she slowly came to realise that they weren't nearly as bad as everyone reckoned they surely were. They weren't the very wives and daughters of Lucifer at all. Most were just like her; girls who had been unfortunate or perhaps unknowingly wicked, and she swore that they didn't deserve punishment at all.

There seemed to be no end to the gentlemen who would come over to Brimston to be 'accommodated' as Mrs Eire called it. They would arrive *at all hours of the day or night, sometimes alone and sometimes in raucous, jeering groups. Always, they would choose one, two or even three of the fallen women or girls, and take them for a while into one of the many little rooms of the labyrinthine farmhouse.*

There was also a room in the barn. It was a big, special room Mrs Eire called the Dungeon, where she kept lots of curious contraptions. The other fallen women and girls talked about the Dungeon sometimes. They hated going in there. Often, when they came out, they would be crying. Sometimes their wrists and ankles would be ringed with angry, red marks that would turn into great purple and yellow bruises. Sometimes they would have bloody cuts and lashes across their back or their legs. She thought they must have been especially wicked if the men had to come all the way up from Harrogate or across from the great cities of Leeds or Bradford to punish them as thoroughly as that.

Mrs Eire herself sometimes punished grown men who had been wicked. Lizzie had not known for sure that grown men could be punished until she heard Mrs Eire telling a gentleman how naughty he had been and how she was going to have to whip him for it. She had taken him alone into the Dungeon for most of the day and when he came out, he was flushed and limping badly. He gave Mrs Eire ten guineas for her help in correcting him with a promise that he would make it twenty next time if she succeeded in rendering him insensible. Lizzie wondered for a moment if Uncle Alfie or Mr James or even Mr Price had ever been rendered insensible.

Mrs Eire told her that she didn't generally believe in medicine for wicked girls. She said it was an unnecessary expense for all but the very frailest gentlemen. Lizzie didn't really need it now anyway. She had found a way of making it seem that what the gentlemen were doing to her was really happening to a different little girl.

When she was taken to one of the rooms of the farmhouse, she could think about playing games with John or doing her lessons with Mary or about going to the churchyard to talk to her dead mama and papa in their grave. She could pray to the Lord Jesus and ask him to let her die and be an angel in Heaven. Then the baby growing inside her belly could die too and be a cherub with them all – with her and with Jesus and with her dear mama and papa. It would save it from being born. Otherwise, the baby in her belly might grow to be wicked, just like her and just like her own mama. Then, like her, it might have to be punished too. But then she worried that if she died now, whilst she was still so wicked and sinful, she might not go to be in Heaven at all. She worried that St Peter might know how bad she really was and that he might send her to Hell to be punished by the Devil and his demons for all eternity.

Uncle Alfie had told her that there was a special place in Hell for seductresses like her. It was called the Eighth Circle and he had shown her it in a poem written by a great Italian scholar called Dante. If she went to the Eighth Circle of Hell, of Dante's Inferno, perhaps her baby might have to go there too. And then, instead of becoming a cherub for Jesus, her baby might become a demon for Lucifer.

But Lizzie worried most of all that her uncle might have been right about her mama; that she might really be in the Eighth Circle of Inferno being whipped by demons and not with the Lord Jesus and her papa at all. Sometimes horrible, horrible pictures of her mama being punished by Uncle Alfie and the gentlemen of the Friday Club would come into her mind. Sometimes she even imagined Uncle Alfie and his gentlemen friends as Lucifer and his demons. She knew Lucifer could change himself into an angel of light. But then, when she imagined that her uncle might be the very Devil himself, she knew just how wicked and ungrateful a wretch she must really be.

Usually, when she made it seem as if the gentlemen were doing things to punish a different little girl, it was easier. The gentlemen that Mrs Eire brought to the Home for Fallen Women and Girls didn't always seem to want to punish her so mercilessly as her Uncle Alfie and his gentlemen friends did. When the gentlemen didn't want to punish her mercilessly, and when they didn't talk so and make a fuss and stop her from going to the special, safe place in her mind, and except from the awful way she felt afterward, it was almost bearable.

But now she was in the big room in the barn with the cold metal shut over her wrists, and her arms pulled tight against the heavy, wooden rack. It was her first time. Mrs Eire had always said that she was excused duties in the Dungeon on account of her uncle not wanting her to be too badly marked. But Mrs Eire had said that today was a day when needs must, and that she had taken the precaution of asking the gentleman to be circumspect with her.

She was pinned fast to the rack, but she could still move her head. She tried again to go to the special place in her mind where she could make it seem as if it was all happening to a different little girl. But again, she couldn't.

She definitely could not. Each time she tried, she remembered how the girls always cried so much when they came out, and she remembered their marks and their cuts and their lashes, and each time she tried, her panic would rise up and spoil it and drag her back to the here and to the now.

There were two other girls with her here and now, in the big room in the barn. One was strapped to a rack just like hers, but face down, so that she could only see the milk white skin of her back with its faint, pink stripes and her smooth, round buttocks. The other girl she knew was little Sarah who didn't like Vikings, even though she couldn't quite see her. She knew it was Sarah by her gentle, despairing sobs.

And then the memory moved on and became a gentleman who had come up from Harrogate. He had especially picked them out to be punished in the Dungeon. She could hear him speaking to the girl with the milk-white skin and his voice was full of hate and relish. It had that awful catch in it that the gentlemen always had when they badly wanted to hurt someone.

All at once there was the sudden, flat crack of a lash and the shrieking, agonised scream of the girl. Lizzie started at the noise. She had let her eyes open by mistake and the image they let in flooded her mind with horror. The milk white skin of the girl's buttocks was flayed into a mess of bloody, red streaks and the gentleman was standing behind her, like a vengeful demon in her nightmare of the Eighth Circle of Dante. He was standing with a great, many-thonged whip in his hand, ready to strike once more.

Then she could hear little Sarah, who didn't like Vikings. Hers was a scream of terror, not of agony, and Lizzie felt a gush of relief for that. But then little Sarah was begging, begging for mercy; she was begging him not to make her do it. Her pleading was getting louder and louder and more desperate and then, it stopped, and there was silence. There was silence except for sounds that were muffled and gagging, as if little Sarah might be choking on something, and the sounds of the bestial grunts of the gentleman.

CHAPTER 16

"Who the bloody hell is Sarah?"

The sergeant was standing in the middle of Elizabeth's tiny cell looking down curiously at her as she hung in her chains like some broken and discarded marionette.

The constable's voice, harsh and echoing in the confined space, came from behind him.

"I haven't a bleedin' clue, Sergeant. She kept asking for someone called Albert on the way here, then Tom, and now it's Sarah. It's all part of a game to make us believe she's mad if you ask me. She's just practicing to pass the McNaughton rules and escape the gallows."

"Is that what you want, Wilson?"

The sergeant's voice was loud and stern and Elizabeth started at the sound of it.

"Who's Albert? Who's Tom? Or do you want Sarah? Who's Sarah? Who's Sarah, Wilson?"

Elizabeth gazed at him and the moisture welling in her eyes seemed to increase the intensity of her gaze. A tear tracked steadily down the line of a deep wrinkle on her face and spread across the corner of her lips.

"Albert Wilson, Sarah Wilson," she whispered, "Where is Sarah?"

"Her only living relative, now that she's killed her uncle that is, is Dr Roberts so far as I know," the constable said. "All the rest of her family are long since dead."

"They're all dead, Wilson."

The sergeant spoke again in his loud, stern voice and Elizabeth looked at him and nodded. More tears followed the track of the first and they dripped and melted into the fabric of her bodice as she began to rock steadily to-and-fro, her bony fingers whitening as they clung to the chains of her manacles.

"Then to the grave," Elizabeth said in a curious, high-pitched voice, almost as if she were singing the words and not speaking them at all.

"Dr Roberts has been to see the magistrate for you," the sergeant continued. "He wants you to go back to live at Sessrum House and not to go down for his granddaddy's murder. Do you hear what I say? He's trying to get you off. You might fool him, Wilson, head-doctor or not, but you ain't fooling McNaughton and you ain't fooling us. You might just be allowed to spend your last few days at home until your trial begins but after that, it certainly will be 'Then to the grave.'"

He made a silent chopping motion on the back of his neck with his hand and nodded theatrically to her before turning to the constable.

"He's welcome to take her 'til then, I say. Then she can piss on his mattresses instead of ours."

"We'll need to burn this one after she's gone."

The constable pulled at the loose sacking at the mattress corner and sniffed his fingers.

"It's piss-wet and it reeks. She's gone and messed herself too, by the stink of her."

He wrinkled his nose in disgust.

"I know; that's why I'll not be too worried if the superintendant lets her go back," the sergeant agreed, "At least until she goes in front of the assizes. She'll have good reason to mess herself then, when she follows this Sarah to the grave."

CHAPTER 17

Sarah, Sarah who hated the Holy Island.

She was back at Brimston, back at the Home for Fallen Women and Girls. The verdant sweep of the hills replaced the cell walls and Mrs Eire's stony face took the place of the sergeant's.

"Where's Sarah? Where's that little whore got to now? I asked you to fetch her directly, Wilson."

Lizzie curtsied clumsily.

"I beg your pardon, Mrs Eire, but Sarah is coming. She can't run fast on account of her just having been patched up again."

Lizzie could feel the warm sweat trickling down her back with the effort of running with the weight of the child inside her.

"Well I've a gentleman waiting for her in my parlour. He asked for a virgin girl on account of him wanting to cure his syphilis, and Sarah's the nearest I've got to one at the present."

The sweat lying on her back turned to ice.

"Please, Mrs Eire, Sarah is still very sore from being stitched back up. The gentleman can have me in her stead if he likes, just until Sarah is feeling better."

Mrs Eire's hard features twisted into an expression of utter contempt.

"You stupid, little brazen hussy; how would he believe you to be a virgin with that great lump in front of you and tits like pumpkins? I've told you he needs a virgin to cure his syphilis. You just want attentions from a gentleman like all you sluts. I believe you haven't even fetched Sarah at all, have you? You're hoping for him yourself."

"I have, Mrs Eire. I have fetched her, just as you asked. Honour-bright I have. Here she is now, but she's ever so sore from just being patched up. The gentleman will hurt her terribly."

"Well she'll have to bear it. It's supposed to hurt, especially when you're fresh. God made it that way in the Garden of Eden so women didn't become the little sluts that you all have. I'll have those stitches out while the gentleman

finishes his tea and muffins and he'll never know the difference, especially if it does truly hurt her and she doesn't need to play act."

And then she was in the workhouse at Starbeck, in the infirmary, with Mary Lovell the new nurse wrapping a freshly washed bandage around and around her arm. Her blood was soaking each layer the instant it touched the one below.

"You've such beautiful skin, Lizzie; why do you disfigure it so? It'll be a twelvemonth before these cuts turn into silver scars and you'll always be able to see them if you look, especially if the sun catches you."

"Miss Lovell, we've a syphilitic just come in. I don' think she's got very long an' t' receiving ward's full, so where should I put 'er?"

Elizabeth looked round at the sound of the words and gasped at the sight of the figure shuffling along painfully next to Old Rachel, the ancient pauper woman who helped Mary in the infirmary.

It was a young woman. Or at least it might once have been a young woman. Now it was part woman, part monster. On one side of its face a soft, brown eye gazed out from above a finely sculpted cheek. There was something disconcertingly familiar about it. But the rest of the face was gone, crusted over by thick red lesions that had coalesced into a single, hideous mask. It was just as if someone had plastered it in thick clay and left it to bake in the fires of Hell. Its hands were covered by the same red blisters and by the painful, aching way it moved, so were its legs and its feet.

"Lizzie, is that you?"

The creature's voice was no more than a muffled whisper, so weak was it and so encrusted its mouth.

"And Mary, Mary the Governess from the Annexe?"

Elizabeth stared, aghast. A crack had opened in the thick lesion by the side of the mouth slit and a thick line of blood inched its way steadily down the crusted surface and dripped onto its shabby coat.

"Sarah? Sarah, is that you?"

The creature nodded.

"Yes, it's me. Oh, Lizzie, what have they done to me? It hurts ever so much. Mary, dear Mary, please can you make it stop hurting? Please can I have just a little time of peace before I die?"

"Rachel, would you kindly take Miss Sarah to the bathhouse and help her to bathe her sores? Use warm water please and then get her changed into a clean uniform and into an infirmary bed for some rest. I'll attend to her presently."

Sister Lovell's eyes were full of anguish but her lips were pursed resolutely.

"Only God can help her now I think," she murmured to Elizabeth as she tied off her bandage. "Poor Sarah has suffered quite enough. You might like to say your goodbyes to her when she comes back, Lizzie. I fear that Old Rachel is right; Sarah has the next world beckoning for her and I pray that she'll find a little peace there at last."

"Should I fetch ye some quicksilver for 'er scabs, Sister Lovell?" Old Rachel called back across the infirmary as she led the shambling creature through the doors to the bathhouse.

"Yes please, Rachel, and some chloral hydrate too if you would. I shall need the large bottle today. She needs some relief."

A little time later, Old Rachel and Sarah returned. Sarah's hair had been cut off and she looked even less human, even more monstrous than before. Between them, they lifted her onto one of the low infirmary beds, although Elizabeth supposed she could have done it easily on her own, so light and frail was she. The warm water of the bath had softened some of the lesions and already the coarse fabric of the workhouse dress was spotted with patches of bright red blood.

Sister Lovell poured out a very large measure of clear chloral hydrate into a tumbler; the neck of the bottle tinkling against the rim of the glass as her hands trembled in their haste.

"Here, darling Sarah," she whispered, her voice warm yet strained, "This will help you."

Sarah seemed to recognise the bitter, oily taste of the medicine. She seemed to know that it would help to drive away the torments of the present, and the half of her face that was still untouched by the disease, that was still beautiful, smiled as her head sank back onto the mattress.

"I'll leave you with Lizzie for now, Sarah," said Mary. "Rachel, I don't think we'll need the quicksilver after all."

Old Rachel nodded and understood. She padded to the window and slowly and gently lifted the sash just a few inches.

"We don' want to be imprisoning any souls in t' place," she whispered to herself, "'Specially ones as I doubt will be a' peace."

She glanced across at Sarah and dropped the briefest of curtsies before following Mary wordlessly through the door.

When they were alone Sarah asked: "Did you have the other baby, Lizzie?" Her sweet, soft voice was beginning to slur.

Elizabeth nodded.

"Yes I did. It was a little girl. I named her for you, Sarah. I named her for you and for my dear mama; I called her Sarah Beatrice Wilson.

Sarah smiled again before the eyelid closed over her beautiful, soft, brown eye, and a kind of serenity spread across what was left of her face.

Elizabeth took Sarah's tiny fingers in her own and leaned forward across her chest until she could feel the coarse, grogram cloth of her dress pressing against her cheek. The faint murmur of Sarah's heart was beating slowly against her ear. She studied the ravaged face and bitter tears welled up for her childhood friend: Little Sarah, who had been sold by her mother for a gallon of gin; Sarah who had been condemned to a short, brutal life of accommodating the gentlemen of Harrogate, and Sarah who now lay in a workhouse infirmary, dying of syphilis.

Elizabeth watched as Sarah's head gently nodded with each tired beat of her heart. The lid of the eye that was still soft drifted open just a little and Lizzie was sure that the gaze of the beautiful crescent of brown had settled on her in return. Sarah was going to die. Please God that her torment would soon be over and she could find solace at last.

The mouth-slit parted slightly and each frightened breath became a rattling, gasping plea to stay in this world rather than the next.

"Don't be afraid, Sarah," Lizzie whispered. "You're tired. It's time to go to Heaven now. You're allowed to die. Nothing will hurt anymore and you can be at peace."

The brown crescent gazed at her in silent assent and a blotch, a single yellow-grey blotch formed on the point of the high, sculpted cheekbone. It was the merciful harbinger of death, and it began to spread relentlessly and unstoppably across the skin of Sarah's face.

And then, as she lay, the nods slowly faded, the gasping breaths grew fainter and at last, the heart beneath the breasts stopped beating. Little Sarah died.

And then the memory moved on again and her bitter sadness became a bitter, bitter rage.

"I don't care if they do find out where I am; my uncle or Mrs Eire can pay for her funeral. It's all their doing and the least they can do to make amends for their wickedness is to give poor Sarah a proper burial. She was only here for a few hours. Why should she be condemned to a paupers' grave?"

"Lizzie, Lizzie," Mary crooned, "There will be no funeral and no grave for Sarah, pauper's or otherwise. The Master has already sold her corpse to

a hospital in Harrogate. They're going to use it to conduct experiments into the treatment of syphilis."

She pulled a stunned Elizabeth into a tight embrace.

"I know, Lizzie, I know, it doesn't seem right. But we have no idea who her relatives are, or even if she still has any, so it's the Master's right to sell her. The workhouse gets five pounds for her body and you never know; Sarah's death might just help other girls to avoid the awful suffering that she has had to endure."

Elizabeth clung to her and sobbed and sobbed and sobbed. Then, when she could cry no longer, she stood back and smoothed the tears from her cheeks.

"At least they've sold her body for the last time, Mary," she said. "They can't do a single thing more to hurt her and I'll never forget her. She lives on in my daughter. As long as I have Sarah Beatrice, I'll always remember her."

CHAPTER 18

And then the other, terrible memory trembled in its secret place, deep in her mind. This was an open, raw memory, one she could never fully quieten and never properly hide. It was surely coming and when it did, it would harrow and it would claw, deep into her very soul itself. Her hands were held fast by cold metal bands and here, in this place, in the still and the quiet, where there was no busy, there would be nothing to keep it away. She rocked and she rocked and she tried to sing the lullaby; she tried desperately to sing it away to sleep but the other terrible memory awakened, it trembled and it came.

She was held tight in Mary's arms, in her bedroom in the Annexe.

"Are you certain, Lizzie? It seems so soon after Baby Albert for it to have happened again."

She nodded against Mary's bodice. It was safe and warm, just like her mama's had been.

"I've missed my curse four months in a row now and I'm sure I can feel a little bump Mary."

She felt Mary's hand move from her shoulder and push between them, felt her fingers gently probe her stomach.

"Your uncle will want you to go to Brimston again, before you start to show properly."

"Oh, Mary, I couldn't bear that, not with Mrs Eire and the Dungeon and all those gentlemen she brings up from Harrogate and not after... after what happened to Baby Albert."

The warm, safe arms tightened around her once more.

"But what alternative is there, Lizzie? Only for you to find some other institution for fallen women and hope that they are kinder there than at Brimston. Or you could live on the streets. But then you'd likely have to whore yourself out to get money and you'd be worse off than now."

"Or there's the workhouse, Mary."

"Go to the poor-law? Oh, Lizzie, surely you're not thinking of that."

"But why can't I? I've been thinking about it for weeks now. I could easily run away to the workhouse. It's not far to go, only down the road at Starbeck, and I could have my baby there. They have an infirmary and nurses, and I would be safe. I've seen the workhouse paupers working on the Stray. They seemed happy enough and I can't see why my baby and I couldn't be too.

Mary, I've been thinking about you too and about when I'm gone. I'm certain you would be fine; you're clever and you're pretty, and you could easily get another situation as a governess or find a nice, kind gentleman and get married. Uncle Alfie might even want you to stay here, to help look after the waifs-and-strays. You can protect them from Mr Otter."

"What your Uncle Alfie might want is just what I'm afraid of, Lizzie."

She felt Mary's arms squeeze her until she thought she might suffocate with kindness.

Was it really just the very next day? All she could remember was the sense of release; the wonderful, mounting feeling of exhilaration spreading through her body as she crept across the lawn, wet with early morning dew. She had the tiny silver cross that her papa had given her after she was born held lightly between her lips, because if ever she needed the Lord Jesus to guide and smooth her way, it was now. And then, with her heart pounding in her breast, she had flitted between the big iron gates at the end of the drive.

And then she was out... Out onto the wide, open freedom of the Stray. It had never seemed so vast. She and her baby were free. Even if Uncle Alfie or Mr Otter saw her now, she could run. She could run and she could scream. They would never catch her, not if they chased her all the way to Hell and back.

She was free and she had a plan. First she would go to visit her mama and papa in their grave. She would tell them what she must do for the sake of her own baby. They wouldn't mind that she had a baby growing inside her, she was sure of that. Accidents happen and her mama never scolded her for accidents; she only asked that she be more careful next time. Her mama only ever scolded her for being bad. But Baby Albert had been an accident – a terrible, terrible accident, and now she was being as careful as her mama could ever wish.

After she had explained it all to her mama, she would find the main road to Starbeck, to the workhouse, to the sanctuary where she and her baby could be safe at last. Safe from Uncle Alfie, safe from Mrs Eire, and safe from all of their gentleman friends.

'In Loving Memory of Albert Charles Wilson, who died 16th October 1830.

Also, of Beatrice Charlotte Wilson, his beloved and devoted wife who followed him in death, 28th May 1843.

And God shall wipe away all tears from their eyes and there shall be no more death neither sorrow nor crying neither shall there be any more pain, for the former things are passed away.'

Her fingertips slowly traced every line of the black, enamelled letters carved deep into the cold marble face of the gravestone. They were St John's words, she knew, from the Book of Revelation. She read and clung to them every single day in her own pocket Bible. How she wished that could be so for her and for her baby too: No more sorrow, no more tears, no more crying... no more pain.

Then she traced other letters with her fingertip, imaginary ones at the bottom of the epitaph but carved no less deeply: 'Also in Loving Memory of Elizabeth Beatrice Wilson and of her perfect, unborn baby who died this day.'

"Amen," she said aloud, "So be it."

But then she crossed her fingers because she remembered all at once that she was still a wicked, wicked harlot. She remembered that St John had written those words for the righteous and for the faithful, that he had written them for good little girls who weren't pitiful sluts like her.

Elizabeth reached out and embraced the slab as if it were real, vital flesh and blood, instead of cold, hard marble, and wept.

She seemed to have been walking for hours down the broad, tree-lined road that led to the village of Starbeck, just to the east of Harrogate. The people going about their business from the farms and houses nearby all seemed to be looking at her. In fact, she was sure now that they were staring at her. The country folk seemed somehow to be able to see deep into her soul; they seemed to know just what a wicked, wicked creature she really was. She could tell by their eyes that they knew exactly what she had made her uncle and the gentlemen of the Friday Club do to her again and again and again. But then they would know that she was walking to the workhouse too. They would surely know that she was walking to the poor-law workhouse with a perfect, tiny bastard baby inside her, and it was little wonder they stared.

The workhouse — but surely she should have got there by now. To quell her mounting panic, she forced herself to count the great beech trees as she passed them at the roadside: ten, fifteen, twenty. Had she missed it? Was there really a workhouse at Starbeck at all? The women at Brimston had said — had promised her — that there was. The icy hand of doubt suddenly gripped her innards. What if they were lying? What if they were just being wicked and really there wasn't a workhouse in Starbeck at all. She couldn't bear the thought of going back to Sessrum House, to her Uncle Alfie and his Annexe, and to the gentlemen of the Friday Club. And she wouldn't, she definitely would not, go back to Brimston and let her baby be taken away again by the baby farmers to die without its mama.

She would have to live on the streets. There would be nothing else for it. But what if she did have to whore herself to live, like Mary had said she would? She remembered how she could make it seem as if the gentlemen were doing things to a different little girl, how she could take her mind, the part that was really her, the real Elizabeth, off to another altogether different place. She could do it if she had to. She could be a whore if it meant her baby would be safe. All of the gentlemen seemed to want her, even the ones at Brimston who didn't say they needed to punish her. They often asked for her by name, which meant that Mrs. Eire could even charge them extra. Just so long as her baby was safe, so long as it could stay with her where she could love it and care for it and be with it always, then that was all that truly mattered.

And then, Glory Be! There it was: the Harrogate Workhouse on the outskirts of Starbeck. She almost collapsed onto the pavement in relief.

'Oh, thank you, Lord Jesus, and thank you Mama, if you really are in Heaven with Papa, and not being punished for all eternity in the Eighth Circle of the Inferno. Thank you for guiding my steps to here. As soon as I'm a good enough girl to be allowed into Heaven, please, please let me die. Please come for me and for my perfect, little baby.'

Prayer of grateful thanks said, she opened her eyes once more and looked. The Harrogate Workhouse was a large and ornate building, set off the main road behind a high stone wall. The towering, pointed facade reminded her strongly of the carved African headdress that her uncle kept in the library. He had brought it back from a trip to Egypt many years ago, and it both fascinated and repelled her. Uncle Alfie had said that the Africans believed that it connected them to the ancestors of their family, whose spirits would either haunt them or protect them, or even, as he said with a rare chuckle, do both.

An elderly, tired-looking woman in a shapeless grey dress and poke bonnet was bent over a gorse brush, sweeping the cobbled yard. She seemed to sense that she was being watched and suddenly glanced up. Elizabeth froze as she stood peering at her through the bars of the big iron gates.

"Come t' gawp at t' paupers, have we, missy? I expect we make a fine mornin's entertainment for a young lady such as ye'self, an' no mistake."

With her heart jumping like a live thing in her chest, Elizabeth walked forward, forward between the gates that magically seemed to part before her, and into the yard.

She was in.

"Please, ma'am, I beg your pardon. I didn't mean to gawp at you. I should rather like to come and live in the workhouse and be a pauper too. I'm not a wicked girl, I'm really not."

The woman erupted in a peel of laughter, which made Elizabeth start.

"Ma'am now is it? Wan' t' be a pauper, do we, with our beautiful clothes and our beautiful hair and our silver necklace around our beautiful neck? It looks like ye've a long way to fall yet, li'le miss, afore ye could ever be a pauper like me."

Elizabeth curtsied politely, just as her mama had taught her to do.

"If you please, ma'am, I am already fallen. I have lived at Mrs Eire's Home for Fallen Women and Girls at Brimston, but I couldn't bear it there. My mama and papa are dead and my uncle and his gentlemen friends are cruel to me, although I know that they are just trying to stop me from being wicked. But I'm not truly wicked, ma'am, honest I'm not."

Something seemed to resonate deep within the world-weary shadows in the old woman's eyes. Her sneer became a gentle smile and she laid her broom down onto the cobbles.

"In that case, come with me, me pretty lamb, and I'll take ye to meet t' Matron. What's thy name?"

Elizabeth stopped to bob a curtsey again.

"It's Elizabeth, ma'am, Elizabeth Beatrice Wilson, but most people call me Lizzie."

"Well, Lizzie, my name is Rachel, and I've lived as an inmate at this 'ere workhouse since i' were firs' built, so most people call me Old Rachel. Ye don' need t' curtsey for a pauper woman like me but it migh' be as well

to do so for Mrs Dixon, t' Matron. She can be stern, but she's a good heart in her. Do ye like hard work?"

"Yes, Rachel, I like hard work very much, thank you."

"Well in that case, ye should get along jus' fine 'ere. Ye say that ye've lived a' Mrs Eire's place?"

"Yes, Rachel, but not for long; it was just while I... just while..."

"Jus' while ye had ye baby?"

"Yes, ma'am, it was just while I had Baby Albert."

"And where is Baby Albert now?"

"He's safe in Heaven with the Lord Jesus and my mama and papa."

"Oh, Lizzie, and ye jus' a child! Who was Baby Albert's daddy, do ye know?"

Elizabeth shook her head quickly and Old Rachel laid her skinny arm across her shoulder.

"We know all 'bout Mrs Eire 'ere, Lizzie."

Her old voice was soothing in a way Lizzie had not truly known since her mama was alive.

"She used t' come t' workhouse now and again, pretendin' t' be an in-and-out."

"I beg your pardon, Rachel but I'm not certain what an, 'in-and-out,' is."

Old Rachel chuckled.

"Such nice manners on thee: An' 'in-and-out's' a vagrant, Lizzie, a tramp, someone who stays 'ere jus' for a night or two and then disappears off on their way. Mrs Eire used t' come in as an in-and-out, lookin' for young mothers and widows, and 'specially young girls t' turn their ear. They would abscond, or discharge themsens with their silly 'eads full o' promises of work or marriage or money or such like. Mostly though, they'd end up in various gentlemen's beds, or be sent o'erseas to work in plantations and in other gentlemen's beds. Mrs Dixon got wise t' her ways, she did. She sent her off wit' sharp edge of her tongue. Warned all t' other workhouses round abou' here too, she did, Ripon and Knaresborough and Scriven. Many a poor, dizzy-headed girl is a lot better off a-cause o' Mrs Dixon, an' many a gentleman's bed t' colder and t' emptier."

"Where does Mrs Eire get the girls from now?"

"All manner o' places, Lizzie; Mrs Eire's not one t' be put off easily. She gets 'em from apprentice houses an' t' shops where t' servant girls run for their errands. Nurse girls are always a favourite with her, I hear; there are always lots on 'em walkin' t' Stray wit' their mistress' bairns in perambulators. She knows fine they're generally on their own an' that they're nearly all virgins. Virgins are where Mrs Eire can get 'er best money. Once t' gentlemen 'ave 'ad their way with 'em, well then... there's always Brimston an' more money t' be 'ad from 'em there."

"I preferred the gentlemen at Brimston to the ones at..."

She clapped her hand to her mouth, mortified at what she had almost let slip. Rachel seemed kind to be sure but she was still virtually a complete stranger.

But Old Rachel swept her into a tight embrace. Inside the cocoon of gnarled, wrinkled old arms and coarse, stiff cloth, Elizabeth felt just a little of the pain of her life begin to seep away.

"Hush, child. I know, I know. With these old eyes, I've seen all manner o' things that shouldn' happen under God's keepin'. I know wha' men can do to a helpless li'le child they're meant to protect an' cherish; aye, and laugh about it too. But ye are safe now, Lizzie. Mrs Dixon an' I'll keep ye safe an' look after ye an' your baby jus' fine here."

"Oh, Rachel, I do believe that you'll keep me safe, I truly do. It's just that I can't seem to get it all out of my head. Everything keeps whirling around and around like a merry-go-round."

"Ye will, Lizzie, ye will, wi' good hard work an' that there baby out of yer belly an' into t' sunshine."

Elizabeth felt the dry, cracked lips press onto her forehead just as her legs threatened to give way as if they had turned to india-rubber.

"How do you know about my baby?" she whispered.

Rachel chuckled again.

"'Cause I work in t' infirmary, me pretty child, and in t' lyin'-in room, and I've delivered hundreds o' babies in t' years I've been 'ere." She sighed deeply. "An' in that time, Lizzie, I'll tell thee straight: I've seen more than a few pretty young lambs like ye, who'd rather come an' sell their soul t' a poor-law workhouse than be ill-used a' home."

She stepped back and forced her lined, toothless, old face into a reassuring grin.

"Look now, girl, ye've gone an' quite crumpled them fine clothes o' yours. 'Ere, let's straighten ye out an' then we'll in an' see Mrs Dixon."

CHAPTER 19

She followed Old Rachel towards the little entrance porch under the great, ornate facade of the workhouse. It was the mouth of the African mask she was so reminded of, and it never moved as it swallowed her whole.

In spite of the warmth of the bright summer morning outside, as Lizzie entered the bowels of the workhouse, she was engulfed by a sudden gloom and icy chill that made her skin creep. And as she gazed about, the chill seemed to penetrate further than her skin; it seemed to seep deep inside her chest and freeze her very heart.

From without, Starbeck Workhouse was a handsome, well proportioned, even grand building, but from within it was bleak, austere and labyrinthine. The floors were of great, cold stone flags, a little like the pavements of Harrogate, but without the warming sun. The walls and ceilings had no plaster, no paint and no hangings; only a thick, smothering layer of stark, white lime-wash, and instead of paintings and portraits, there were terse, official notices prescribing what every part of her life was now going to be.

"Jump in 'ere, Lizzie, while I fetch Matron or t' Master."

Rachel was pointing through a doorway into a little room beyond. A polished, brass plaque on the wall announced it as the 'Receiving Office,' so wide-eyed and obedient, she walked inside.

The Receiving Office was a small and very square room, with a large sash window on one side looking out over the part-swept front yard, and the great stone boundary wall beyond. The wall seemed so much further away, yet so much higher, from in here. After the dark of the corridor, the room was oppressively bright.

Several notices punctuated the wall opposite, and the sight of one of these in particular flooded her instantly with cold, visceral dread. It was headed by the words, 'Punishments for the Misbehaviour of Paupers,' and Elizabeth's eyes swept quickly down it. They swept down it so fast that she could pick out only the occasional word, almost as if somehow, those words might not be as real, might not be as true, that way.

Her eyes searched in horror for anything that might hint at the punishments Uncle Alfie or his gentlemen friends meted out. And there it was. Dear Lord there it was. Amongst all of the withholding of cheese and butter, or tea or sugar; amid all the warnings of various confinements in the refractory cell, there were the words: '...the pauper may be publically whipped.' She shivered as she remembered once more the big room at Brimston and the mess of blood and wheals that was the fallen girl's back. That memory changed instantly into a terrifying image of her mama, tramping despairingly around the Eighth Circle of Hell being whipped on and on by demons. Then she saw herself, stripped naked in front of Old Rachel and hundreds of other paupers, and chained to a rack. There would be no circumspection. They would surely all see her lumpy belly, see its faint, pink marks where it had once been stretched so tight and they would know for certain what a wicked, wicked creature she really was.

"Acquainting ourselves with the rules and regulations already, are we?"

She started and whirled round. A small, intelligent-looking man was standing in front of her, regarding her shrewdly. Old Rachel was behind him smiling a smile of encouragement with her lovely, toothless old face.

"I am Mr Dixon," the man continued, "And I am the Master of the Harrogate Workhouse. Rachel here has told me that you entertain some notion of admittance as an inmate?"

"That is quite correct, sir."

Elizabeth bobbed her nervous curtsey. The Master's eyes followed her movements with rapt attention.

"If I may say so, Miss..."

"Elizabeth Beatrice Wilson if you please, sir."

She curtsied once again.

"If I may say so, Miss Elizabeth Beatrice Wilson, you are not in our usual line of inmates."

"Am I not, sir?"

Dread took a cold grip on her gullet.

"No indeed. However, Rachel has told me that you are an orphan and that you wish for relief to escape your uncle's cruel punishments. Is that correct?"

His eyes seemed to bore into hers, and instinctively, she reached up and caught her silver crucifix between her fingertips.

"Yes, sir, if you please."

She was watching the Master's eyes, waiting for them to begin to creep down her body as all men's eyes did. And then they did, and dread took her in its hands and squeezed and squeezed and squeezed.

"How old are you, Elizabeth?" the Master asked.

"I am fifteen years old, sir."

"That is convenient; I thought perhaps you might be older. Rachel, would you have a bath prepared for her? Cold taps first, mind you and ninety-five degrees by the thermometer. I shall be supervising her myself as she's not yet sixteen. Mrs Dixon is occupied at present and can't be broke off. After that you may see to her hair and clothes, and then take her up to the receiving ward for the Medical Officer to examine her."

"Aye, Mr Dixon," said Rachel, then: "Come, Lizzie, let me take ye t' Ablutions Room; I'll get t' men to fill thee a bath."

She could feel her body trembling, feel the myriad pinpricks of goose flesh pimple her naked skin. The hem of the Master's jacket brushed lightly against her thigh as he stooped across her and she shuddered and cried out.

"A little over ninety-three degrees, Rachel, so that will do quite nicely for her."

Mr Dixon stood and flicked a drop of bathwater deftly from the bulb of his thermometer. He turned and his eyes slid once more down her naked body. She shuddered again and shielded herself with her arms and her hands, writhing in her humiliation like some worm caught in a salt pit.

"Very well, Wilson, into the bath you go. I don't suppose for one moment that you actually need one, but regulations are regulations."

Old Rachel's horny fingers steered her into the water. It was just tepid, and she could feel it creeping inexorably up every inch of her skin as she lowered herself down into the tub.

"I bath every Saturday, sir," she ventured nervously, "And wash my face and hands each morning."

The Master chuckled and held out a large, red block.

"I don't doubt it, Wilson, but not with this though, I'd wager. Take it; it's carbolic soap."

He held the block out to her, then, just as her fingers peeled from her skin to take it, he pulled it tantalisingly out of reach.

"Take it," he repeated, grinning horribly.

Elizabeth hesitated; she so needed to be admitted; for her baby to be safe.

The Master raised his eyebrows and scowled, and she vacillated for just a second longer before she reached out and snatched it from his hand. The chill air of the room wafted against her naked breast, where her hand had been a second before. The Master chuckled again, and this time she sensed the catch in it, that awful catch that gentlemen have when they intend to be cruel. She curled up tight and began to rock gently to-and-fro in the water, waiting for the brutal touch of his hands, of his mouth, of...

"Make sure she uses the carbolic, Rachel. You know how the Medical Officer likes to smell it on his new arrivals."

Then the door clicked and he was gone.

"Don' mind 'im, Lizzie."

She started violently as Old Rachel's fingers touched her back. They were slick and lumpy with soap, and her nose was filled with the sudden pungent aroma of the carbolic.

"Mr Dixon likes ye t' know that he's t' Master 'ere an' that ye be only an inmate, but upon my soul, 'e would never touch ye."

Elizabeth sat patiently in the bathtub as Rachel washed the fine perfume and powder of Sessrum House from her skin and replaced it with the coarse, brutal stench of carbolic. And then she sat patiently on a stool as her long, blonde tresses were carefully cut away.

"We'll get a pretty penny for these, Lizzie," Rachel cackled as she laid the handfuls of hair carefully onto a sheet of new, brown paper.

"You'll sell it, you mean; you'll sell my hair?" Elizabeth was astounded.

"I winnet, child, but t' poor-law will. It'll go to be made into wigs for t' fine, old ladies o' Harrogate to make 'em look pretty."

Elizabeth glanced into a small, round looking-glass fixed to the wall under a blanket shelf, and saw what looked to be a delicate young boy with bright, piercing blue eyes staring back at her through the film of dust. She smiled and the boy smiled back, but his smile seemed somehow hollow, somehow filled with pain. And when she looked through his eyes and deep into his soul, she shivered.

"I'm glad, Rachel; they can have it. They can be pretty instead of me. I don't want to be pretty anymore. It just makes gentlemen think that you're wicked."

"Hush, child, don' talk so. Thy hair'll grow back soon enough an' then ye'll be beautiful again and some kind gen'leman will come an' make ye a handsome husband." Her eyes dropped for a second to the tiny bulge on

Elizabeth's naked belly. "Anyway, le's get thy uniform for ye. Ye pretty clothes'll be cleaned an' disinfected in t' sulphur cupboard an' then nailed safely ont' t' wall until ye leave. Not that they need disinfectin', mind ye; it's just tha' t' regulations say tha' they must."

"I don't want them, Rachel. If you like them, you can have them."

The boy in the mirror shook his head frantically and the sudden glistening tears in his eyes made him seem even more delicate, yet more fragile.

Rachel's wizened old face appeared next to it.

"Thank ye, Lizzie, but God himself couldn' fit me into them clothes in a month o' Sundays, no, nor half o' t' women in this poor-law. An' if he did, we'd look nothin' but a troop o' music hall turns. No, me lamb, we'll be nailin' them up safe for ye, else they'll be a-disappearin' down t' pop-shop — th' pawnbrokers t' ye — afore we know it. That way, when ye do want t' leave wi' ye kind gen'leman and ye little baby, well then, they'll be still there waitin' for ye, won' they? Ye won' want t' go out still in ye workhouse uniform an' 'ave everyone stare an' shout names an' t' boys throw stones a' ye, now would ye?"

The boy shook his head and Elizabeth felt a gnarled hand gently pat her shoulder.

"There's a lamb. So 'ere's thy new uniform then."

She pointed to what Elizabeth had taken to be a pile of old blankets stacked on the shelf above the mirror. The boy in the mirror looked up and Elizabeth noticed a vivid yellow bruise just below his ear. In her other life, she remembered carefully and shamefully arranging her hair so as to cover it, and a single memory of Mr James fell from its place and made her flesh writhe as if it were crawling with maggots. For a moment she felt his suffocating weight on her back and his teeth, sharp as Mr Price's, biting into her neck.

The hand patted her shoulder once more and the memory fled.

"Oh, Lizzie, I dare say t' clothes aren't wha' ye are used with, but they'll not be so bad, once ye ge' accustomed to 'em. They last well enough in 'ere, anyway. Ye pretty clothes would be turned t' rags in no time.

Look ye here; ye've got a good, strong grogram gown for every day, two shifts o' calico, a petticoat an' a pretty gingham dress for church on Sundays. T' blue'll set ye hair off lovely when it grows again, an' this day cap'll hide it until it does. There are worsted stockings for ye pretty legs an' slippers for ye feet."

As she spoke, she dropped each item into Elizabeth's naked lap. The rough grogram scratched the skin of her legs, softer than ever from the bath

---

100

water. She reached down and felt the cloth between her fingers. It was coarse and stiff. Uncle Alfie's gardener, she realised in horror, put better clothes on the old scarecrow that stood in the kitchen garden.

She looked up and saw Rachel smiling at her in the mirror.

"Look sharp now an' get thee dressed. Mr Wright t' Medical Officer will need to examine ye afore ye can start work."

The Reception Ward at the Harrogate Workhouse was empty, save for a single wizened old hag who occupied the farthest of a long line of wrought-iron beds. She was trembling and gently sobbing, as she lay curled on her thin flock mattress in what must have been a deeply tormented sleep.

"What is your name, please?" said a sudden, deep voice to her left, which made Elizabeth start and almost cry out in shock.

She turned to see a gentleman in a top hat and heavy cape coat bent over a desk in a shadowed corner of the room. The nib of his pen was scratching rapidly across a sheet of paper and he hadn't looked up.

"Elizabeth Beatrice Wilson, if you please, sir."

Elizabeth curtsied and felt the rough, stiff material of the uniform resisting the movement.

The scratching stopped abruptly at the sound of her voice and the gentleman looked up. His eyes roved languidly down her body and she hid her sudden discomfort in another, nervous curtsey.

"My name is Mr Wright," said the man at last, "And I am the Medical Officer for this workhouse. It is my duty to examine you before you can gain any relief here."

"Yes, sir," said Elizabeth.

Mr Wright pointed the nib of his pen towards the nearest of the beds.

"Lay there, Wilson and take off your slippers and cap; I'll be with you presently. Rachel, you may wait outside. I'll call for you once I have completed my examination."

The bed was narrow, crude and uncomfortable, and like the princess in the fairytale, she could feel every one of the narrow iron struts pressing into her back through the thin mattress. The door clicked shut behind Old Rachel and she looked up. Mr Wright's long, black silhouette was looming over her. Blind, visceral panic gripped her and began inexorably to overwhelm her senses. Lizzie watched as his hands lifted and reached down for her. They were big hands, as big as Mr Price's, and they were overpowering and unstoppable. She wanted to beg him to still them, beg him to let her go, to let her flee this bed, this ward, this workhouse, but the words she needed choked unuttered in her throat. She wanted to turn away, to push him back but her leaden limbs refused to heed the shrieking, shrieking screams of her brain.

"You've a nice manner and a quite beautiful face, Elizabeth," Mr Wright purred as his fingertips trailed along the smooth line of her jaw. "Have you ever thought of going into domestic service?"

"No, sir," Elizabeth whispered.

She needed him to stop talking to her. If he was quiet, if she didn't need to listen to him or think of answers to his questions, she would be able to take herself away to her safe and special place, where it would seem as if all of this was going to happen to a different little girl.

"In this workhouse, Elizabeth, we discourage idleness by means of austerity, discipline and good, hard work. It can be a very, very cruel place for poor little girls like you."

His fingers drifted down the length of her arm and slowly encircled her trembling hand.

"Your hands are so soft and so warm. I can think of a much better employ for them than hours and hours of scrubbing floors or picking oakum."

He let her hand fall gently back onto the mattress and his hands floated to the hem of her dress.

"I know several gentlemen in Harrogate who would willingly employ a nice, pretty girl such as you, Elizabeth."

Elizabeth closed her eyes tight as the coarse material of her dress scratched its way along the length of her shins, brushed her knee, lifted from her thighs.

"Those gentlemen are very wealthy. They would happily pay you pounds and pounds if you would play a special game with them."

'Please, Lord Jesus, please, Mama, please send your angel to make us die right now. Please take my baby and me into Heaven to be angels with you.'

"You have marks on your body, Elizabeth, that suggest that you've had a baby already."

She opened her eyes straight into Mr Wright's as he leered down at her with an expression somewhere between triumph and bitter disappointment.

"Yes, sir, I had a baby; it was Baby Albert but he was only little and he died."

"Did you kill him, Wilson?"

"Oh lordy, no, sir; Mrs Eire took him away because she said that a boy was neither use nor ornament to her or anybody else, and she gave him to a *lady friend to fetch up. But Mary told me that he'd died and gone to be with his grandmama and grandpapa in Heaven."*

"I see."

She felt his hand cup her breast, felt his fingers pressing into her.

"You have a heavy bosom for one so young."

Another hand pressed hard on her stomach and then there was a sudden, sharp pinch on her nipple that made her yelp out in pain.

He said: "You're due to have another baby soon aren't you, Wilson? That's what has brought you running to our door begging for relief. In that case, to use our friend Mrs Eire's words, you're neither use nor ornament to me either. My friends only want chaste, virgin girls around them, not some shameless harlot with someone's bastard whelp growing inside her."

She felt her dress being dragged back over her legs.

"She's having a baby."

The wizened old hag from the bed at the end of the ward suddenly appeared next to the Medical Officer, peering down with startlingly bright eyes from the shadows of her shabby poke bonnet.

"Hold your tongue, woman," Wright growled without looking round.

"She's having a baby," the woman repeated.

She cackled and began to sing in a high, trill voice.

"Hush-a-bye baby, on the tree top,

When you grow old, your wages will stop.

When you have spent, the bit money you made.

First to the poorhouse, then to the grave."

"Will you hold your tongue, woman?" Wright roared, "Or do you wish to start your time in the workhouse in the refractory cell?"

"Her baby died so she's having another," the woman persisted.

She knew it would come: the memory, the very worst memory of them all.

She knew it was surely coming to hurt her again and there was nothing she could do to stop it. The panic that had been waiting to overwhelm her ever since she had first felt Wright's shadow falling across her started to rise still further. She didn't have her Bible with its comforting Book of Revelation; she couldn't run to Mary, she was just lying here, on a bed, trapped beneath a man who was surely going to punish her. He had already hurt her nipple, and she could still feel it stabbing with pain. She closed her eyes, and concentrated with all her might on the hurt, on the pain, letting it flood her consciousness, letting it block out everything else.

*And the worst memory of all didn't come. This time — mercifully —
it stayed. It remained festering in that remote part of her mind she kept
especially for it and for its foul and loathsome kin. This time, it didn't come
to hurt her as it always did. The only pain she knew was the throbbing ache
in her nipple and it was oh, such a relief.*

"Bless me but t' child's fallen asleep!"
She opened her eyes. It was Old Rachel.
"I'm not a wicked girl, Rachel, truly I'm not."
"O' course ye aren't, Lizzie."
"The Medical Officer said that I was. He said that I was a shameless
    harlot."
Old Rachel slowly eased her body down until she was perched on the edge
of the narrow bed frame opposite.
"Well we both know t' truth of it, don' we?" she murmured. "An' God
knows t' truth of it, and Jesus knows t' truth of it, an' ye mammy an' daddy
know t' truth of it, so why do ye worry abou' what t' Medical Officer thinks?"
Elizabeth smiled and blinked back sudden tears and Old Rachel patted
her stomach.
"Ye jus' be a-worryin' 'bout this little 'un, child. They say there's enough
worry a-comes from one little child to last their mammy a lifetime. Now, rouse
thyself, I'm to take ye to t' girls' ward an' old Leah there to t' refractory cell
for t' night. Oh, an' Mr Wright 'as ordered that ye wear one o' these." She
held up a stiff, grogram jacket. It had been dyed to a bright yellow colour.
"But why would he wish me to wear one of those, Rachel? I'm getting
quite used to the chill and the colour — well it would make me look just like
a little duckling. No one else wears one."
"I know, me lamb, but t' jacket ain't t' keep thee warm, it's... well, it's t'
show that ye're not a chaste girl, Lizzie. Mr Wright said that t' other girls
needed warning abou' ye 'lack o' moral virtue.'"
She mimicked his voice perfectly and chuckled.
"But don' worry, it be more t' other way about, an' none o' t' other girls
won' take any notice o' 't anyway, not really."

CHAPTER 20

It had seemed longer – much longer – than the three hours the library clock had tried to pretend it had been before at last they heard Dr Roberts' voice echoing beyond the hallway door. It was answered almost immediately by a woman's – Mary Lovell's – speaking in equally urgent, muffled tones.

Lucie Fox quickly closed the thick tome on phrenology she had been using to help pass the time and mirrored the lurcher Gladstone as he pricked up his ears and stared intently at the green baize lining of the door.

"He's returned from the magistrate's at last," Atticus said, carefully setting down a large African tribal mask he had been examining.

The brass handle of the door rattled and twisted and Roberts burst in, followed by a tearful and strained-looking Mary. Gladstone gave a great bark and bounded to his feet.

"Hello, old fellow."

Roberts bent and rubbed the dog's shoulder for what seemed like an age before he stood straight and tall again.

His face was unreadable and he said: "Thank you for your patience Atticus, Mrs Fox; I'm so sorry to have been away for so long."

"Never mind that," Atticus snapped, "What did he say?"

Roberts' face broke into a grin. "He said – and the police superintendant didn't object one bit – that Aunt Elizabeth may stay here at Sessrum House in my care and keeping until he decides whether or not she must stand trial."

"That's wonderful news." Lucie beamed too. "But surely there can be no question whether she's fit to stand trial?"

Roberts' grin tautened and became as strained as Mary's.

"I'm afraid that's where the superintendant and I did disagree. Apparently the constable who accompanied Aunt Elizabeth to the police station swore that she gave signs of perfectly understanding what he was saying to her. He's pushing for her to stand trial anyway and to let the judge and jury decide what happens to her."

"But that's preposterous," Atticus roared.

"I know, Atticus," Roberts said, "But that battle is for another day. At least she's coming back here for the present. Mary is going to fetch her from the police station presently, and walk her back across the Stray. I won't have her ride in a carriage; she's done enough of that already to last a lifetime. Then, once she's safely home, we can push for the McNaughton rules to be applied, and if we can achieve that, I cannot see any other outcome but that she will live out her final days here, in peace."

CHAPTER 21

"Here's the Stray, Lizzie; do you remember the Stray?"

Mary and Elizabeth looked like just another pair of elderly ladies taking the light exercise that, along with the taking of the mineral-rich spa waters, comprised such an important part of 'The Harrogate Cure.'

"The whin bushes are pretty," Mary added. "Look at the whin bushes, Lizzie."

Elizabeth turned and gazed in the direction in which Mary was pointing, toward a dense thicket of bright yellow gorse.

"Am I to help Rachel?" she asked.

Mary sighed wearily.

"You don't understand one word of what I say, do you, Lizzie? Rachel's long-since dead, my love; she's dead and buried in her grave. I'm Mary."

"The Master mus' like ye, Lizzie," Old Rachel cackled as she handed her one of a pair of heavy implements she was carrying. It consisted of a large, brutal-looking blade, attached to a stocky wooden handle, and Rachel called it a 'slasher.' It looked to Lizzie like one of the great medieval weapons her Uncle Alfie was so fond of collecting, and that he kept mounted in their dozens on the walls of his hunting lodge in Northumberland.

"E's sendin' ye out wi' me to cut whin bush on t' Stray," Rachel went on. "We're to go out an' cut it an' then t' men will haul it back 'ere at t' end o' t' day."

She looked carefully round and then whispered: "It's a hard job an' yer pretty arms will get scratched t' bits on t' spines, but we're out o' t' workhouse an' oftentimes, t' overseers will let them that's been a-doin' it go to t' Stray horse races as a reward."

She looked around again and cackled merrily before she winked and added: "Sometimes they even let us 'ave a little drop o' gin too, while we're on."

"What do you do with whin bush, Rachel? Is it for table vases?"

Old Rachel stared at her, her expression fluid as quicksilver.

"For table vases?" she stammered at last, "For flowers ye mean?"

Lizzie nodded.

Rachel seemed to suddenly be having some kind of fit, and Lizzie worried if she should be running for Mr Wright or the Matron. Rachel's face went puce, her eyes began streaming with tears and she stooped, hanging onto the handle of her slasher as her ancient shoulders shook and shook.

"Oh, me poor, innocent lamb," she gasped at last, and Lizzie realised she had been laughing, "Table flowers in t' refectory is it?"

She doubled up once more and cackled as if she would never stop. But then she did and she took a hold of herself.

"We use t' whin bush for animal food mainly, Lizzie. T' farms 'ereabouts buy as much as we can cut. But we use it for makin' brooms as well, an' for a-dressin' the soil in t' garden. Th' flowers go to make pretty yellow dye, so by then, there's generally nothin' left for t' table vases." And then she erupted into peels of laughter once more.

It was very curious feeling, to walk with Old Rachel back up the long road to Harrogate – almost as if she were entering a strange town for the first time; a town that she had previously known only in picture books. Everything looked the same; the great beech trees that lined the road, the cottages and the farmsteads, the Stray itself… But it was also all strangely different. True, she was dressed as a pauper girl now in her stiff grogram gown and day cap, and the bright yellow jacket she wore seemed to attract all manner of attention, from disdainful stares to outright hostility.

It had taken quite a long time for her to realise that it was the jacket that was the cause of the attention, and not just the sheer fact that she was a wicked pauper girl with a precious bastard baby in her belly. Women hustled their children into their houses or hid them behind their skirts and they would call, 'slut,' or, 'harlot,' or 'whore' as she passed. Men would shout from passing wagons, asking how much for a kiss, and would she meet them in the tavern after dark. One man even broke away from a whistling, jeering group of farm labourers to run across the road and grab at her. She let her body fall limp and her mind flee as his rough stubble raked across her face until Old Rachel beat him off with the thick handle of her slasher. But even as her mind took off and fled to her special, secret place, Elizabeth realised that her uncle and Mrs Eire had been right all along; everyone knew, everyone could see even without the yellow jacket she was wearing that she was a nasty, sinful little harlot who needed to be punished and punished and punished.

"No ye aren', child," Rachel had said, just as Mary had said before her. "Ye've jus' been terrible unfortunate, that's all. Take that there jacket off an' I'll hide it in a tree for ye 'til we come back. No-one need be any t' wiser. Mr Wright can't see us when we're away from t' poor-law an' what he can't see winnet hurt 'im."

Elizabeth took it off, but she knew that it would change nothing. She knew for certain that she was wicked – that she was a wicked, wicked creature who would surely go to Hell, and who deserved no mercy. She deserved the shouts and the insults, and she deserved for the men to attack her. As she watched Rachel wind her jacket into a tight roll and push it snugly into a fork of a roadside tree, she hoped with all her heart that the spines of the whin bushes would scratch her and scratch her, and scratch her to death.

It had taken quite a long time for her to realise that it was the jacket after all that had been the cause of the attention. But she walked now with no heavy jacket, listening to Rachel's chattering and her stories of the workhouse, and even her heart seemed to grow lighter. She had just the weight of her perfect, unborn baby in her belly, and the slasher in her arms. People still stared at them to be sure, but now no-one shouted, no-one jeered, and no-one came to hurt her.

Not long after her poor mama had left her to go to Heaven, and she had been taken away to live in the Annexe, Mr Otter, the steward of the Friday Club, had suddenly burst into her room where she had been sitting in a chair reading to John.

John was a full three years younger than she, but she remembered how brave he had been that day. He had picked up the wooden sword he had recently taken to carrying with him everywhere and he had brandished it at Otter like a gallant knight to an ogre.

Mr Otter had laughed as he had plucked the sword from John's grasp, and he had laughed again as he had smashed it to pieces over his knee. But he had seemed deadly serious when he had said, more to Lizzie than to John: "You want to be very careful with me, you do."

"You aren't allowed to touch us, Otter. I heard Papa tell you. We're gentlemen's children and we're not to be interfered with."

John's scream was a scream of rage.

"You're only allowed your pick of the downstairs children, and even then, only after the Friday Club has finished with them."

"You're both to come with me right now," Mr Otter had growled in reply. "Mr Roberts wants to show something to you on the Stray."

Curious, but still wary enough to leave a respectful distance, they had followed him obediently through the Annexe's smoking room and down the stairway beyond. But when he reached the big door at the bottom, he had turned on them with a suddenness that had both frightened and surprised them for such a big man.

"If I were ever to touch you, Miss Elizabeth," he growled, *"If I were ever to come to your room and drag you from your bed and take my fill of you, you can be certain that neither of you would live to tell the tale of it."*

His laughter had echoed horribly in the empty void of the stairwell and, when he turned and pulled open the door, neither Lizzie nor John doubted the truth of his words for a moment.

They were almost relieved to find Uncle Alfie waiting impatiently for them by the columns of the portico.

"John, Lizzie, come with me; I want to show you both what happens to disobedient children and to those who run away."

He led them along the carriage drive to the big, stone gateposts marking its end. There he pointed.

They looked. A little way across the Stray one of the great, old trees by the roadside had fallen in the night. A large group of people, men, women and children, were crawling over it like the colony of ants John kept in a jam jar under his bed.

"Those creatures are paupers," Uncle Alfie announced, *"From the poor-law workhouse at Starbeck. They have come to clear that tree for firewood.*

I want you to look hard and pay heed to their misfortune. Workhouse paupers are the most miserable wretches in Christendom. They are naturally idle, indolent and feckless. That is why, in an attempt to drive the more godlike qualities of industriousness, abstinence and humility into them, they are starved, beaten and worked as hard as they can bear.

Now if you should wish to avoid the fate that has overtaken those poor unfortunates, you must always, always do as your betters instruct you, and you must never run away. If you are being hard punished, I remind you that it is for the sake of your immortal soul. Do you hear me, Lizzie?"

She nodded. She had heard the words her uncle had spoken, certainly, but as she watched the paupers laughing and chattering and calling to each other as they worked, she barely believed the truth of them.

The pauper women and girls — for they looked to have women and girls just like ordinary folk — were all dressed identically in heavy grey dresses. She was reminded suddenly of Halcyon, the house where she had lived with her mama before she went away to Heaven, and of the family who lived next door. They had three children, all girls, and they were always dressed exactly the same — just like a row of little ducklings, as her mama used to say. They had always seemed happy too; they were always laughing and chattering just like the paupers. How she wished and wished that she could be a little duckling, following her mama wherever she went. How she wished she could be a pauper and laugh and chatter like them. They were like a family; one great, big, happy family, with brothers and duckling sisters and even, dear Lord even, warm, living mamas.

CHAPTER 22

"I can't believe it. I just can't believe it. How utterly stupid must the man be, Atticus? Shouldn't a magistrate be blessed with at least a spark of intelligence?"

Dr Roberts was utterly distraught as he paced back and forth in front of Sessrum House.

"Doctor, we only came over to tell you that your aunt's lawyers are preparing the papers regarding her inheritance, but we seem to have walked into a veritable brouhaha. Whatever is the matter? You look fit to explode."

"The matter is, I've had a letter from that fool magistrate. Here, read it for yourselves."

He thrust a ball of crumpled paper across at Atticus, who caught it, and with a deeply apprehensive glance to Lucie, opened it out and smoothed it against one of the big stone columns.

"She's failed the McNaughton test," he said after a moment, "Due to the absence of any evidence of madness and the sworn testimony of the police. She's to stand trial at the next assizes."

"Surely not," breathed Lucie, "But how could she?"

"That imbecile of a police superintendant swore an oath that she could understand perfectly well what was being said to her whilst she was in their custody. It's utter poppycock, of course; she's senile. She hadn't the first idea what was happening to her in there."

"Absence of evidence is not the same as evidence of absence," Atticus added.

"But you're an eminent psychiatrist," Lucie said, "Won't they take your sworn word as evidence too? Your oath is as good as his."

"They've an idea I'm in on it!"

Roberts' eyes seemed to bulge from their sockets.

"Can you believe it? They spoke to that fool Liddle at the workhouse and he told them that I'd been there many times to see their Medical Officer. So now they think I might have conspired with Aunt Elizabeth to kill my grandfather. They think I might have coached her in how to behave like an imbecile, so she could get away with it scot-free!"

"So when are the next assize sessions?" Lucie asked hurriedly, to forestall the question she could sense was already forming on Atticus' lips.

Roberts looked at her grimly.

"Next week," he said.

"Then, *Quo Fata Vocant*," said Atticus, neatly folding the letter and handing it back to Roberts, "Whither the Fates Call. We need a plan of action."

"Very well," said Roberts, "I'll have Petty send up some tea. We'll meet Mary in the Annexe for a council of war. It'll be private there, and Aunt Elizabeth will be having her mid-morning nap."

A few minutes later, they were back in the smoking room of the Annexe under the malevolently watchful gaze of Freya and the ghosts of the Friday Club.

"I'd forgotten quite how oppressive this place is," Lucie whispered after the doctor had excused himself to summon Mary.

Atticus nodded.

And then Mary Lovell duly appeared, and when she did, they were appalled at the sight of her. It might have been Elizabeth Wilson herself shuffling after Dr Roberts through the door, so stooped and broken did she look. Her face was crumpled and worn, and the gloom of the Annexe accentuated the deep black semi-circles beneath her eyes. It seemed as if she hadn't slept a moment in the days and nights since they had last seen her, and that those sleepless days and nights must have worn her down like so many years.

"You've heard the news I take it?" she whispered, as she collapsed onto a seat opposite them and fell against its arm.

"We have," Lucie confirmed.

"And they're here to help us plan a course of action if this travesty of natural justice is to be avoided," Roberts added.

"There is no way to avoid a trial, then?" Atticus asked.

Roberts glanced at Mary, and Mary shook her head.

He said: "I'll engage a lawyer, the very best lawyer I can find to fight for it – of course I will – but the magistrate says not, especially when the sessions are so close."

"Then we must think about a defence for her," Atticus replied.

He tapped his chin with a forefinger.

"I've been giving all of this a lot of thought, and it seems to me that although it is conceivable by the letter of the law that Miss Elizabeth might hang, in reality it's most unlikely, most unlikely indeed. Very few women are executed for murder these days, and those that are, are either the ones who have shown clear and wicked malice aforethought, or the ones who have gone completely against their natural, maternal instincts; child killers for example.

Miss Elizabeth had only been here for a matter of hours that day, and she had no prior notion that she was going to be fetched here at all, no matter what the police might suspect. Also, remember that it was your grandfather who paid the visit to her bedroom, and not the other way about. No, I could quite imagine her being sent to an asylum or even perhaps, to a prison, but I certainly can't see her being executed."

"Mr Fox," Mary said, her voice no more than a whisper, "Incarceration would be a thousand times worse for Lizzie than execution."

"Worse? But how could it possibly be worse, Miss Lovell?"

Atticus was astonished.

"Her mind is gone as you all agree. So as long as she was warm and adequately fed, surely she wouldn't know the difference?"

"In short, as long as she was kept caged, like the meanest animal, that would be fine, Mr Fox? Is that what you're saying?"

Mary Lovell's words dripped with venom.

"No, no of course I didn't mean it like that, Miss Lovell," Atticus replied hastily, "It's just..."

He paused to select his words carefully.

"It's just that she surely wouldn't feel the pain of imprisonment as keenly as an ordinary person would, someone who had a full command of their faculties."

"You're quite wrong, Mr Fox."

"Excuse me, but how so?"

"Because her thoughts and memories torment her far more than you could possibly imagine. She's in purgatory every single, waking hour. I believe Dr Roberts has already told you how she takes a knife to her arms and breasts so that the pain of her wounds can distract her from the pain of her soul. Before her dementia, she used to tell me continually how she could never quite drive the demons from her mind. Every day for nearly fifty years she has wished herself dead, Mr Fox. She has spent every single day yearning to die, and the only things that have stopped her from taking her own life have been sheer good fortune, and a fear of going to Hell. You see, she believed that she was so wicked, so utterly loathsome, that if she died, she would surely go straight to Hell and be tormented for eternity."

She hesitated.

"And there was one other thing."

"Which is what?"

She hesitated again, her eyes pained with fear and doubt.

"You must tell us everything, Miss Lovell, if we are to help her," Lucie urged. But instead of Mary Lovell, it was Dr Roberts who answered. His rage had all but subsided, and instead had given way to exhaustion and resignation.

"May I tell you both something in the strictest confidence, something you must never divulge to another, living soul?"

"I can't guarantee anything, Dr Roberts," Atticus answered cautiously, "But we pride ourselves on our discretion."

"Very well, I can't ask for anything more, I suppose."

Roberts took a long breath and raised up his head, as if it were he that was about to face the gallows and not his aunt and said: "In plain terms, Atticus and Mrs Fox, my grandfather was nothing less than a monster."

"A monster," Atticus exclaimed, "But how can you call him that? He may have been a little overbearing perhaps, bombastic even, but in spite of that, he was still a great philanthropist. Or like Miss Lovell, are you saying now that he wasn't even that?"

Roberts shook his head and Mary stared stoically at the tea tray.

"That's what he would have had the world believe."

He took another long, deep breath.

"It was Lord Acton I think who wrote that: 'Power tends to corrupt and absolute power corrupts absolutely. Great men are almost always bad men.' Alas, how true those words prove to be. We British are undoubtedly a great and powerful nation, Atticus. It's just unfortunate that, as a consequence, we have produced a disproportionate number of great, but corrupt and ultimately bad men. We think that with the genius of our engineers, the wealth of our industry, and our sheer military might, we can do almost anything we choose. Tragically, too many of those same corrupt men believe that they can indeed do anything they choose, and get away with it. Tell me: Have either of you ever heard of something called the 'Defloration Mania'?"

Atticus shook his head. He glanced at his wife, who was staring at Roberts in what might have been horror.

"It's also been called, 'The Maiden Tribute of Modern Babylon,' I believe." Roberts added.

At that, a great wave of comprehension swept over Atticus Fox. It left him cold, dazed and wet with sweat.

"Stead," he hissed at last; "W. T. Stead, the editor of the Pall Mall Gazette. I read about his articles a few years ago – the 'Maiden Tribute' articles – if that's what you mean. I thought that Stead was just a sensationalist, just someone trying to sell copies of a newspaper. I mean to say, thousands of young, innocent girls entrapped or bought like slaves on the streets of Britain for the perverted pleasure of the wealthy classes. I can't see how all of that could have been going on under our very noses. Surely it would have raised Hell itself?"

"I do indeed mean Mr Stead's articles, Atticus, and yes, I do mean the procurement of vast numbers of very young girls – virgin girls – in order to forcibly deflower them. Mr Stead's claims were, and still are, entirely accurate. I will concede that you're right when you say it should have raised Hell. But it happened here, in this Annexe, for years and it didn't even raise the servants.

I'm deeply ashamed to admit to you both that my grandfather and his select circle of friends in the Friday Club rejoiced in the vanguard of Harrogate's very own defloration mania."

They glanced as one at the picture high on the wall, and the smirks and leers of the faces there betrayed the stark truth of his words.

"Then thank Providence that's all the Friday Club is now," Lucie said, "Just awful memories and an old photograph on a wall."

"We're all very glad too, Mrs Fox," Roberts agreed. "Those men are all either dead now or at least are very old and frail. But remember this: Mr Stead wrote those articles – his 'infernal narrative,' as he called it – not fifty, not twenty, not even ten, but just five short years ago. There have been some reforms to be sure; the age of consent for girls has been raised from thirteen to sixteen years for example, but you can be certain of this: The Maiden Tribute is still being paid to this day, in the dark places of every town and city in the realm."

Roberts shook his head despairingly.

"When my Aunt Elizabeth came to live here directly after her mama's death, she was thirteen years of age. My grandfather was her only living relative. He couldn't believe his luck. His niece, his sister's daughter, a beautiful, young, innocent girl, had been dropped completely into his power. In his own words, she would have cost him a clear two hundred pounds if he'd bought her from a procuress but there she was, a free gift of the Fates.

Forgive my indelicacy, Mrs Fox, but he used her wretchedly. Her mama hadn't even gone cold in her grave before he took Elizabeth's virginity, and for the next two years, he used her as nothing more than a plaything. Worse than that, he allowed, in fact he encouraged, the other gentlemen of his Friday Club to do the same. Often they would sedate her with chloral hydrate or laudanum to prevent her resisting, especially if one of the older, frailer gentlemen was having a turn at her. Perhaps in coming back here, to this house, to this Annexe where much of it happened, it triggered memories of her life of Hell here. Perhaps that's why she killed him."

Lucie was the first to recover and her voice was both steady and calm.

"Then that would certainly explain her apparent battle fatigue, but if she left before you were born, Doctor, how is it you know all of this?"

"There was the inevitable talk amongst the servants. My grandfather thought it was all a closely guarded secret but they knew; they knew or at least they suspected what was going on. I overheard their conversations many times as I played here."

"But I knew for certain."

Sister Lovell turned back at last from the tray and her face was ashen white.

"I was Elizabeth's governess. I knew that he, and the beasts-of-the-field he called his gentlemen friends, were taking advantage of her, and of all the other poor young girls that passed through this wretched Annexe; the girls the whole world thought he had rescued from poverty and was sending on to a better life."

She turned and stabbed a finger at a large tapestry hanging on the wall opposite.

"Freya, Mr and Mrs Fox, was the Viking goddess of love and beauty."

She stared at it in contempt.

"Beauty certainly; they much preferred their girls, and occasionally boys, to be beautiful, but love – hah – the only grains of love they had were for themselves. And people thought them philanthropists! Dear God, what philanthropy is there in procuring virgin girls from the streets and from the workhouses and even from their own poor mothers, and in plain terms, bringing them here to be raped? Tell me that, Mr and Mrs Fox."

"And not just raped."

Roberts' voice broke the ringing silence that followed Mary's words.

"They were raped as violently and as painfully as possible. Do you remember the words carved over the door downstairs: 'Abandon all hope, ye who enter here'?"

Atticus and Lucie nodded together.

"They used to show them those words as they brought them in. They wanted the girls to be terrified even before they began. And when they did begin, when they viciously and sadistically deflowered them, they would delight in being as hard and as brutal as they could – just like the Viking barbarians they idolised. That, Atticus, and that, Mrs Fox, is why the walls and the doors of the Annexe are so thick, and why the carpets are doubled. It was to muffle the sounds of the girls as they screamed and begged for mercy, and it was to deaden the sounds of the boys being buggered."

The ringing silence enveloped them once more.

"What happened to the girls... and the boys then? What happened after they were finished with them?" Lucie whispered, aghast.

Mary Lovell answered.

"Any number of things, Mrs Fox. Many of the girls were taken to a farmhouse not far outside of the town, at Brimston. It was run by a procuress who called it a Home for Fallen Women and Girls. But don't be fooled for a moment by its charitable name; it was really nothing more than a brothel. She would use the women and the girls she kept there to accommodate a gentleman's every desire, his every fantasy, no matter how depraved that might be. Mr Alfred also used the procuress — Mrs Eire she was called — as an abortionist, and to sew the girls' maidenheads up again after they had been deflowered so that they could be violated once again. She would sew them up again and again until they were too cut up to allow it any more.

Other girls were sent to France, to work in brothels there, and others to the Orient. One of the Friday Club gentlemen — Mr James — was a ship owner you see, and he would transport them like slaves with no questions asked. The Arabs in particular prized them for their fair skin and for the fact that they were British. They fetched an excellent price in the slave markets. Mr James wasn't averse to buying up native girls there either, and bringing them back to Harrogate. The boys were generally thrown out onto the street."

"Did they never say anything? Did they never tell anyone?" Atticus asked.

"No, Atticus, they never did."

Roberts took up the tale once more.

"Remember that these were young girls and boys, anywhere from ten years of age upwards, who had been separated from their families, or who never had any families in the first place. They had been sullied and they had been brutalised. Society's attitude towards unchaste girls is bad enough now; forty or fifty years ago it was harsher still. And if they had managed to speak out, if they had told someone about any of it... Who would have believed them anyway? What would the word of one little whore girl have been worth against the solemn oaths and reputations of some of the great philanthropists of Harrogate?"

He laughed, harshly and mirthlessly.

"And the boys would always stay silent."

He nodded his head towards the door to the stairway.

"And do you remember the words written above that door there?"

"I do," Atticus replied, "'Freya is the receiver of the slain. Lördag cleanses your body and your tongue,' or something very much like it."

"That is exactly correct, Atticus," Roberts confirmed. "Your memory remains quite excellent. Those words were put there to remind the children – and the gentlemen of the Friday Club themselves – that anyone who breathed a word of what went on in this Annexe to the world outside would be in mortal peril. Lördag is Saturday; it was the traditional Viking day to bathe. Not only were the gentlemen supposed to cleanse their bodies of the debaucheries of the night before, they were supposed to cleanse their minds too. They were supposed to wash away even the memories of what they had done, so that they could never spill the awful secrets afterwards."

"Did they never tire of Miss Elizabeth, once they had deflowered her?" Lucie asked.

"Far from it," Mary retorted. "She was a very beautiful girl and that held their interest all the while she was here. And because she had perfect manners and spoke very well, she would always be the one they took back to their houses and their hotels rooms with them, passing her off as their niece or their daughter or some other relative to anyone who bothered to enquire."

"What about Mr Alfred's wife?" Lucie asked Roberts. "Where was your grandmother when all of this was happening?"

"She was where she always was, Mrs Fox – alone in her bed with her green faeries – her bottles of absinthe. My grandmama was another of my family's sordid secrets; drunk, incapable of coherent speech most of the time, and on the brink of madness. It was how she dealt with it all you see. It was the only way she knew of coping with the terrible knowledge of what my grandfather and his friends were doing.

A chambermaid was well paid to tend to her. In other words to feed her and to fetch her drink, and to empty her chamber pot. But most of all, to keep her mouth shut."

"But the servants knew, or they suspected anyway," Atticus countered, "And you knew, Miss Lovell; you said so yourself."

Mary was staring again at the tea tray the parlour maid had left for them on the side table. She reached over and turned the teapot a fraction, and three sets of eyes silently followed the movement.

"Yes, Mr Fox, I did know. I cannot deny it. Lizzie confided in me exactly what her uncle and his friends were doing to her and to all the other children. But I knew anyway; the screaming and crying, the begging to be out was quite harrowing. There is not a day that goes by when I don't hate myself for my cowardice in not speaking out.

Dr Roberts is kind. He reminds me that I was hardly older than Lizzie myself at the time and I suppose if truth be told, I was afraid for my life too. Maybe I convinced myself that if I had told someone, I would have brought shame on Lizzie; that she would have been blamed as being the seductress of the great, good Mr Alfred Roberts. Perhaps, if I had said what was going on in here, people might have guessed that they had deflowered me too."

"Oh, Mary," Lucie cried.

"You don't need to tell, Mary," Dr Roberts said gently.

"I do, Doctor, I do," Mary replied, dabbing her eyes with a pocket handkerchief. "Mr and Mrs Fox need to know exactly what it was like here in Alfred's day."

She dabbed at her reddening eyes a little more and said: "Mr Alfred usually told the other gentlemen and that ogre of a steward he had to leave me alone. He was afraid that, because I was a servant of sorts, then if they attacked me, word would get out to the rest of the household. But one night, in August I think it was, they got especially rowdy and very, very drunk. Mrs Eire had only managed to procure one or two virgin girls that week, so once they had finished with them, once they had 'buttered' them as they used to call it, they were still howling and shouting for more. Lizzie had run away to the workhouse by then, or she surely would have been 'buttered' too.

Then they saw me, finishing off some dainty-cakes for them in the scullery.

'Why you've a lithe, tender young lamb tethered over there, Roberts,' roars Mr Price, pointing at me through the door. 'The hounds are still ravenous hungry, so how about throwing your pretty young governess to us then?' The others started shouting and crying, just exactly like dogs baying at a fox-hole, so I dropped my dainties there and then, and ran out towards the main house. But the steward, Mr Otter, was blocking the way, and he caught me before I was even half way down the hall. I was picked up and thrown onto Lizzie's old bed, held down whilst I was given a dose of chloral hydrate to stop me struggling, and then, Mr and Mrs Fox, then I was stripped of my clothing and brutally deflowered. I was raped by each and every one of them in turn – including Otter – while the rest of them looked on and jeered.

I resigned my position the very next day of course and fled the house, but even now, I still wake in the night feeling them on me, hearing their jeering and having that awful, bitter taste in my mouth.

Mr Alfred naturally tried to stop me from leaving. He offered to pay me handsomely if I would stay and take up procuring girls for them in place of Mrs Eire. He said that Mrs Eire hadn't really been much good since she had been indiscrete and was barred from the workhouses. When I refused – I could never put another child through what I'd suffered – he promised that if ever I breathed a word about them or about what they did to a single living soul, he would send Mr Otter to hunt me down and rip my tongue from my head. I heard afterwards that he'd spoken to Mr James about having me drugged and shipped out to the Sudanese slave markets, but I never gave him the chance.

I knew that when Elizabeth ran away, she would have likely gone to the Harrogate Workhouse, which was in Starbeck at the time. It was before the parish unions, you understand. More than ever, I was racked with guilt that I had never said anything to help her, so I determined to track her down.

She had indeed gone to the workhouse as I thought she would. I sought and was given a position there as nurse, and I've spent the rest of my life watching over and caring for her and the other little children. It's my penance you see. It's the very least I can do to make amends for my months of silence."

"Did you tell the magistrate any of this?" Atticus asked.

Roberts looked horror-struck.

"No, Atticus, and please, I would greatly prefer not to. The scandal, you know, and the shame on Aunt Elizabeth and Mary and... Well, the scandal would be unbearable.

I can only hope that if my lawyer can't persuade that fool magistrate to reconsider his decision, then surely the judge will see that her trial is a mockery of justice. If that fails and the trial goes ahead, then I'll say that in killing my grandfather, Aunt Elizabeth was acting, in a way, in self defence; that it was a natural reaction to the two years of horror she suffered at my grandfather's hands."

"And then what, Doctor?" Lucie asked.

"Then I'll press to have a guardianship order passed to deliver her back into my care and keeping. Mary can continue her life's work in caring for her and yes, she can be seen to be guarding her too, if that's what they want. Aunt Elizabeth in her current state will know no difference anyhow and she can eke out her few remaining years in comfort. It's the only just and fair way.

Aunt Elizabeth might be locked in this Annexe awaiting trial for murder, but for the first time in nearly half a century, she's free, just as Mary and I are now free. Did you see how content she looks? She knows that he's dead; that he's gone forever. One part of her torment is finally over."

"One part of her torment is over?" Lucie repeated, "You mean there is more to it yet?"

"Oh, yes," Roberts said quickly, as if he had been expecting, maybe even hoping for the question. "There is much more to it yet. Do you recall when you first brought Aunt Elizabeth back here, that I said I had two further tasks for you? The first was to restore her mother's inheritance to her. The second, however, is of much greater importance given the present situation. I'll ask the parlour maid to bring us some fresh tea whilst Mary checks on my aunt. Then, I shall tell you all about it."

CHAPTER 23

"Ye'll be able to see t' magpies on t' Stray, Lizzie. Ye like to watch t' magpies, don' ye?"

Elizabeth turned and looked into Old Rachel's eyes, full as they were of concern. She desperately wanted to speak, desperately wanted to say, 'Yes, I love to watch them. I'd love to be a bird myself, free to fly wherever I choose, free to fly to my mama,' and, 'Thank you, Rachel, for being so kind when the rest of the world despises me for being a whore.'

But the blackness, the deep, impenetrable blackness, held her fast.

"It will be a lovely day, Lizzie, wit' t' fine racin' hosses gallopin' across t' Stray."

The blackness pressed still closer.

"An' t' overseers 'ave said ye may take yer yellow jacket off while ye're out."

The blackness dissolved just a little, became perhaps a fraction less dense. It eased just enough for her to whisper "Thank you," and for her almost to fall to the floor in relief.

"Tha's better, Lizzie; I thought t' cat 'ad run off wit' ye tongue. Ye need 'ave no jacket on so there will be no-one a-calling ye names."

Lizzie nodded, and the sneering, disdainful faces of the other inmates flashed through her mind, one after another, like so many magic-lantern slides. In public, they all taunted her, mocked her, calling her 'hedge whore,' 'trollop,' and 'Lizzie-leap-a-bed.' They would bump into her in the corridors, and knock her brutally against the hard walls; they would spit onto her newly polished brass, or smear mud across her clean-swept floor. In private though, when she was alone, the men would creep near her and brush against her. They would push their rough, dirty hands into her shift and whisper. They would whisper the things, the horrible things, that they longed to do to her, into her ears, and leave them to seep into her mind.

And then she was outside the workhouse, jacketless, in her best gingham dress.

The sun was shining. It was shining brighter than the yellow jacket, brighter even than the whitewash of the walls, now that the blackness had dissolved, and the other paupers, even the men, were just ignoring her; all, that is, except Old Rachel.

"Ye look as pretty as a picture, Lizzie," she said. "Ye'll be a match for any o' them fine ladies o' Harrogate."

"She'll be hoping that she gets ridden as well as the horses, Rachel," a woman's voice cackled from behind them.

"Don' mind wha' she says, Lizzie," Rachel retorted, her voice raised and her tone acid, "She's jus' envious o' how pretty ye are."

Lizzie waited for the woman's own retort, waited to hear more of how slatternly even the paupers thought she was. But it never came. Instead, the two short lines of inmates suddenly straightened and stiffened, as rigid as the ash-wood handles she spent so many hours binding with whin bush to make brooms. A smart black carriage with two liveried coachmen swept between the stone gateposts and arced gracefully to a halt outside the workhouse porch.

"It be one o' t' overseers," Old Rachel whispered.

Lizzie didn't reply. Her whole body, and the very spirit within it, was trembling uncontrollably. She knew that glossy black carriage only too well, as too she did the arms painted proudly below the window; the gold shield with a black lion rampant. One of the coachmen clambered from his seat and pulled the carriage door respectfully open. The black lion moved and seemed suddenly to be stalking her. A walking cane appeared — a familiar, black walking cane — followed by an even more familiar arm. It was an arm she knew, only too well, was overpowering and unstoppable, and her trembling grew worse. She wanted to cry out, she wanted to beg someone — anyone — for mercy, but the words gagged in her throat. She wanted to turn, wanted to flee to the sanctuary of her bed, but her limbs had turned to cold, heavy lead, and they refused to heed the shrieking, shrieking screams of her brain.

'Oh Lord Jesus, please don't let it be him; please let it be someone else, anyone else. Please don't let them have found me at last.'

But even the Lord Jesus refused to hear the anguished cries of her mind. It was him; it was another of the great philanthropists of the Friday Club, greeting the Master and his wife, and all of them had smiling, laughing faces.

'Please don't know him. Please don't let him be your gentleman friend too,' she begged. But she remembered how her flesh had crawled when the

workhouse Master – her master – had first looked upon her nakedness. She remembered the gleam of lust in his eyes, and she knew how it must be.

"Mr Price," she whispered.

"Do ye know t' O'erseer, Lizzie?" Rachel sounded astonished. *Lizzie could feel her intelligent old eyes lying on the back of her head, but the blackness was beginning to bind her once more and she couldn't speak the words.*

Mr Price was talking to Mr Wright, the Medical Officer, as if he were an old friend, and all the while his eyes were searching the ranks of the inmates, surely seeking her out. And then Mr Wright pointed directly at her. Mr Price looked and the black lion rampant looked, and her heart stopped beating.

"Are ye ailin', Lizzie? Ye've gone as pale as a ghost."

It was Old Rachel again, but she could hardly hear the words she was saying for the blood pounding and pounding and pounding in her head.

"Very well, inmates," *the Master called, and the spell was broken.*

"This day at the Stray races is a reward for your cheerful undertaking of various disagreeable tasks. You will conduct yourselves properly at all times, and normal workhouse rules will apply. Any breaches of those rules will be met with punishment in the usual ways."

'Will be punished in the usual ways, will be punished in the usual ways, but how can that be?'

Memories cascaded over her of the way Mr Price usually did punish wicked little girls. She remembered him towering over her as she knelt before him, remembered his arms coiling around her like some huge serpent; remembered his crushing weight and his little, sharp teeth biting into her flesh.

Something grabbed at her arm and she gasped, crying out in fear. But it was only Rachel, grinning toothlessly, and she breathed once again.

"Come along, li'le Miss Daydream, we don' wan' to be left behin' now, do we?"

The two whispering ranks of inmates became two laughing, chattering files. Like one huge family, they began walking up the road behind the Master and Mr Price. Mrs Dixon ambled along just behind them, and Elizabeth walked in silence, just as these days she always walked in silence, with her eyes fixed on the broad back of the Overseer's frock coat.

And then they were part of the laughing, chattering crowds at the racecourse, and she could see him no longer amongst all of the other gentlemen in their own frock coats.

'*Where did he go? Where is he now? Dear God, where is he now?*'

She had relaxed, just for a second. *How could she have let him disappear like that? How could she have let herself be distracted so? How could she have been such a stupid, stupid girl?*

"*Miss Elizabeth Wilson, how delightful it is to see you again.*"

Her limbs turned instantly to cold, heavy lead and kept her there, held her there in front of him, trapped in his mocking smirk like a tiny snared rabbit caught in a poacher's lantern light.

'*Rachel!*' she wanted to shriek, wanted to scream for all the world to hear.

But the word refused to pass her lips, and Rachel was gone. She was alone — alone with Mr Price, amid the laughing, chattering crowd.

His hand crept around her fingers and held them tight.

"*Your Uncle Alfred will be very pleased indeed that I've met up with you, Miss Elizabeth.*"

He squeezed her fingers viciously and then gently lifted them to his lips. She felt the rough scratch of his whiskers as they raked across the soft skin of her hand.

"*He was very concerned indeed as to where you might have got to,*" he continued, his tone as mocking as his eyes, "*And what you might have said.*"

He squeezed her fingers once more, crushing them cruelly and she gasped.

"*You haven't said anything, have you, Miss Elizabeth, about Mr Alfred or about the other members of the Friday Club?*"

"*No, Mr Price,*" she whispered.

A woman in a fine, silk dress looked inquisitively over at them for a moment. '*Please come!*' Lizzie tried to beg, tried to plead with her eyes. '*Please come and help me; please come and make him go away.*' The woman shook her head in contempt and turned away.

"*The Medical Officer tells me that you're with child again.*"

Price was smiling but he had the smile and the voice of a serpent.

"*Yes I am, if you please, Mr Price.*"

"*Have you been whoring yourself since you left Sessrum House?*"

"*No, Mr Price.*"

"*It is against the law of the land to whore yourself. Shall I call the constable and have you thrown into prison, Lizzie?*"

"*Please no, sir.*"

"*So you have been whoring yourself?*"

"*Yes, sir; I mean no, sir. No I haven't.*"

"So is the baby mine?"

She stared at him, not comprehending the words. Surely it was her baby, hers to love and to hold and to be with always.

"I asked, Miss Elizabeth, if the child is mine."

"I don't know, sir."

Price crushed her fingers again and she cried out in pain. His smile grew wider and more fixed, like the villain of a magic lantern show.

"How can you not know whose it is, you stupid child? It must be mine. It must be from the time I took you up to Alfred's hunting lodge for the week. Hell and Damnation! How could you have been so careless, you silly little hussy?"

He stared at her for a moment longer and said, "Damnation!" again.

"Are ye a'right, Lizzie?"

It was Rachel.

'Oh, thank you, thank you Lord Jesus for sending her to save me.'

Rachel peered at Mr Price and at his massive hand, as it lay coiled tightly around Elizabeth's fingers.

"Lizzie, are thee a'right?" she repeated.

Price released her fingers but his smile remained.

"Miss Elizabeth and I were just renewing our acquaintance, pauper," he said stiffly, "Not that it is any concern of yours. I was assuring her that I don't need to tell her uncle where she is, just so long as she promises to be very careful."

He paused to allow Elizabeth to comprehend the full meaning and import of his words, and in that time, it seemed somehow as if he had to come to a decision.

"And what's more, like her uncle, I am a philanthropist. I will personally ensure that she and her baby are cared for properly in the workhouse, and that the child, if it lives, is given every opportunity to better its situation."

CHAPTER 24

"She's still sleeping in her chair," Mary Lovell whispered as she returned to the smoking room of the Annexe, as though her voice might yet awaken Elizabeth.

"How is she?" Dr Roberts asked.

He was whispering too.

"She's terribly unsettled, Doctor. She's been crying out for Rachel in her sleep again."

"Who's Rachel?" Roberts asked.

"She was an old pauper woman who used to help me in the workhouse infirmary at Starbeck," Mary replied. "She's long dead now, of course, but she was a good friend to Lizzie in the early days at the workhouse, when it was especially hard for her."

Dr Roberts nodded and carefully poured the fresh tea the parlour maid had brought. As the tea tinkled into the fine porcelain cups, the feeling of anticipation around him steadily built.

"I fear I have a second missing person for you to find," he announced at last.

Atticus and Lucie exchanged startled glances and Atticus said: "Another missing person?"

"Yes, indeed," replied Roberts, handing him a cup. "I should very much like you to find my cousin. I've never had the pleasure of meeting her, but her name is Sarah. Sarah Beatrice Wilson was, or rather is, Aunt Elizabeth's daughter."

"Elizabeth was expecting a child – her second child – when she eventually fled to the workhouse," Mary explained. "It was born, a beautiful baby girl, a few months later. I delivered her myself, with Rachel helping. Elizabeth named her Sarah, after a friend she had as a girl, and Beatrice, after her late mama."

"If Sarah was her second child, what became of her first?" Lucie asked.

"Her first child, little Baby Albert, died at only a few weeks old," Mary replied.

She sipped at her tea.

"I was the one who had to break the news to her."

She sipped at her tea again.

"He was almost certainly murdered."

"Murdered?" Atticus exclaimed, his face flushing with alarm, "How do you mean, 'He was almost certainly murdered'?"

"I mean it in the plainest sense of the word, Mr Fox. You see, if the gentlemen of the Friday Club had the misfortune to put one of their girls with child, they had them sent straight away to the Home for Fallen Women and Girls at Brimston."

"The brothel you told us about?" asked Lucie.

Mary nodded.

"Whilst they were there, they would either be given a rough-and-ready abortion, or if they were allowed to have their babies, they would be made to prostitute themselves to Mrs Eire's gentlemen visitors until they were too far gone. Then, once their confinements were over, their fate was the same as the other girls who'd served their purpose to the Friday Club. They'd either continue to be whored out at Brimston, or they'd be sold on elsewhere. Mr Alfred much preferred them to be sent abroad. He thought it was cleaner that way.

If the baby was a girl and the mother had been reasonably pretty, the infant would be brought up at Brimston – by its mother if it was lucky – and then sold into the Friday Club at whatever age it was deemed fit. The baby girls whose mothers weren't so pretty and the baby boys, well, they were generally sent out to a baby farmer."

"Oh, dear Lord no," Lucie groaned.

"Yes, Mrs Fox, I'm afraid that's invariably what happened. Mr Alfred or the Club would pay twelve pounds for the infants to be taken care of, permanently. I found out later that most of them would be kept quiet with laudanum whilst they were slowly starved to death on a mixture of lime and water. Elizabeth never knew that that was what almost certainly happened to her baby, to Albert. The coroner's verdict was 'debility from birth,' and she just thought that he had died of natural causes, but even that – even that was enough almost to kill her.

When she fell pregnant for the second time, she was desperately afraid that her new baby would be taken from her and that it would die too. That was the reason she ran away to the workhouse. She believed they would allow her to keep her baby and to bring it up safely."

Lucie shuddered.

"And did she?"

Mary pursed her lips.

"No, Mrs Fox, alas she did not. That is why Dr Roberts' is engaging you both to find her."

She turned her head.

"Lizzie, have you awoken, my angel?"

Standing silently in the hallway, her lips forming unheard words, was Elizabeth.

"Come and have some tea with us, Lizzie, as a special treat. We have guests today. You remember Mr and Mrs Fox don't you?"

Mary stood and gently led Elizabeth into the group of chaises longues.

"Dr Michael has asked Mr and Mrs Fox to find Sarah Beatrice for you, Lizzie. You'd like to see Sarah Beatrice again, wouldn't you? You'd like to see her before you..."

Sarah — Sarah Beatrice — Baby Sarah! The other terrible memory stirred once again in its special, secret place and trembled against the fragile bonds that held it.

"Lizzie, we 'ave a new nurse in t' infirmary to 'elp Mr Wright."

Old Rachel's eyes were almost bursting with excitement.

Elizabeth's own leaden ones crept around to meet them, and she wondered how Rachel could always seem so happy. She was old, and she had been forced to endure so many long years of life, yet still she smiled, still she was able to laugh.

"It's someone ye know," Rachel continued.

Elizabeth forced a single word through the blackness. It was, 'Who?', but it sounded strangely hoarse and unfamiliar to her ears.

"Ye see, ye're speakin' again, an' I haven' even told ye who it is yet. She'll be a-helpin' me to deliver yer little-un in t' lyin'-in room."

Rachel glanced down at the great mound under Elizabeth's grogram gown and grinned.

"Lizzie, it's thy old governess, Sister Lovell."

Sister Lovell? The name sounded strange, but at the same time somehow familiar. Lovell?

"Mary?"

The voice sounded much more like hers once more.

"Mary Lovell?"

Rachel's grin widened.

"Aye, Mary Lovell, but ye mus' call 'er, 'Sister,' now, or 'Ma'am.' Come wi' me; I'll take ye t' see her."

And then she was back in Sister's, in Ma'am's, in Mary Lovell's arms; sobbing as if she would never stop.

"Lizzie, you're huge," Mary exclaimed, "I can hardly get close to you."

Elizabeth nodded.

"And Rachel tells me that you never speak these days, and that you hardly ever properly eat. All you do is make up brushes out of whin, and then wear them out on the floors."

Elizabeth nodded again.

"Well, we're together again now, Lizzie, and I promise – I promise you now – that I'll look after you always. I've found a situation here as nurse, so Rachel and I will be delivering your baby and not Mrs Eire."

The very worst memory of all; the memory of little Baby Albert also began to twist and tremble against its bonds, and reach out for its twin.

"They hurt me, Lizzie; all of them. They hurt me just like they used to hurt you and John and all the other children. Then your uncle wanted me to go and find them more girls for the club. They wanted me to become a procuress like Mrs Eire. So I did what you did, Lizzie, and I ran away from there."

And then the other, terrible, terrible memory, the one that could never be hidden properly away in the secret places of her mind, broke free.

Mary and Rachel's faces were there, brimming with love and compassion.

"Almost there, my lamb," Rachel crooned.

Another great wave of pain engulfed her, overpowering, unstoppable. She cried yet another cry of agony, pain tore once more through her body, and then she gasped, gasped in blessed relief.

Another cry replaced hers. It was the cry of new life, of a newborn baby; of her baby. Its cries thrilled her, and Mary held out its tiny, perfect form.

"It's a lovely baby girl, Lizzie, quite as beautiful as its mama," she said.

"Sarah," whispered Elizabeth, "Sarah Beatrice Wilson; A granddaughter for my mama, and a little sister for Albert. They won't take her away, Mary; they won't ever take her away, will they?"

And she cradled her baby, Baby Sarah, and rocked her just as she remembered her own mama rocking her. And just like her own mama, she sang as she rocked:

"Hush-a-bye baby, on the tree top,
When the wind blows, the cradle will rock.
When the bough breaks, the cradle will fall,
And down will come baby, cradle and all."

And then she thought about the words she was singing to her baby and a terrible, visceral chill gripped her. The cradle will fall... and so will the baby.

Baby Sarah will fall, just as she had fallen, just as her mama had fallen, and had needed to be punished.

She suddenly wished with all her soul that she had not sung the words because the words were surely a curse. She wished now that they had both died, died as Rachel told her many women did, in childbirth.

And a second set of words came into her mind, as she sat rocking to-and-fro, clinging to her baby. They were the words that the old crone Leah had sung to her when she was first admitted to the workhouse:

'Hush-a-bye baby, on the tree top,
When you grow old, your wages will stop.
When you have spent, the bit money you made,
First to the poorhouse, then to the grave.'

The other memory moved on in her mind, and two years flew past in the time it took for her to rock to-and-fro, clinging to her baby.

"Taken her, taken Sarah Beatrice? Who's taken her? Taken her where?"

"Calm yourself, girl, there is nothing to be alarmed over. Your daughter has been taken away to be adopted by a wealthy local family. They will bring her up with every privilege. You should be very pleased."

They were the words, the words she had dreaded with each and every one of her long waking hours. She could hear them still, inside her head, filling it, creeping through her body, through her arms, through her legs, turning them to ice.

"Who's taken her, Mrs Dixon? Who's taken my Baby Sarah? Please tell me."

The matron's irritation effervesced and boiled over into anger.

"Wilson, one of the workhouse overseers kindly took it upon himself to arrange for Sarah Beatrice to be adopted into one of the best families in the whole of the West Riding of Yorkshire. I do not know their name and nor do I need to, but I am assured that they are very respectable indeed. Your daughter will be raised in grace and comfort. That should be more than good enough for you."

It was happening once again. Mrs Dixon's face seemed to drift away as if down a long, black tunnel. Her baby — Baby Sarah — had been taken away and she would never see her again. The worst thing of all was happening again. Little Sarah was going to die. She'd be starved to death and found in the still, black waters of a ditch; wrapped up in an old newspaper, to save the expense of a doctor being called to pronounce that she was properly dead. That's what the old crone Leah had said had surely happened to her little Baby Albert.

A picture of little Sarah's perfect face with her beautiful, beaming smile exploded into Elizabeth's mind.

"Mama," the vision of Sarah said, and giggled.

But then she heard her cry, and her cry was a scream of terror. From deep inside the dark places of her mind she could hear her uncle's voice echo once more:

"Welcome to Sessrum House, Baby Sarah. You're a bad, wicked child, and I want you to beg me for mercy, just like your mama, and your poor, dead grandmama begged and begged and begged."

Elizabeth could see his face, that loathsome face, and see the beast in his eyes. He was framing the words — those words — the ones that haunted every one of her nights, when the bad things happened.

"In my experience, little girls who beg for mercy seldom deserve it."

And then Sarah screamed once more, but this time her scream was a scream of agony. It lingered, then all at once began to fade and die and the whole world seemed to fade with it, until finally, it all turned to blackness.

"Lizzie... Lizzie... Wake up. Wake up, my lamb."

Mary was off her seat and frantically shaking Elizabeth's skinny shoulders.

Elizabeth's eyes flickered open and she stared back, her face expressionless.

"Oh, thank the Lord she's come round," Mary gasped, "I thought that she'd had a fit."

"It certainly looked like it."

Lucie was kneeling next to her, pressing her fingertips gently between the gaping bones of Elizabeth's wrist.

"And it was certainly a shock when she cried out like that and collapsed. Her pulse is racing. What do you suppose it was?"

Mary straightened Elizabeth's crisp, white poke bonnet.

"I think she just had a bad dream. That's all it was. She was having a dream."

"Lizzie... Lizzie... Wake up, darling!"

Someone was shaking her, calling for her. It was a gentle voice, full of warmth and compassion. Was it her mama, come for her at last? No, she decided, it wasn't her dear mama. Then who was it? Could it be Mary; Mary who'd come to watch over her, come to make sure no one hurt her ever again?

But then she remembered that she had been hurt. They had taken her baby, and when they had, they had ripped away part of her soul too. Her eyes snapped open and the memory of the Matron's words overwhelmed her once again.

"Oh, thank t' stars, she's a-come 'round," said another voice.

It was Old Rachel.

"Lizzie... Lizzie... it's us. It's Mary and Rachel. You fainted and now you're in the infirmary."

Mary's face appeared above hers and she felt warm fingers entwining her own.

"Mary, they've taken Sarah away. I don't know where she is!"

"Hush, Lizzie, I know, I know. Mr Price arranged it all. He said that she'd been adopted into a good, local family. Don't fret; I've checked with Mr Petty at Sessrum and no one has seen a little girl that young come through the house — recently anyway. I don't suppose Mr Price would have taken her to his own house to hurt her there either because of his wife. She adores children although she can't have any of her own. Anyway, Sarah Beatrice is too little — even for him."

"Find her, Mary. Please find her and bring her back to me!"

Little pricks of light were beginning to fill her vision, and she felt as if she was beginning to float; almost as if she'd just been given some of her uncle's medicine for wicked girls.

"I will find her, Lizzie, I promise."

Mary's voice was distant now.

"I'll find her. I'll find her if it takes me a lifetime."

CHAPTER 25

"Please find her, Mary."

The four of them: Atticus, Lucie, Mary and Dr Roberts, stared in disbelief at the old woman now singing 'Hush-a-bye, baby' softly to herself, as she rocked to-and-fro.

"Good Lord," Roberts exclaimed, his teacup frozen in mid-air, "She spoke to us. That was as plain as the nose on my face. She understood everything we just said."

"It's no wonder the police wouldn't entertain the McNaughton rules," Atticus added.

Mary shook her head.

"I don't think so. Sometimes she seems to understand a little of what's being said to her. Occasionally, on a good day, she even makes odd remarks like that which seem perfectly sensible. Most of the time though, in fact, almost all of the time, she might as well be on the moon."

She took Elizabeth's hand and held her fingers.

"Lizzie, do you know where Sarah might be?"

Elizabeth stared down at their hands and rocked.

"One and eight and eight and one is Eighteen Hundred and Eighty-One," she sang.

"Do you know where her daughter might have gone, Miss Lovell?" Lucie asked, after a respectable amount of time had passed.

"Surely the workhouse records would show the name of the adopting family?"

Mary shook her head once more.

"When the parishes combined into the union and the big new union workhouse was built at Knaresborough, a lot of the old records disappeared. I'm not even certain there was ever a record kept in the first place. I've searched and searched over the years, but I've never found anything. I suppose no-one saw a need to keep an adoption record of a dozen years previous."

"Damned sloppy," interjected Roberts, and Atticus grunted in agreement.

"All I can recall," Mary continued, "Is that one of the overseers at Starbeck arranged for Sarah to be adopted just after her second birthday. It was by coincidence, Mr Price, the ringleader of my rape in the Annexe. You can see him on the photograph there: He's the one standing next to Mr Alfred."

As one, they glanced up at the photograph and picked out his image. There he was; a broad, powerfully built man, with one massive arm crooked over Alfred Roberts' shoulder.

"Is he still alive, do you know?" Atticus asked.

Mary said: "No," and Roberts added: "Thankfully not. He died a few years ago of a heart attack. Not that I would have believed for one minute that he actually had a heart, but I remember reading it in his obituary so it must be true. He was another great Harrogate philanthropist, so it said."

"That's a pity; he might have been able to remember where Miss Sarah was adopted. Does he have any close relatives, do you know?"

This time Roberts nodded.

"He has a wife, Anne Price. She's still alive, although she's very old and frail now. I believe she lives over in Low Harrogate, to be near the Pump Rooms."

"Anne Price was a lovely, kind-hearted lady," Mary added, the warmth of the memory forcing her to smile.

"She used to bring all kinds of sweets and toys for the workhouse children when she visited with her abomination of a husband. She couldn't have any children of her own, so she would come over and spend hours and hours with the pauper children instead. We quite missed seeing her when we moved to Knaresborough and we had the new parish guardians instead of the old overseers."

"I can't see how it's likely she'll remember what her husband did with one little girl though, Fox," Roberts said, voicing all their thoughts.

"He must have moved dozens of girls on, most of them into misery, and it was over forty years ago."

They all had the same, terrible thought, and inevitably, it was Atticus who voiced it.

"Was she brought here, do you think – to the Friday Club?"

Mary winced and glanced at Elizabeth. Thankfully, she seemed unaware of the conversation going on around her.

"We can only pray not, Mr Fox. Sarah was only two. I checked at the time with one of the servants here, and he told me that no-one had seen a girl that young come into the Annexe."

"So then why adopt her out?" Lucie asked, "Why take her from her mother, when her mother could quite easily ruin him in an instant? Did he sell her abroad do you think?"

Mary shrugged.

"Who knows for sure? But the Matron told me that Sarah was still in the West Riding and she had no reason to lie. Lizzie told me that Price believed he was the girl's father. Around the time Sarah would have been conceived, Price had taken Lizzie with him up to Alfred's hunting lodge in Northumberland. He raped her there many times, so it's quite possible, I suppose, that he was. I wouldn't have thought he'd have wanted to ship his own daughter abroad, but then at the same time, I could very well understand a monster like him wanting something as incriminating as an illegitimate daughter well out of the way."

Elizabeth had stopped singing her lullaby. She had stopped rocking.

Mary reached over and wrapped her skinny fingers around a teacup. Elizabeth looked down at it, and her mouth gaped like a nestling's.

Mary said: "Mr Price took you to Budle Tower didn't he, Lizzie? Mr Price took you to Northumberland."

Elizabeth nodded, and the teacup quietly dropped and vomited its contents across the carpet.

The shrill whistle shrieked along the length of the express train and dissolved into the chill of the afternoon; dissolved everywhere, that is, except within her soul. There it compounded with the silent screams of her anguish; with Sarah's; with John's; with little Peter Lovegood's... And grew louder and louder and louder.

She concentrated her whole being on the rhythmic clicks of the carriage wheels as they glided over the joints in the tracks. She closed her thoughts to everything except her urgings of the train to slow, to stop, to falter somehow, so that she need never set foot again in Northumberland, in that accursed county where forever a little boy floated face down in the rank black waters of her mind.

Mr Price was taking her to Budle, Uncle Alfie's hunting lodge, far to the north. It wasn't far from the Holy Island, John had said. They were supposed to have stayed there after the game of Viking Marauders that had gone so horribly wrong, when little Peter Lovegood had drowned and Sarah had screamed her scream of terror. But, after the cleansed sands of the causeway had reappeared once more, Uncle Alfie had ordered that the coach take them straight back to Newcastle and the fast train to Yorkshire. So she had only ever seen the big, square tower at Budle as a charcoal sketch.

John had said it was a peel tower; a fortified house built hundreds of years previously, by the wild Reiver clans. He said it was full of the brutal pikes and swords and maces that Uncle Alfie was so fond of collecting, and that if you went to the very top and gazed out over the battlements, you could see for miles and miles and miles across the sea, far beyond even the Holy Island. He swore that he had once seen Denmark.

But that was before the game of Viking Marauders, and that was before Mr James had taken him alone up to Budle. Now, he wouldn't talk about it at all.

Her first glimpse of Budle Tower rather surprised her. It surprised her not because it looked in any way dissimilar to the charcoal sketch that hung between the windows in the library at Sessrum House; it surprised her in that it looked so exactly like it.

Budle Tower was built of grey-black whinstone, and founded solidly on a grey-black, featureless drift of the same hard rock. Behind it, the cold, slate-grey Northumbrian sky was reflected perfectly in the cold, slate-grey waters of the North Sea.

Uncle Alfie kept only two servants at his hunting lodge, neither of whom she had met; a gamekeeper and a housekeeper. On the day that Mr Price first took her up to Budle Tower, the gamekeeper had gone off for the day to Berwick to fetch his new apprentice boy. Mr James was bringing a hunting party up for the following week and he would certainly be needed for that.

Miss Pearce was the housekeeper, and at the sound of the horses' hooves clopping and sliding on the smooth, hard rock of the lane leading up to the tower, she had slipped through the great front door and stood as attentively and as patiently as a spider in its web to welcome her special guests.

When Lizzie saw her standing by the door, with her hands clasped respectfully in front of her pure white apron, she again found herself not a little surprised. The servants at Sessrum always seemed to be sharing smirks or conspiratorial winks whenever Miss Pearce's name was mentioned, and Lizzie had always assumed that there must be something quite peculiar about her. But that certainly seemed not to be the case. She seemed perfectly normal, quite pretty even, if in a rather mannish way with long auburn hair and a ready, careful smile.

When Mr Price had been talking to her on the long coach journey from Newcastle, Lizzie had begun to hear the catch in his voice; that awful, breathless catch gentlemen get when they are thinking of punishing some poor little girl, and it had become more and more pronounced the closer to Budle they came.

She had hoped it was just the pure, clean air of Northumberland catching in his lungs, but then his enormous hands with their short, stubby fingers had begun to move. They had slipped inexorably towards her every time the only other passenger in the coach, an ancient gentleman with long, white whiskers, had drifted off into one of his frequent, fitful dozes. She was very glad indeed that there was another woman at Budle.

When she thought about it, she was especially glad that it was Miss Pearce at Budle. She knew that Miss Pearce must be some kind of entertainer – a turn. Perhaps Miss Pearce might somehow entertain Mr Price through the long, lonely nights, so that the shadows behind her door might stay mercifully still, and he might not come and slip into her bed.

She was sure Miss Pearce must be a very accomplished performer. Several times each year, Uncle Alfie would arrange for her to be brought down to Harrogate – a not inconsiderable distance – to do a turn with Mrs Eire in the smoking room of the Friday Club. All of the gentlemen members would be sure to attend their performance. Sometimes they would bring other gentlemen as guests too and on those nights, Mr Otter the steward would quite have his work cut out.

She wasn't altogether sure what form Miss Pearce and Mrs Eire's performances took. No one seemed particularly inclined to talk about it. But in spite of the thick walls and deep carpets of the clubroom, there was always a constant sound of rumbustious merriment. In fact, as her cousin John once remarked, they seemed to be raising Merry Hell itself in there.

There always seemed to be more than the usual number of waifs and strays in the Annexe on the nights when Miss Pearce and Mrs Eire were performing for the gentlemen. And when they had finished and the guests had gone home, the waifs and strays would be roused. They would be dragged up the iron stairs, one after another, and taken away by the gentlemen to be punished. Mr Otter certainly did have his work cut out then. The gentlemen always seemed to be having their work cut out too. And the girls would scream and scream and scream.

Night was when the bad things happened. But here, in the utter solitude of Budle, where the days were as quiet and as lonely as the nights, she worried whether perhaps the bad things might happen by day too. And so she had climbed to the very top of the spiral stairway that wound its way up one corner of the tower. It was horribly like the great stairwell of the Annexe at Sessrum House, but with the added terrors of the silent, unmoving suits of armour watching her from the shadows of every corner.

Each and every one of the stone steps had been worn down by the centuries of feet that had trodden the very same route that she now took. She wondered how many of them had pounded them in fear and mortal dread. What horrors had these ancient stones witnessed since they were first laid down by their Reiver founders?

She was jerked from her thoughts by the sound of Mr Price's harsh laughter echoing up the stairwell. She could feel it echoing inside her head. Perhaps Miss Pearce was entertaining him already? Yes, that would be it. Miss Pearce would be performing and making him laugh. But another part of her mind, an insistent, disquieting part told her Mr Price wasn't here for laughter, or the pure, fresh air. He was here for her.

At the very top of the stairs, just as at Sessrum House, there was a door. But unlike at Sessrum House, when she timidly pushed it open and peered through into the world beyond, there was no overpowering stench of tobacco, no ravenous leers and no raucous, mocking laughter. Here there was only silence, and the glorious scent of the sea. Instead of the terrible, terrible screams of the girls, there was only the far distant screech of gulls.

She crossed to the parapet and looked out over the broad whinstone drift. She gazed across the broad, flat sands of the bay to the black, black waters of the North Sea beyond. Except that the waters weren't black at all. The clouds had parted now, and they were a deep, sparkling blue. They reflected perfectly the glorious blue of the sky above them, and Lizzie realised all at once that they were there simply to do the bidding of the Heavens. They would mimic the Heavens in their colour, and they would follow it in their tides. It was the tide that had drowned little Peter Lovegood, but it was the Heavens that had seen his wretched terror and had taken pity on him. It was the Heavens over Lindisfarne – the Holy Island. They must have known that he was really a good little boy. They must have known that it was better to be drowned in the black, black waters of the North Sea than to be drowned in the suffering and cruelty that Mr James and her uncle meted out.

She watched as the waves became myriad points of light, reflecting the sun as it slowly arced over her, and gradually, she began to fill with dread. She felt a sickening fear of the time when the orb and the far-distant Cheviot Hills would finally kiss, knowing that night would surely follow, that bad things would happen and that Mr Price would surely come.

She could flee! She could run and run and run to where Mr Price and her uncle would never find her. She could run across the Pilgrim's Causeway to the Holy Island, and plead to the Heavens there. It was a holy island, and the Heavens would be merciful, just as they had been merciful to a little boy from a workhouse.

But then she remembered the great iron-studded door of the tower, and that it had been locked fast behind them. What had been built to keep out armies of raiders would surely serve equally well to keep in one little girl; one wicked little girl, whose mama had left her for Hell.

Could she fling herself from the high battlements and dash out her life on the hard, bare rocks below? For several long, delicious seconds she immersed herself in the relief, the wonderful, blessed relief that this would surely bring.

And then she remembered Dante, and his Inferno and how wicked she still was.

And then the orb and the hills did kiss, but there were no sweet dreams, and bad things did happen.

Miss Pearce had eaten with them. That too was surprising, startling even, because for a servant to have eaten with them in the grand dining room at Sessrum House would have been utterly unthinkable. And then she, Elizabeth, had been given wine at the table. It was a fine French wine that suited the meal perfectly, and Miss Pearce had laid out the crystal and poured her a large glass – a very large glass – as if she were a grown lady and not a little girl at all.

That too was startling. Never before had she been given fermented drink where she hadn't been held down on her bed and the liquor forced down her gullet.

A lot of Uncle Alfie's best wine was consumed with the dinner. Miss Pearce was smiling and attentive with the bottle and, with the strength of the wine and the heat of the fire-basket, all too soon Elizabeth's head was spinning and her ears were pounding. And then she had to weep for being a wicked, little seductress and for poor lost Peter, and for her dear, dead mama.

Miss Pearce told her that she had been born on the Holy Island. Like the Heavens, she had seen her despair and she had come like an angel of mercy to comfort her. Miss Pearce pulled her into a tight, warm embrace. She stroked her hair and kissed her forehead. Safe in her warm, strong arms, it was almost like having her dear dead mama back again. Lizzie tried to swing her legs, tried to swing them like she did when she was a very little girl, but her heels caught on the hard, stone flags of the floor.

And then, with a grinning nod of permission from Mr Price, Miss Pearce lifted her gently from her chair and led her back up the worn, spiral stairs. Round and round, round and round. Miss Pearce and Mr Price became no more than shadows driving her on. Lizzie knew that she could easily throw herself from the rooftop now; that she could at last make it all stop. She needed so much just to sleep forever. Like the Heavens, Miss Pearce knew that too. She kissed her once more and gently pulled her, dizzy and unsteady, into her bedchamber.

"The wine was a special treat for you," Miss Pearce whispered huskily, "I hope it wasn't spoiled?"

Elizabeth shook her head and the room spun... round and round, round and round.

"Good, because I wouldn't want to have my special treat spoiled, or Mr Price's."

Elizabeth tried to focus on her face, tried to focus on her words.

"Our treat," Miss Pearce continued, easing her down onto the bed, "Is to have you with us, Elizabeth."

That was kind, she thought, the sort of sweet thing her dear mama would have said before she left her for Hell.

Miss Pearce's hand lifted. She reached over and pulled at the blue velvet ribbon in Lizzie's hair that set off her hair so nicely. It loosed and fell away and Miss Pearce smiled. She began to caress her hair, to stroke it down tenderly over her shoulders and Lizzie remembered the time before her mama died, when her mama would brush her hair exactly fifty times before she kissed her goodnight. They would count the strokes of the hairbrush together. But Lizzie could see that Mr Price was in the room; that he was sitting on a low settee beside a large, dancing fire, watching as if entranced. He seemed to have fire dancing in his eyes, but Lizzie wasn't worried; bad things wouldn't happen this night, because Miss Pearce was there to protect her, just like another mama.

"You're very beautiful, Lizzie."

Miss Pearce's fingers were cool behind her neck and she kissed her cheek with such tenderness that Lizzie didn't even notice them slowly reaching for the clasps of her gown. It was her dear mama kissing her goodnight to protect her against all the bad things. The touch of her lips surprised her just a little as they reached out once more and met her own. It was surprising to be kissed by lips that were so soft and so gentle, that had no reek of tobacco, no taste of hard liquor, and no rake of stubble.

She felt her dress being pulled from her. Her mama was undressing her for bed.

"But Mr Price is watching," she mumbled, trying to protest.

Her brain seemed as heavy as lead, her thoughts as sluggish as the shadowy waters that rolled and lapped at the shore outside.

"Shh, Lizzie, never you mind what Mr Price is doing."

Miss Pearce seemed a little breathless now. It must be the heat of the fire. Lizzie nodded and allowed her leaden, leaden eyelids to fall shut. Under them the room seemed to be spinning once more, faster and faster and faster. It was a curious sensation.

And then there was another curious sensation. She was being kissed again, she was sure of it; not brutally as she usually was, with hands mauling her and grabbing her and making her hurt, but softly and tenderly. She felt something hot against her skin and she shivered. There was another part of the curious sensation too, a part that she couldn't quite comprehend with the room spinning so, but it was of Sessrum, of the Annexe and of cruel, cruel punishment.

She awoke. Miss Pearce was there, leaning over her. She was naked – stark naked – with the curves of her smooth and flawless skin rippling orange in the firelight. She was naked and she was touching her, caressing her, stroking her. Her touch was light but her eyes were ravenous. She had Lizzie's hand in her own and she smiled the smile of her uncle, as she pulled it against the softness of her breast. Horrified, she felt it swell against her fingers like a live thing. The wine vanished from her blood and she shrieked.

"Hush, Lizzie, don't struggle so, I'll show you what to do," Miss Pearce purred, reaching for her hand once more, spreading her fingers.

"No, no — please don't!"

Lizzie snatched away her hand, curling into the bedcovers, hugging them as if she were a tiny, tiny child and not a grown girl at all.

A shadow; a great, black shadow crept across the flickering wall above her head. It was large and squat, and it held in its hand, if hand it was, the paler shadow of a bottle through which the light of the fire cast swirling shapes and eddies. Its voice had a deep, familiar catch.

"I'll settle her down for you, Pearce. Roberts gave me this for her in case she struggled. He calls it her medicine."

Lizzie felt hands taking hold of her. They were big, muscular hands; hands she knew were overpowering and unstoppable. Her head was forced back and the hard, cold rim of a bottle pushed against her face. She felt cold liquid over her lips, across her cheeks, in her mouth. There was an acrid, bitter taste. She gasped and then there was more liquid. She spluttered and choked. The liquid was running cold around her neck, like Miss Pearce's icy fingers. Two faces, blurred, almost preternatural, appeared over hers and a voice spoke, too deep and too slurred to understand.

She awoke the next day to the sun's rays streaming flat and bright through the narrow window slit of her room, and to a suffocating wave of nausea. The pillow was soaked under her cheek, as if in the night she had cried tears enough to quench the flames of the Inferno itself. But then, as she lay on the clammy wetness, the memory, the raw, unbidden memory of the night before came back and the scab was ripped from her mind. She remembered that the wet under her cheek was the spilt, choked medicine for wicked girls, and oh, how wicked she had been.

She remembered Miss Pearce and how she had tried to... to arouse her, to seduce her. That was it; those were exactly the right words. Miss Pearce was a woman, but she had tried to somehow seduce her, and Mr Price had been watching her do it. He actually seemed to have been enjoying it, with the flames dancing in his eyes.

She was certain Miss Pearce would go to Hell, to the Eighth Circle of Hell where Uncle Alfie always said her mama had gone. She wondered if Mr Price had punished Miss Pearce for her wickedness as she vaguely remembered now he had punished her. Yes, she could feel the ache, deep in her belly where he always hurt her, and the stinging on her neck where he liked to bite her with his little sharp teeth.

She thought again of her mama, and just for a moment, just for the briefest moment, she hoped that her mama really was in Hell. For the briefest moment, she hoped with all of her heart that Uncle Alfie was right and that Mary and John and the words on the gravestone were wrong. Because if her mama really was in Hell then the broad whinstone drift beneath them would have blocked her view of the bad things that had happened in the night. Her mama would not have seen just how wicked she truly was.

She thought again of the roof, and of flinging herself onto the rocks below. She thought of the long, sandy causeway to the Holy Island, and of sitting there, singing her favourite lullaby as the waters rushed in to drown her. She imagined herself, face down, being pulled into a fishing coble. She pictured the fishermen looking at her, examining her, seeing that she hadn't been punished nearly enough, and dropping her back into the cold, bleak waters to sink down into Hell.

And if her mama was in Hell, she would see her again – today – now.

But she knew the instant the thought seared a path across her mind that she couldn't do it; she couldn't do any of it. Because maybe Mary and John were right after all, maybe her mama was in Heaven with Jesus. Perhaps she had seen everything that she had made Miss Pearce and Mr Price do to her.

She knew then that she had always to be an especially good little girl, and do everything exactly as she was told, so that her mama would come for her soon. Then she could explain that she had never, ever meant to make them do that, that it was all a frightful, frightful accident. She could explain that she really would be more careful from now on, and that she really never, ever meant to be a wicked girl at all.

Her thoughts were interrupted by the big gong calling her to breakfast. She ignored it. The lingering effects of the wine and the lingering image of a woman with firelight dancing on her naked skin drove her instead to seek the sanctuary of the battlements.

For the rooftop was a sanctuary. It was somewhere she could be safe, and somewhere she could be alone. The whispering of the waves calmed her spirit and soothed her mind, and the gentle breeze purged it of the wine. And if ever Mr Price or Miss Pearce were to happen upon her; if they were to seek her out with their ravenous, lascivious eyes, then the welcoming rocks below would be glad to receive her.

So Lizzie sat by the parapet and gazed across the bay.

To her left was the Holy Island, where Miss Pearce had been born and where, just a few short months earlier, a game had gone horribly wrong and a terrible, terrible thing had happened.

She glanced away lest that memory should come, bidden by name. To the right of the bay were yet more islands, rugged and bleak against the pure blue of the sea. John had told her that these were the Farne Islands, formed from pillars of the same black rock as that on which this very tower stood. He had also told her there was a lighthouse there, from which just a few years before, the great North Country heroine Grace Darling and her papa had rowed a little wooden boat − a coble − almost a mile through a terrible storm. They had rowed through the storm and rescued no fewer than thirteen shipwrecked sailors from certain death.

Grace had recently died, John had said, from tuberculosis, and as she watched those same seas, so calm and serene now, Lizzie felt a stab of envy. Grace had lived, cut off from the world, in a lighthouse − in a tower − built on whinstone, and so here was she, cut off and imprisoned no less. But Grace had had her papa with her, and she had performed a deed of such goodness and heroism that the Lord Jesus had looked down and rewarded her. He had rewarded her with death after just twenty-seven years of endurance on this earth. Pray God Lizzie could be rewarded some day too.

A huge grey gull soared above her, riding the winds that rose over the tower. When Mr Price or her uncle, or the other gentlemen of the Friday Club were punishing her in the Annexe, or in their carriages, or at their grand houses in the town, she could almost make it seem as if she wasn't there at all. In her mind, she would be playing games with John, or taking her lessons with Mary, or talking to her dead mama and papa in their grave. The men were content to punish her sinful body, and they would leave her spirit, what was really her, to wander as freely as it chose; as freely as the gull on the breeze or the magpies on the Stray. But here, at Budle, was Miss Pearce. Miss Pearce didn't want to punish her body. Miss Pearce was tender and soft, and she treated her body almost as if it were something holy.

Miss Pearce wanted her soul.

At night, when she came to do terrible things, she would never hurt her like the gentlemen hurt her. Miss Pearce would stroke her and caress her; she would whisper soft and tender things into her ear and tell her how she was quite lovely. Miss Pearce would try to possess her. And each time she did, Lizzie would be dragged back from her safe and special place to cling desperately to her very soul itself.

CHAPTER 26

The spa of Harrogate contained some eighty-eight distinct mineral springs, of which no two were exactly alike. No fewer than thirty-six of these springs were contained within the gardens of the Bogs Valley of Low Harrogate, the greatest concentration of such medicinal wells not only in England, or even in the Empire, but in the world.

Such an abundance of health-giving waters served to attract vast numbers of the sick, the infirm, and the elderly. It was said that anyone could be cured at Harrogate, just so long as they were wealthy enough, and it was to one of the large, opulent town houses overlooking the Bogs Valley Gardens that Atticus and Lucie Fox were bound.

The Price house was perhaps not quite as large or as stately as Sessrum House itself, but it was very comfortable nonetheless. They paused outside as Atticus took out his silver calling-card case and lifted out one of their thick, embossed cards. One of the corners had already been carefully folded over and the word, 'affaires,' — matters — neatly written on the little white triangle it formed.

Lucie felt strangely exposed as they trod the short path up to the prettily-painted front door of the house, but then suddenly they were there, and Atticus had already rapped on the knocker.

The die was cast.

The ornate knocking-iron was cast in black iron in the shape of a snarling cat's head. It seemed to be silently challenging them as they listened for sounds of movement within. Then, the door-knob twisted and a young woman in a crisp maid's uniform appeared. She curtsied politely and said: "Good afternoon."

Atticus smiled what he hoped was a warm and winning smile and politely raised his hat.

"Good afternoon. Perhaps you might be able to help us? We are Atticus and Lucie Fox, and we wish to leave our visiting card for Mrs Price."

The maid took the card and curtsied once more as she showed them through the vestibule to a large, tiled hallway beyond.

"I'll see if Mrs Price is at home," she said.

As the sound of the maid's footsteps faded, Atticus grimaced at Lucie.

"That sounds hopeful," he whispered. "It would save us a lot of time if she sees us today."

Lucie put her finger to her lips, like a school mistress before morning prayers. It was utterly vital that they spoke with Mrs Price. She was the last, in fact she was the only, firm link with little Sarah they had, and it would be ridiculous to offend her even before they began with a silly, thoughtless whisper.

Atticus mouthed, 'Sorry,' and the maid returned. She was beaming.

"Mrs Price has asked that I show you into the drawing room," she announced.

"She would be delighted to receive you."

They are looking at her. They are staring at her. They are staring through her. Everyone is laughing at her.

'The poor little whore of a pauper girl has lost another of her bastards.'

'Why won't anyone help? Why don't they tell her where she is?'

She stops everyone. She grabs their clothes. She drops to her knees and pleads and pleads and pleads with them.

"For the love of God, have you seen Baby Sarah? Tell me! Help me find her, please."

But they turn away, shaking their heads as if she's some kind of madwoman. An old lady looks at her; her mouth moves, speaking words she cannot hear. But her eyes are hard; her eyes say she doesn't know, or won't tell, and Lizzie runs on.

"Sarah!" she screams, "Sarah!"

A man in a shabby waistcoat and battered bowler hat grins like a fiend. He moves and blocks her way.

'Lord Jesus, please don't let him hurt me, or if he must, please make him do it later, after I've found Sarah. Please, please don't make it now. Please don't let him stop me from finding my Sarah.'

"I've lost my baby, sir. Please help me find my baby."

He grins again, and points to a ginnel.

"Oh, thank you, thank you, sir."

She runs into the alley.

"Sarah, it's me. It's your mama. I've come to fetch you. I've come to love you."

The silence presses on her ears. The walls seem to close in. The ginnel is empty, save for an upturned crate, a part-drunk bottle, and a clump of white-blanched nettles, clinging to life in the gloom.

"Sarah, my darling, where are you?"

A shadow moves. The world surges past her and the hard, stone wall of the ginnel slams into her back. Through her shock, she sees a bowler hat and the grinning face of a fiend; a fiend with eyes full of cruelty. Something is gripping her arm, gripping it hard. She is dragged through a doorway and thrown to the floor. For an instant she feels relief that the floor is smooth and wooden and not more, hard stone. Something lashes across her face and she tastes blood. A hand clamps her mouth. Her body freezes but her mind shrieks and shrieks and shrieks. It screams a scream of terror and flees to that place where it seems as if it is all happening to a different little girl; a different little girl whose body is being mauled and pawed under the suffocating weight of a lust-crazed monster; a different little girl whose grogram gown is being dragged away from her, and a different little girl whose eyes are clenched tight shut, whose limbs are numb as lead as she begs the Lord Jesus and her dead mama to make him be finished with her.

And then he was.

"Breathe a word o' this and upon my oath, I will kill thee. I can see what you're wearing; ye're a yellow-jacket slut from the workhouse, so I'll know just where to come looking for you."

The gruff voice drags her back, shrieking again, from her safe and special place. She realises that what has happened hasn't happened to a different little girl at all. It has happened to her; to little Lizzie Wilson.

She lies there, not daring to move – not able to move – for an age, thinking about his words. Then she remembers her gown and her nakedness and she pushes its heavy, comforting weight back over her legs.

He knew how wicked and how sinful she really was. He'd had no learning, no schooling and he was as drunk as her aunt, yet even he knew as soon as he saw her that she was a dirty, fallen slut. He'd said so. He knew to push her into a ginnel and to... She struggled with the words for what he had done. Was it seduction? Was it punishment, or did he just hate nasty, little sluts like her with their yellow jackets and their black hearts?

He said that he'd kill her if she told anyone. The wonderful, wonderful promise carved into her mama's gravestone drifted into her mind: 'And God shall wipe away all tears from their eyes, and there shall be no more death, neither sorrow, nor crying, neither shall there be any more pain, for the former things are passed away.'

'Please, God, please send the man in the waistcoat back — please send him back to kill me. And please let Baby Sarah be dead too so that she doesn't ever have to fall and have men hate her and punish her and make her seduce them in dark ginnels. Please, please let her be dead.'

"Where have you been today, Wilson?"

Mrs Dixon's waspish tones swept down the long workhouse corridor and stopped her heart.

"I asked you where you'd been," *she repeated an instant later,* "And how in God's name have you come to be in that state?"

Elizabeth turned and the briefest expression of shock flitted over the Matron's face.

"Please, Mrs Dixon, please, ma'am, I've been up to Harrogate. I've been looking for my little Baby Sarah."

She curtsied and a fresh wave of pain stabbed her below her belly.

"And who gave permission for you to be up in Harrogate?" *the Matron demanded.*

Elizabeth curtsied and grimaced once more.

"No one, Mrs Dixon," *she whispered,* "But I had to find my Sarah. I truly did, ma'am. She'll be crying for me. She'll be frightened. She needs her mama to look after her and to rock her and to sing her to sleep."

"But I've already told you, Wilson; your daughter is with a fine, new family. Why don't you understand? She will have a proper nursery to sleep in now and not a workhouse ward. You must forget about her because by now, she will surely have forgotten all about you."

"No, she can't have…"

"She will, Wilson. She has a new mama now. One who can care for her properly and one who isn't a yellow-jacket inmate in a poor-law workhouse. Now, more importantly, you have broken a thousand rules today in absconding from the workhouse without permission from an officer, and what's more, you've done none of your work."

"Please, Mrs Dixon, I was only looking for Sarah."

"Don't take me for a fool, Wilson. Your clothes are dishevelled, you have dirt on your back, and you have a clear hand-print upon your bosom. It's plain what you were in Harrogate for, and it's abominable."

"But, Mrs Dixon…"

"You're a slut, and if another brat results from this day's escapade, I'm not sure that the people of this parish should be made to pay for it. I thought your mother might have brought you up better than this, Wilson. I'm sure she wasn't a slut. Or was she? You will spend the night in the refractory cell with the hope that in there, you will have plenty of time to think, and to reflect upon your actions today, and to beg God for forgiveness."

"No, please, ma'am, please not that. Don't make me be on my own. I'll do anything you want. I promise never to go out again. Please, Mrs Dixon!"

The door slammed shut behind her and cut off all the light; all, that was, except for a thin, bright strip above the flagstones of the floor. The bleak, whitewashed walls of the tiny refractory cell reflected just enough of this meagre light for Elizabeth to make out a low, brick bench covered by a blanket and next to it, a slop pail. The air was thick with the acrid, gagging odour of sweat and stale urine.

What light there was would soon be gone, and then there would be only silence and blackness and the horrors of her thoughts. Panic exploded within her. It was panic that would not be stilled however hard she rocked and however loudly she sang, 'Hush-a-bye-Baby.' She needed to hurt herself. She needed a different hurt to the terrible hurt in her mind, which would drive her this night to the edge of insanity and perhaps beyond. She needed a different hurt; one she could feel, one she could control and one she could think about with all her might. She might just be able to get through the night then; she might just be able to get through to the morning if she didn't need to remember the terrible, terrible things.

And then she looked at the pail again and she sobbed in relief. The jagged, iron edge of the rim was so sharp, and her skin was so soft.

Mrs Anne Price was already in her drawing room, cocooned under a rug in a large, comfortable-looking tub chair, when the maid showed Atticus and Lucie through. Behind her an empty wicker bath chair stood under a large portrait of a smiling, be-whiskered gentleman. It was the very same man who leered down from the photograph into the Annexe at Sessrum House.

"Mr and Mrs Fox, please forgive me for not coming straight out to greet you, but as you can see, I am an invalid. I need a bath chair to get about, and that is rather inconvenient inside the house."

Mrs Price's reedy voice plucked their attention from the portrait.

"Mrs Price, there is no need to apologise. We are very grateful indeed that you have received us today."

Atticus felt curiously insincere in his cordiality under the watchful eyes of the monster on the wall.

Mrs Price smiled warmly.

"Not at all, not at all; I'm very honoured to be meeting Harrogate's very own Sherlock Holmes and Doctor Watson, and most especially so as you are real people and not just some ink-and-paper creations."

She chuckled infectiously and smoothed out the rug across her skinny lap.

"I'm leaving to visit my daughter and my young grandchildren in Northumberland tomorrow, so I wouldn't otherwise have been able to see you until my return. That might have been several weeks from today, so your timing is fortuitous. Now, I believe you have... *matters* that you wish to discuss with me?"

The maid entered the room, and Atticus and Lucie smiled and waited patiently as she poured the tea. The smiling and the waiting had become almost unbearable by the time the maid finally curtsied and left and Atticus was able to say: "We do indeed have very important matters to discuss, Mrs Price."

"Is it a murder investigation?" Mrs Price asked conspiratorially, her intelligent eyes twinkling with excitement.

Atticus was completely wrong-footed: 'She must know about the baby farmer,' he thought incredulously, 'And she's laughing about it.'

He glanced up at the portrait and her dead husband suddenly seemed to be laughing too.

Lucie filled the awkward vacuum of his silence.

"I'm afraid that these particular matters are no more exciting than the simple tracing of a missing person, Mrs Price, but no less important for that. We are trying to trace a missing child who by now will be a grown woman."

Atticus relaxed as Mrs Price's face dropped in disappointment.
"Not a murder?"

Lucie shook her head and smiled apologetically.

"We are only commissioned investigators; we rarely get involved with anything so glamorous as a murder."

"I see. Well, never mind; how can I help you both?"

"I believe that your late husband was one of the overseers of the Starbeck workhouse before it was replaced by the present one in Knaresborough?" Lucie ventured.

The old lady looked intrigued now.

"One of quite a large number of overseers, Mrs Fox, yes, but that was over thirty years ago now. Why do you ask?"

Lucie smiled her warmest and most radiant smile.

"The lady we have been asked to find was adopted as a small child from that workhouse into a wealthy local family. Your husband was the overseer who arranged it all, but unfortunately there were no records kept. We wondered if you might remember anything about it."

Mrs Price turned and gazed for a few moments at the portrait on the wall.

"Dear Barty," she said, "Always helping the poor, little children. He was a good friend of Alfred Roberts in his time, and something of a philanthropist in his own right."

"We had heard something of the sort," Lucie said, with a sharp warning glance to her husband.

Mrs Price took a handkerchief from her sleeve and dabbed at her eyes.

"Please forgive me; Barty and I were together a long time and I do miss him dreadfully. He couldn't have been a better husband."

"Of course," Lucie threw another glance to Atticus.

"By chance, it's Alfred Roberts' grandson who has asked us to find this lady."

Mrs Price looked up, her eyes moist and shining.

"Really? How strange. Then of course I shall do my very best to help you, although I never really got involved with the day-to-day running of the workhouse. Keeping proper records was never one of Barty's strongest cards."

She made a noise somewhere between a laugh and a sob.

"Tell me about this little girl then, Mrs Fox."

Lucie looked visibly relieved.

"She was called Sarah, Mrs Price. Sarah Beatrice Wilson, and she was adopted out at the age of two. It would have been around Eighteen Forty-Eight."

Then, after a moment she added: "Her mother is a relative of the Roberts family."

Mrs Price stared into her teacup and slowly shook her head.

"She was a very pretty little girl by all accounts, with fair hair. Her mother was called Elizabeth Wilson – Lizzie."

Mrs Price had begun to rock gently backwards and forwards in her tub chair. It reminded them sharply of Elizabeth herself.

Lucie pressed her.

"Do you remember Sarah, Mrs Price, or Lizzie?"

The old lady nodded, slowly and precisely.

"I remember her," she said. "Her daughter was born out of wedlock, wasn't she?"

"Yes," Atticus confirmed.

"Her mother had been taken advantage of," Lucie added, her eyes sharp, her tone measured and even.

"Actually, in plain terms, she was raped. She was repeatedly raped by several men over the course of many months. She finally fled to the workhouse to escape them."

Mrs Price looked as if Lucie might just have slapped her. Her eyes closed tight and she stopped rocking, and instead seemed to reel against the thick leather sides of the chair.

Atticus frowned. Surely his wife had been too graphic, too brutal for the old lady's sensitivities. But Lucie knew well what she was about, and reassured him with the shadow of a nod, and a quick and fleeting smile.

At last Mrs Price was able to recover herself. But when she opened her eyes once again, some of the pain of the words seemed to have lodged itself deep within them. Her voice too seemed weaker, and somehow diminished.

"I am truly sorry to hear that, Mrs Fox. But young women of that age do say all manner of things to cover up what they've done. As I said, I do remember Sarah, and I do remember her... mother; Lizzie, did you call her?"

Lucie nodded.

"Very pretty girl – beautiful even, and quite well spoken too as I recollect. I cannot say where my husband had her girl sent. I only remember now that it was to a respectable, loving home and that they cherished her and brought her up as their own. Any base morals from which her mother may have suffered were thankfully not passed on to her child, and Sarah is a model of respectability. You may tell Mr Roberts' grandson and whomever else it may concern exactly that, if it will help to settle their minds."

"Mrs Price, I'm afraid the reason for our commission is a little more complicated than that..."

"Mr and Mrs Fox."

The old lady's twinkling eyes and warm smile were gone. She banged her teacup onto its saucer with a clatter.

"You may have been asked – commissioned, or whatever it is you call it – to find Sarah, but tell me this: How do you know that she actually wants to be found? What if she has a new life? What if she has a husband and a family of her own now? What if she has no notion that she was ever adopted at all, that she's really the illegitimate child of a workhouse whore? Why, after over forty years, should I turn her life topsy-turvy? My husband was a great philanthropist. If he left no parochial record of where she had gone, then you can be sure it was for a very good reason. It was most probably to remove a lovely, innocent, little girl from the clutches of her harlot of a mother. Now, if you will excuse me, I need to rest now. I have a long journey ahead of me tomorrow and I have said all I wish to say on the matter."

CHAPTER 27

"I have said all I wish to say on the matter. It's out of my hands, Wilson. The overseers want you to be a pauper apprentice to Walton And Company, and so that is precisely what will happen. They have just taken over the linen mill at Knaresborough. Mr Walton has grand plans for it and he needs lots of skilled workers."

"But please, Mrs Dixon, I need to see Mr Price – I need to ask him about my Baby Sarah."

"Not that it is any of your business, Wilson, but it was actually Mr Price who paid them the three pounds they needed to take you off our hands. He paid it out of his own pocket too, hark ye. They usually take smaller girls than you as apprentices, so you can think yourself fortunate that Mr Price is such a kind philanthropist."

Her stern expression softened a little.

"I'm sorry, Elizabeth, but there is no point in you being a burden on the parish when you can pay your own way in a mill. You've no daughter to worry yourself about now, so you will leave the workhouse today."

And then she had been fetched, along with a pauper boy of around ten who made her think of little Peter Lovegood, by an enormous man called Tom. Tom was the foreman at Messieurs Walton and Company of Knaresborough, and he had a big, round face and twinkling eyes that reminded her of Old Rachel.

She gasped. Rachel!

She hadn't had a chance to say goodbye to Old Rachel or to thank her for being her only friend in the world until Mary had come back to her. Nor to Mary! They had just found each other again; surely they couldn't be separated now without a word. And she needed Mary; she needed Mary to make Mr Price let little Baby Sarah come back to her, back to her mama where she belonged and back to where she would be safe from all the bad things that would surely happen.

She turned back, instinctively, desperately, just as the great front door banged shut.

"Where are ye going lass?" Tom had asked in his deep, measured voice, that sounded to her like the tick-tock of a grandfather clock.

"I can't go, I can't!"

Elizabeth dropped the brown paper parcel which had her clothes neatly folded inside it and hammered on the solid timber with her fists. She drummed until each blow began to leave a little smudge of red on the fresh, white paint. But the door stayed shut. The mouth was closed. It remained as it ever was; silent and unmerciful. It had witnessed too many tears and too much heartbreak over the years, and now it refused to heed her shrieking, shrieking cries of despair.

She felt a huge arm encircle her waist and she froze as it plucked her easily away.

"Come with me, little lassie; you'll be all right."

The huge arm set her gently onto her feet and through the mists of her terror she heard the deep voice speaking once again: "We're not going to eat you, lass," it said, "We only want you to come and spin yarn for t' linen."

She stared at him as he smiled amiably down at her, and through the mists of her mind, his words ticked and tocked, and ticked and tocked, and raced, and grew louder and louder and louder.

'We only want you to spin yarn for the linen; we only want you to spin; we only want you; we want you, we want you, we want you...'

And she could think only of what would happen when the day's work was done, when it was night. Night was when they would want her, when they would do bad things to her. Night was when the shadows on the door would begin to move, and they would come to her bed. Night was when they would take her away to be punished. Tom was bigger and stronger even than Mr Price, and she was sure that he would punish her terribly.

She seemed to float down the road to Knaresborough as light as a gossamer thread. In the far, far distance, she could hear the boy who reminded her so much of little Peter Lovegood chattering excitedly to Tom about the Castle Mill; about the spinning machines and the great power-looms and about how he would earn tuppence a week for his very own. She could hear Tom laughing his deep, belly laugh in return. She could hear him as he patiently explained about retting and scutching, about how the spinning machines and the power-looms worked, and how they turned the flax into linen.

But she thought she could also hear an echo of Mr James as he made polite conversation with her cousin John in the Annexe, with that awful catch in his voice. And then she heard echoes of her cousin John, screaming and screaming as Mr James laughed and dragged him away.

"I don't want to have to repeat myself, Mrs Fox. I've told you; that is all I have to say on the matter."

Mrs Price carefully smoothed her rug again. Then she looked up and glared at them defiantly, as if daring them to stay.

It was all or nothing, and with a silent plea to the Fates, Lucie Fox shook the die once again.

"Lizzie Wilson was no harlot, Mrs Price."

The old woman's defiance boiled up into anger. Under the heavy rug on her lap, she stamped her foot.

"How dare you contradict me in my own home? She was most certainly a harlot. You will leave – now – before I summon the gardener and have you thrown out."

Lucie ignored the tantrum, and the threat. She cast the die.

"I believe your husband was a member of a gentlemen's club, Mrs Price; a gentlemen's club called the, 'Friday Club'?"

Mrs Price froze.

"My husband was a philanthropist, Mrs Fox. He was a celebrated philanthropist. It was a philanthropist's club."

Lucie shook her head.

"It was from various, shall we say, philanthropists, of the Friday Club that Lizzie Wilson fled. The father of her baby was one of those very gentlemen, who had raped her."

"No, Mrs Fox, you're quite wrong; everyone knows that they were great and good men."

The fury had gone and the old lady's tone was imploring.

Lucie sounded calmer now too, reasonable and persuasive.

"Mrs Price, I have spoken with another person in the last few days who was also ill-used in the Friday Club. She too was a young girl at the time, barely older than Elizabeth."

"No. No, you lie. They were philanthropists. They did many good works."

Once again, Lucie ignored her pleas.

"Alfred Roberts had a wife, Mrs Price — Agnes Roberts — who by all accounts spent her later life entirely in her bed. She coped with her husband's, shall we call them, proclivities, only by living in a permanent stupor enabled by the drinking of absinthe. If I may say so, your denial is your own absinthe."

"You may not say so. You are a vile and a wicked woman and you may not."

She stamped her foot once more.

"What I naturally need to be sure of, and what our client needs to be sure of, is that little Sarah Wilson didn't fall prey to those very same proclivities as her poor mother."

"Get out of my house, both of you. Get out!"

Mrs Price's face was a twisted mask of hatred and of fear.

"Get out, get out, get out!"

CHAPTER 28

A thick shroud of mist had settled at the foot of the deep gorge of the River Nidd, where it skirted the ancient town of Knaresborough. The throngs of people bustling about their daily business along the riverside seemed to Elizabeth almost like angels walking on clouds.

"Old Mother Shipton's cave is ower yonder," she heard Tom tell them, and he waved his arm towards the riverbank. "She was a prophetess who was born in the cave hundreds o' years ago and she foretell'd the future. This bridge ower t' river 'ere," he pointed to a broad, stone bridge just ahead of them, starkly black against the pure white of the mists. "The High Bridge it's called. Owd Mother Shipton said that if it was ever to fall down three times, it'd mean t' end o' the world was upon us. Now I'll tell thee both truly; it's fallen twice afore already."

The boy looked thunderstruck.

"Aye it's true," Tom continued, looking solemn, "An' she said when it would happen too. She said: 'The world to an end shall come, in Eighteen Hundred and Eighty-One.'

Now there's some that believes it, and then there's some, like Mr Walton, the owner of t' mill that don't, but she said that the world would end in Eighteen Hundred and Eighty-One and every one o' her other prophesies has come true."

Elizabeth felt a tiny surge of hope. Eighteen Hundred and Eighty-One! Eighteen Hundred and Eighty-One was thirty-four years away. So even if her mama didn't come for her before then, even if the Lord Jesus said she couldn't be like Grace Darling and be allowed to die young, then she would still see her dear mama again, and Baby Sarah, and Baby Albert, before she was fifty-two years old. But fifty-two was so old, and so far away. She would be old then, old and wizened and not worth a tramp's farthing, never mind two hundred pounds. How good, how wonderful that would be. And then, then she could die at last, because everyone would die at the End of the World. Even Uncle Alfie and Mr James and Mr Price would die at the End of the World, along with Mr Otter and all of their gentlemen friends.

Suddenly, she realised that Knaresborough, with its river of mist, its narrow, twisting streets and its rows of ancient cottages, was surely the most beautiful place on earth.

They crossed over the High Bridge and turned into the narrow riverside lane that footed the immense crags reaching up out of the gorge to an old, ruined castle.

"What are they a-building there, Tom?" the boy asked pointing ahead of them.

Lizzie looked. Four great, flat columns of stone, laced all about with scaffolding and swarming with men, seemed to be racing each other to get to the sky.

"That," announced Tom, "Is a new viaduct that they're building."

"What's a viaduct, Tom?" the boy asked.

Tom laughed his deep, slow laugh.

"It's a bridge, Peter; a special bridge for t' railway to go ower."

Lizzie started; the boy was called Peter too.

"Knaresborough," Tom continued, "Is going to get a railway line."

They approached the nearest of the columns and a whistle seared a shrill, burning path through her mind. The noise of the men working; the chiselling, the hammering, the rattle of the blocks-and-tackle, all abruptly stopped, and the whole world seemed to be holding its breath and looking at her. Lizzie dropped her head and stared at the broken rocks that littered the crag bottom, wishing and wishing that more would fall and bury her from sight.

'Please Lord Jesus, please don't let them look at me; please don't let them look at me and see me for what I am.'

But she knew that they would look, and she knew they would know, just as they always looked, and they always knew; and she waited for the shouts and the jeers that would surely follow.

A shout – a mocking, jeering shout stopped her heart. Her ears didn't need to make sense of the words because the laughter that followed told her exactly what they would be. She cringed yet deeper and turned her head in shame.

There was a flash of movement. Tom had picked a workman from the pulley-chain he was holding and pitched him bodily into the river. The mists parted and swallowed him, and it seemed an age of raucous shouting and *laughter later that he emerged coughing and gasping from the unseen waters. Tom stabbed an enormous finger at him.*

"Don't ye ever insult a lady again," he bellowed.

And then, as they walked, the sounds of laughter and of ridicule slowly faded. They faded everywhere, that is, except inside her head. There they compounded with the silent screams of her anguish and grew louder and louder and louder.

But there was a new sound too; a distant sound of gushing water, a sound that also grew louder and louder until it became a muffled roar. It was a weir, she heard Tom explain to Peter, who made her remember the Holy Island and a game that had gone terribly wrong; a double-weir with a mill-race that powered the machines which made the flax into fine linen. The waterwheel it fed already had the power of twenty-five horses, but Mr John Walton, the new owner of the mill, had a grand plan to install a steam engine. He had already built an engine house in readiness for it with a short, square stack. Only a modern steam engine, Tom told them, could provide enough power to drive the rows of looms that would soon fill bay after bay of the celebrated Castle Mill.

And then the muffled roar became deafening, and she saw at last where she'd been sold into apprenticeship. It was a huge, square, grit-stone building, with rows and rows of small-paned windows, just like those of the workhouse. But unlike the workhouse, Castle Mill had no pretence of ornamentation or finery. It rose, plain and austere, like the old, ruined castle in whose shelter it worked.

CHAPTER 29

Atticus Fox was a firm believer in the medicinal benefits of the Harrogate spa waters. In particular, he took care to drink several glasses of the iron-rich chalybeate water each and every day. By so doing, he was able to maintain his brain in first-rate order, and his brain, after all, was the principal tool of his profession.

This particular morning however, Lucie was with him as he stood outside the sumptuous spa Pump Rooms, and they were both peering anxiously into the crowds that were gathering to have their own prescribed waters dispensed into large glass tumblers.

"I see her here every morning, and she's usually quite early," Atticus said over the rousing music that had suddenly erupted from the bandstand up the way.

Lucie shouted over the music, "I just hope she hasn't already left for her daughter's house."

Atticus nodded gravely and they turned to peer through the crowds once more.

"There she is!" Atticus exclaimed, and several people turned to frown at them, understandably indignant at the shock he had caused to their delicate constitutions. But he was right. There, wrapped snugly into her wicker bath chair, with both hands firmly gripping the tiller handle, was Mrs Price. A hired bath chair man was pushing from behind, or rather he was pulling heavily on the handle, to prevent the chair rolling away from him down the sharp slope of the pavement. Mrs Price caught sight of them almost as soon as they had seen her, and she swung the tiller wide. The bath chair turned sharply towards them.

"Good morning, Mrs Price," said Atticus, a little stiffly.

The old lady raised her gloved hand and the man heaved the heavy chair to a halt.

"Good morning, Mr and Mrs Fox," she replied in a voice that sounded exhausted.

She stared resolutely at her hands still gripping the tiller-handle for several long seconds before she spoke.

"The girl's mother – the one we spoke about yesterday – is she the Elizabeth Beatrice Wilson in the papers, the one who murdered her uncle?"

"She is," Lucie replied.

Mrs Price nodded in acknowledgement and looked up at them at last. Her eyes were as red as the tartan rug tucked neatly around her legs and they had deep, dark circles beneath.

"I hadn't immediately connected the two, you see. The Lizzie I knew at Starbeck was only a slip of a girl. I never knew her as Elizabeth, or as an old lady."

She examined her gloves once more.

"If what you say is true, then God forgive me, but I can understand her wanting to murder Alfred. I wanted you to know that. But as I said yesterday, how can I tell you where her daughter is now?"

She lowered her voice to a whisper.

"How can I risk Sarah finding out that she is the bastard offspring of a rape – maybe of an incestuous rape at that? It would kill her as surely as her mother sticking her knife into Alfie Roberts' chest. I'm sorry, Mr and Mrs Fox, I truly wish I could, but I cannot possibly help you."

"There's a fortune too, Mrs Price," Lucie murmured, and the bath chair man glanced across.

"There is a fortune of several thousands of pounds that's of no use now to Elizabeth. All she has ever wanted since we first met was to see her daughter once more. And after the life she's had, I think that's the very least that she deserves."

"Money is of no consequence," Mrs Price answered quickly. "Her new family is very well-off, very well-off indeed. They are industrialists. She has no need for any outside inheritance."

"But Elizabeth's lawyers will still want to know what to do with it after she's gone. They will have to advertise the fact in the newspapers."

Mrs Price raised her hand once more and the bath chair man leaned obediently against the handle.

"I don't want to miss my train," she said. "My answer is unchanged. Do your worst, Mrs Fox, and may you and your husband and your infernal lawyers be damned for it."

They watched the wretched, old figure in the little, wicker bath-chair trundle along the pavement until the crowds swallowed her up. Then Atticus shrugged and said: "What now?"

Lucie stared at him.

"Mrs Price is very well off," she said.

"I know," Atticus replied.

He gestured along the line of elegantly dressed people waiting patiently to take their waters.

"But then so is most of Harrogate."

"I know, Atticus, but think back. Didn't Mary Lovell say that Mrs Price liked to spend time with the workhouse children because she couldn't have any of her own?"

Lucie's eyes were dancing with tiny explosions of revelation.

"But now she tells us that she is off to see her daughter."

Atticus gasped.

"You're right. So you think that it was the Prices themselves who adopted Sarah?"

"Yes," Lucie said, "I'm very much afraid that I do."

CHAPTER 30

It had been agreed with the Master of the workhouse that Elizabeth would be paid the sum of tuppence each week as a pauper apprentice. Tom, in his capacity as mill foreman, reminded her of this as he caught her alone on the great stone stairwell of the mill that reminded her so much, both of the Annexe, and of Budle Tower. She stood trembling as he spoke, waiting for him to drag her off to Hell. She barely heard him say that he had now agreed with Mr John Walton, the owner of the Mill, that as well as her lodgings in the apprentice house over the way, she would now be paid no less than sixpence each and every week. She had, he explained in his capacity as the mill foreman, impressed everyone. She had impressed them with her diligence and quick learning, with her sheer industriousness, and with the fact that she often worked, unbidden and unpaid, far beyond the twelve hours a day that a girl of her age was allowed to be employed tending the looms.

Tom smiled and reached out towards her. His hands were massive and overpowering; they were utterly, utterly unstoppable. She wanted to beg him for mercy, to plead with him to leave her to her work, but the words gagged unspoken in her throat. She tried to turn, tried to flee back down the dark, winding stairwell, but her leaden limbs refused to heed the shrieking, shrieking screams of her brain.

His hand found her shoulder, and her soul cringed as he gently squeezed it and smiled, saying "Well done, Lizzie," before he turned away.

Sixpence – what did she care for sixpence? Would any number of sixpences bring back little Baby Albert, or Baby Sarah, or her poor, dead mama? She worked, not for all the sixpences in Threadneedle Street, but to keep those awful, awful memories locked away, shut off in the foul, festering depths of her mind.

When her mind was full of looms and yarns, of shuttles and spinning, it had no space for anything else. It was only at the end of the day, when the sun had kissed the side of the gorge and when she was too exhausted to work any longer, that the memories would slip their bonds, and would come to hurt her. Night was when she always remembered the bad things that had happened.

But she had also remembered the hurt in her nipple, when Mr Wright had first examined her at Starbeck, and she remembered how it had so eased the hurt in her soul. Now she had a knife. It was a sharp knife, with an edge that shone with all the colours of the rainbow, if you held it up to the sun. Tom had given it to her to shave off the stray threads from the linen cloth. She kept it as sharp as a razor. Stroking the edge over and over and over again with the whetstone somehow seemed to sooth her mind; somehow make her feel a little calmer. But at night, when she remembered the bad things that happened, she could slide the blade under her nightdress and think only about the long, stinging lines on her breasts.

She sometimes wondered if there would be enough skin on her breasts to last until the End of the World – until Eighteen Hundred and Eighty-One, when she could at last be with her babies and her mama once again.

Eighteen Hundred and Eighty-One; it was such a special number. When she wrote it down, and she wrote it down very often, it always looked the same – it always was the same – whichever way she held her paper. And when she counted up the numbers – one and eight and eight and one – they added up to eighteen. She was eighteen now – eighteen years old. And then she had wondered: Was it possible; dare she hope that she didn't need to wait until Eighteen Hundred and Eighty-One before she could die at all? Perhaps the End of the World would come in Eighteen Hundred and Forty-Eight instead, because Eighteen Hundred and Forty Eight was when she was eighteen and one and eight and eight and one was eighteen too. Could she, like the brave Grace Darling before her, be granted an early relief from her life? One and eight and eight and one was such a special number, and whichever way you reckoned it, it always, always added up to eighteen.

Mr John Walton of Walton And Company knew that it would have been commercial folly to bring in workers for his mill from the great industrial conurbations of the West Riding. To do so would have involved building every single worker his own tiny cottage to live in: an expense of over one hundred pounds per head. So instead, Mr Walton had built a single large apprentice house over the way from his mill. It had cost a good three hundred pounds to build – a not inconsiderable sum – but for that, he could house no less than eighty child apprentices. And Mr Walton knew that if he then filled his new apprentice house with pauper children, not only would the *workhouses pay him to apprentice them in the first instance, but he could also employ them at a wage of just tuppence each week.*

Beyond the finish of her shift each night, when Lizzie finally became so exhausted that she could work no longer, she would hurry across the way to the apprentice house. There she would go straight to the girls' dormitory, and the sanctuary of her cot.

She was lucky with her cot, because Tom had arranged with the mill manager that she could have one all to herself. The other girls had to sleep in pairs in the little wooden boxes they jokingly called 'coffins.' That was much warmer, but Mr John Walton had known that it would have been commercial folly to have had the cots made any bigger than the little children really needed. But Lizzie was tall, almost too tall to be a little girl at all. So she had been allowed a cot entirely to herself. It was cold to be sure, but she really didn't mind being cold at all. In fact she preferred it, because lying there, cold as death in the little wooden box, she felt somehow closer to her mama.

The cots were built in stacks four high in the dormitories to save Mr Walton valuable floor space, and she was lucky because hers was a topmost cot and that meant that there was only the thin slates of the roof between her and the Heavens above.

Because hers was a topmost cot, she didn't suffer from the apprentice boys creeping in from their own dormitory next door and gawping and probing at her whilst she slept. There were no boys and there were no demons to peer into her coffin or to carry her away. The little wooden cots had needed no bell; no bell that would ring and ring and ring as the demons slipped inside and dragged her down to the Eighth Circle of Hell.

She didn't mind the cold either, because it helped to keep her from sleeping. It was whilst she was sleeping that the memories would come. They knew somehow when she was too exhausted for busy or for her knife. They would come and they would spill into her dreams and turn them into nightmares. But if she succumbed, if she could hold off sleep no longer, Lizzie would often – mercifully – be awoken, and not only by the cold. She would be woken too by the little girls as they whimpered and cried from being hurt in the mill, or by the stench of their greasy, unwashed bodies, or, as was more usually the case, she would be woken by her own nightmares.

One Sunday, when she couldn't be busy in the mill because God had said that no-one could be busy on that day, whilst she was soothing her mind with her whetstone and her knife, a memory spilled into her daydream. And because that day was a day of rest, when even God couldn't be busy, the memory was of a demon. On that day a demon did peer into the coffins of the apprentice house.

It had come with a gentle knock on the door of the dormitory. The blade of her knife had trembled against the whetstone even though she knew it must be Tom who had knocked, because her Uncle Alfie never knocked.

"Girls," he had said in his deep, slow, tick-tock voice, "And Lizzie," (just as if she was a proper grown woman and not a little girl at all), "I would like all o' ye to pay attention. I have a nurse here who has come from t' other side o' Harrogate to tend to thy injuries."

Lizzie peered over the edge of her topmost cot and saw a thin, black shadow standing next to Tom; a thin, dark shadow blocking the light of the doorway.

She shuddered.

"Mr Walton 'as agreed it. A lot o' ye 'ave been getting hurt in t' machines an' this lady has come 'ere as a philanthropist to help ye. She's been visiting all o' t' 'prentice houses round Knaresborough and doing it all from t' goodness o' her heart. She won't be charging thee or Mr Walton or anyone else a farthing.

She'll be a-coming round your beds to inspect all o' ye for injuries so ye must speak nicely and respectfully and take care to do exactly as she says."

Lizzie fell back flat against her mattress, her heart pounding like the big steam engine that churned and throbbed in the shed by the river.

'She mustn't know I'm here. She mustn't see my cuts. She mustn't ever stop me from cutting myself.'

Instinctively she pulled her shift tight against the stinging lines on her breasts, shielding them with her hands and lay, as still as a corpse, horrified at the thought of a life where there could be no more pain.

The sound of the woman came closer, growing louder and louder and louder. She was moving from cot to cot and the poor little girls were calling for her, begging for her to go to them, begging for the nurse — for the angel of mercy.

Little girls who beg for mercy seldom deserve it.

The angel passed along the coffins, peering in. It was checking the girls, examining them, sorting them. It was like an angel on the Day of Judgement, like an angel in black — an Angel of Death.

It was down there now — examining the girl in the cot just below her. She closed her eyes and stopped her breath and waited.

"You're a pretty little thing," the angel whispered to the girl in the cot below her. "Do you like working here? Answer me truly, my dear."

"Yes, ma'am," the girl in the cot below dutifully answered.

"The mill only pays you tuppence a week I believe. How would you like to earn pounds and pounds?"

Like an abscess bursting, the worst memory of all, the very worst memory and all of the other memories, every one of the foul and loathsome horde, poured from the secret black places of her mind. A great billow of dread rolled over her as she lay in her coffin and her brain shrieked and shrieked and screamed the name of the angel, of the Angel of Death:

'Mrs Eire.'

Old Rachel had told her of her other name as together they had slashed the whin bushes on the Stray. Old Rachel had said that Mrs Eire was nothing more than a common procuress.

Her brain shrieked and shrieked and Lizzie whispered the word: "Procuress."

"I know some nice gentlemen with big houses in Harrogate who would love to have a pretty little thing like you..."

"PROCURESS!"

Her brain shrieked and screamed and now Lizzie screamed. She screamed the name, the other name that Rachel had taught her as they pretended that the dense, spiny stands of whin bush were Mrs Eire and they slashed and slashed and slashed.

"SHE'S A PROCURESS, A COMMON PROCURESS!"

Over the edge of her topmost coffin, Lizzie could see Mrs Eire, the common procuress staring up at her as the girls around them jumped up and screamed too. Her eyes were like Uncle Alfie's eyes when he had stood in front of the empty black waters of the North Sea, slipping silently past the shore of the Holy Island. They were the very eyes of the Devil.

"You!" she hissed like a serpent. "It's you, Alfred Roberts' two hundred pound whore. So this is where Barty Price had you sent, is it? To spend your days weaving linen? That's good. The Friday Club needs lots of fresh, clean linen for their beds, Lizzie, so they can..."

"HELP," she screamed, "Tom, please help us. She's taking the girls away for the gentlemen's beds."

And Tom had come. He hadn't knocked, but neither had he crept in like a shadow, as Uncle Alfie or Mr Otter might have done. He had burst through

173

the door as a saviour, into the shrieking, shrieking screams of the girls. And Mrs Eire, the common procuress, had fled. The demon had paid visit, and now, mercifully, it had gone.

Afterwards, when the girls had stopped screaming and her mind had stopped shrieking, Lizzie had begun to feel like a heroine. As she lay in her topmost cot in the apprentice house and watched the rainbow colours slide up and down the edge of her blade, she remembered Grace Darling. Grace Darling had been a heroine too; she had saved thirteen lives that surely would otherwise have been lost. Lizzie might not have saved the lives of the little girls sleeping, safe and quiet now in the cots all around her, but she had certainly, certainly saved their souls.

Just a few nights after she had begun to feel like a heroine, she had awoken in her little cot in the apprentice house to find a dead moth lying beside her on her mattress. Someone had told her that it was a mother shipton moth, named for the witch who had been born in the cave just over the river. They had pointed out the curious pattern on the wings, like two hags' heads facing each other, and Lizzie had been thrilled. But now, the more she thought about it all as she lay awake in her topmost cot and watched the rainbows slide along her blade, the more she was convinced that it must have been Old Mother Shipton herself who had sent it.

For the moth was surely a messenger, bringing the word that everything would be fine, that the End of the World was coming, just as she had said it would, and that she, Elizabeth Beatrice Wilson, a heroine just like Grace Darling, could die at last.

She had asked more about the witch — no, surely not a witch — the prophetess. Tom had called her a prophetess and not a witch, and Tom seemed to know everything.

Old Mother Shipton — Ursula Shipton, she was told — had made many other startling prophesies during her lifetime. And every single one of them, she was promised, just as Tom who knew everything had promised, had come true.

They also told her that many people had thought Old Mother Shipton wicked whilst she lived. In fact, many had thought that she was a witch. They thought that her mama, Agatha Sontheil, was a wicked and sinful woman too, even that she was a harlot. They said that Mother Shipton had no mortal papa and wondered why they both hadn't been thrown into the witch pool to see if they drowned.

But maybe, Lizzie thought as she lay awake in her topmost cot, maybe Old Mother Shipton wasn't wicked at all. Maybe she was good and in Heaven at that very moment with the Lord Jesus and her own dear mama. Maybe she felt sorry for her, Lizzie Wilson, as she looked down from Heaven. Perhaps she even felt, just as Lizzie herself felt, that they were so very alike, with everyone thinking them wicked, with harlot mamas and with no papas. Maybe, just maybe, Mother Shipton wanted to help her.

One day, Tom told them that the great viaduct, built high over the River Nidd, was almost finished at last. The temporary wooden falsework arches supporting the spans were to be dropped clear, the rails laid, and Knaresborough was to be joined to the railway. He said that Mr John Walton intended to use the railway to take his famous 'Knaresborough Linens' to the big cities across Yorkshire and even to London to be sold. It would of course be commercial folly not to.

But then, on March the Eleventh, as she could never forget, as she was fastening a broken thread for what seemed to be the hundredth time that day, there was a rumble exactly like that of thunder over the constant roar of the looms. The weavers, their work forgotten, ran to peer through the little grimy windows, and Lizzie ran with them. There was nothing outside but clear, blue skies. But there had definitely been a rumble exactly like thunder and she wondered, she wondered with all her heart, if it could be — if it could really be the End of the World.

A wave, a great boiling, angry wall of water surged round the curve of the river, dragging its arms along the banks and sweeping everything aside. Behind it, a grey, billowing storm cloud — no, not a storm cloud, a cloud of glory — was filling the gorge and smothering everything in its path.

Lizzie fell to her knees and sobbed in grateful relief.

'Oh, thank you, thank you, Mother Shipton.'

Old Mother Shipton had smiled on her from Heaven. She had sent her moth and Lizzie was not afraid. She gave thanks that this was surely Armageddon, and the Lord Jesus was coming at last in His Clouds of Glory.

People were running. Everywhere, people were running and screaming and shouting. Then the word went round, from window to window, from bay to bay:

'The viaduct has collapsed. The railway bridge has fallen into the river!'

It was true. Even before it was finished, Thomas Grainger's great viaduct had fractured and collapsed, and been swallowed up by the Nidd.

Hadn't it been foretold? Had Ursula Shipton not prophesied that once the high bridge fell, the End of the World would surely come? The viaduct was the highest bridge of all. One and eight and eight and one made eighteen. She was eighteen. One and eight and eight and one was the same whichever way you looked at it. She could hear her cousin's voice – John's voice – echoing through her mind.

'It's symmetrical, Lizzie. Look, it has a central line of symmetry.'

The moth was the same, the moth that she was sure Ursula Shipton had sent to her – it was symmetrical too. And so was the bridge. Dear Lord, so was the bridge. It was perfectly symmetrical with four pillars just like the four numbers, two small at either end, two large in the middle. And more: When the perfect, round, falsework arches had reflected in the waters of the Nidd, they had formed the number eight. The pillars were number ones. The viaduct had formed an enormous number, just as Ursula Shipton had foretold: It was one and eight and eight and one, and now – now the bridge had fallen. It wasn't the road bridge Mother Shipton had spoken about in her prophesy, it was the rail bridge – the viaduct. The viaduct was – it truly was – the highest bridge of all.

She reeled, almost overwhelmed by the waves of sudden realisation that were sweeping over her:

'Carriages without horses shall go,
And accidents fill the world with woe.'

Those were her words. Railway carriages had no horses and there didn't seem a day could go by when there wasn't a railway accident on some line or other... or bridge. And this bridge –the viaduct – was the highest bridge of all.

'The World shall End when the High Bridge is thrice fallen.'

Tom had told her – had promised her – that the old high bridge had fallen twice already. And now there was a new high bridge, and now it had fallen too. They were thrice fallen and the world was going to end.

She closed her eyes and hung her head, trembling in an obeisance of excitement and anticipation.

'Oh, come for me, Lord Jesus. I am ready and I am waiting for Your loving embrace. There shall be no more death, neither sorrow, nor crying, neither shall there be any more pain, for the former things are passed away. Amen'

The waters of the Nidd turned black. They writhed and boiled and filled with the detritus of Armageddon itself: crushed and splintered falsework timbers, shredded canvass shrouds, chattels washed from the riverbanks, and a boy.

A boy!

Lizzie opens her eyes. She looks and sees him; she sees a boy lying face down in the icy waters of the North Sea, being pulled into a fishing coble, and she hears again Little Sarah's scream of terror. It compounds inside her head with the shrieks and the screams of the End of the World and with the clattering of the looms, and grows louder and louder and louder.

'There's a boy. There truly is a boy in the water.'

She runs. She runs through the weaving shed to the stairwell beyond. Round and round, down and down the spiral stairway, as fast as her legs and the panic deep in her belly will let her. She heaves open the door at the bottom and runs out into the yard. The air, thick now with the Cloud of Glory, fills her mouth, her throat, choking her heaving lungs.

She kicks off her slippers and dodges and pushes her way to the engine shed, to where the river is grasping and clawing at the swarming crowd.

"Where is he?" she screams, "The boy, where has he gone?"

'Oh, please, Lord Jesus, please don't let him have drowned. He is so very little.'

The people from the mill have heard her and they look too, pressing around her, jostling like hydrangeas for a better view.

'But why are they just standing there, staring but doing nothing? Why won't they help? Why don't they tell me where he is?'

She runs along the bank, pleading with them.

"Please, for the love of God, have you seen Peter Lovegood? No, not Peter Lovegood, the other boy." she means. "Can you see him? Tell me! Help me, please?"

A white shape turns on the surface of the water and slides into the current of the old mill race. It's him! She leaps. The current, overpowering and unstoppable with the strength of twenty-five horses, pulls her down and suffocates her. It spins her around and pushes her into the narrow channel too. She sees him just ahead of her. Like something preternatural, the shape that is the boy twists and loops in the surging current, rushing further and further away. She reaches out, straining to catch it. The mill race bottoms; the shape slows, and becomes languid in the exhausted current, and she has it. She has it grasped in her hand – no, not it; him – she has him tight in her grasp. Her foot strikes something hard and she kicks against it. There is fresh, cool air on her face. She gasps at it and feels it rush into her lungs.

And then a power that is not her own takes hold of her and she ascends from the water. It is the Lord Jesus come for her at last.

But no, it's not the Lord Jesus; it's Tom, just Tom, in the water with her. He has Peter Lovegood – no, not Peter Lovegood – the boy; he has the little boy in his hands too, and he lifts both of them up onto the riverbank. The boy is coughing, coughing and vomiting out river water. He's alive.

'Oh, thank you, Lord Jesus for letting him be alive. He is so little, too little to be dead, and far too little to be lost to his dear mama.'

Because the next day was Sunday, that accursed day of rest, Mr John Walton himself invited her up to his big house outside the town. Tom was there too. He was there in his capacity as mill foreman, dressed in his very best Sunday clothes. They were to take tea with Mr Walton as a special treat and to celebrate her famous deed of courage.

Mr John Walton himself had declared that she, Elizabeth Beatrice Wilson, was a true North Country heroine. She had not of course saved as many lives as Grace Darling had done, but she had been very courageous nonetheless, considering that she was just a workhouse apprentice girl. And Mr John Walton had declared that if there had been a shipload of little boys in the Nidd that day, then Elizabeth surely would have saved them all too.

Grace Darling had saved thirteen souls from certain death and she, Elizabeth Wilson had saved just one, and he was very little. But she knew, and Tom knew that she had also saved the souls of the little girls in the apprentice house, and she knew, and perhaps Tom knew too, that she had saved a mama the agony of having her precious little boy taken away to Heaven.

It turned out that no-one except Tom and Mr John Walton had realised that she was a heroine, just as Grace Darling had been, and she was glad of that. She was relieved because with the collapse of the viaduct and the damming of the river and the flooding of the town, her famous act of heroism hadn't been reported in the Harrogate Advertiser at all.

Uncle Alfie read the Harrogate Advertiser, and she shuddered to think how he might have read about her and her famous deed of courage, and how, in a philanthropic moment, he might have come to seek her out once more.

She didn't suppose the Lord Jesus read the Harrogate Advertiser, because as she had learned at Sunday school, He was omniscient. So she was sure that He would have known about her famous deed of courage, and so would her mama and Old Mother Shipton. Mother Shipton had sent her moth to tell her that the End of the World would surely come. One and eight and eight and one made eighteen and the bridge had fallen. Now she had saved a boy and the souls of the girls and she was a heroine, just like Grace Darling had been a heroine and Grace had only to endure life until she was twenty-seven.

Elizabeth wasn't omniscient, but she still knew deep in her heart that the Lord Jesus would come for her in her eighteenth year. She would have to endure no more than that.

'Hasten Thy Second Coming, Lord Jesus. Let there be a time soon when, "there shall be no more death, neither sorrow, nor crying, neither shall there be any more pain, for the former things are passed away." Amen.'

CHAPTER 31

"So Price adopted her himself!"

Dr Roberts looked squarely at Mary Lovell, whose crushed, shocked expression exactly mirrored his own.

"Ye gods: I wonder how old she was when he first crept into her bed."

"Or brought her to the Friday Club, to pass around his friends," Mary spat.

Roberts looked away as her eyes closed over the horror of her own, brutal imaginings. He turned back to Lucie.

"Are you sure of it?"

She nodded.

"I think so. Price's wife wouldn't admit anything of course, but then I remembered she couldn't have children of her own."

"That's quite right," Mary confirmed. "She asked me many times if there was anything, anything at all, that she or I or Mr Price could do to help her become pregnant. I suggested in the end that she adopt one of the workhouse children, although I never dreamed for a moment that she would take Baby Sarah. Respectable people usually avoided illegitimate children in case they'd inherited the moral corruption of their parents."

"She had no inkling what a morally corrupt monster her own husband was then?" Roberts asked.

"Who knows for sure," Lucie replied. "She kept telling us over and over again that dear Barty was a great philanthropist."

She shrugged.

"But then again, she said it a little too earnestly and a few too many times for my liking."

"The lady doth protest too much, methinks," Atticus agreed.

"So what do we do about tracing Sarah now?" Roberts asked. "We don't have long until my aunt goes to trial."

"Mrs Price told us that Sarah is married now, that she has a young family of her own, and that she is totally unaware of her history," Atticus replied. "To trace her should be quite easy. The real question is whether we wish to upset all of that? Mrs Price begged us not to."

Roberts frowned. He turned to the nurse.

"What do you think, Mary? Do we send Mr and Mrs Fox to speak with Sarah directly, or do we not?"

"We do."

Mary didn't hesitate for a second.

"To know the truth is always the best. What if she finds out later through some other means – when it's all too late? What if somehow, she knows already?"

"Mary's right, Atticus," said Roberts. "Find her!"

But the Lord Jesus did not heed her prayers and there was no end to her sorrow, or to her crying, or her pain, and the former things did not pass away.

Elizabeth's eighteenth year rolled into her nineteenth, and as it did, it was only her own world, her own precious hope, that was ended.

She slid open the matchbox where she kept the long dead mother shipton moth and stared at the faces on its wings. But they did not look back. They just kept gazing at each other across the moth's tiny, fragile body, as if sharing one huge private joke. Mother Shipton must after all have meant the year Eighteen Hundred and Eighty-One. Dear Lord; Eighteen Hundred and Eighty-One was thirty-two long years away. She would have to endure every day and every night for the next thirty-two years before the End of the World did come, before she could at last have blessed relief. She pushed the matchbox shut. It was too long.

There was a strange and magical spring on the far side of the river, close to Mother Shipton's cave. It was called the Dropping or the Petrifying Well, and it was a natural curiosity; a well that slowly turned objects into stone. Tom had once offered to take her to it one Sunday after church, but she hadn't dared to go with him. One of the spinners had quipped at the time that she looked more petrified at the thought of going with Tom than anything the well could have done. But now, it seemed as if its waters must have touched her after all, because her heart felt just as if it might have turned to cold, heavy stone.

She thought of the viaduct. It was being rebuilt, and already the four huge legs were reaching high out of the valley once more, spreading their wings towards one another like giant angels ascending. Tom had told her that the deck of the bridge was almost eighty feet above the river; high enough to carry the new railway line from one side of the gorge to the other; high enough to be one of the most spectacular railway bridges in the whole of Yorkshire; high enough to kill her.

Six days each week, the bridge swarmed with men, hauling block after block up into the sky and setting them securely into place. On the seventh day they rested and prayed to God that He would bless their labours and the bridge would remain. On that day, the scaffold and the ladders were of interest only to the pigeons and to the crows, and to a little girl with a heavy heart, whose mama had left her for Heaven.

She stood at the foot of a leg and gazed up its immense side into the bright, blue sky. Fluffy white clouds drifted past the tip and with a sudden, gripping angst, she wondered if perhaps her mama or if Baby Albert might be cocooned safely on the other side. The jagged tip of the leg seemed so close to the clouds she could almost imagine herself standing on its edge and reaching up to touch them.

But then, in the dark places of her mind, she heard the bell on her mama's coffin ringing and ringing, and growing louder and louder and louder. She imagined how the shadows under the coffin lid must have formed and moved as the demons crept inside to take her soul, to tear it out of her body and to drag it down to the Eighth Circle of Hell. Was she there, being tormented and punished still, or was she in Heaven with the Lord Jesus, at peace at last?

Would those same demons come for her? When she lay lifeless and broken beneath the part-formed arches of the viaduct, would they surround her body with their beastly, ravenous eyes and drag her down to Hell? Was she still wicked? Was she evil? Was Ursula Shipton, who had once sent her a moth, evil? Was she a seer or was she a witch? If Ursula Shipton was a witch, and she had sent her a messenger, then surely she must be evil too?

And then all at once the answer came to her, and it was the simple answer to everything.

The witch pool!

She had once overheard Tom, in his capacity as mill foreman, telling some of the old women about a place just a few hundred yards upriver where the

Nidd crashed off a shelf of rock into a deep, plunging pool. Here was where the ancestors of the townspeople had thrown those they suspected of witchcraft, bound and helpless, into the water. If they happened to drown, then their innocence was proven beyond dispute before man and God. But, if they lived, then such was the power of the pool that they could only have done so with the aid of the Devil himself.

She knew then what she had to do. If she threw herself into the pool, and if, please God, if she drowned, then she must have been a good little girl – good enough to die – and she would be called up to Heaven at last.

But what if she lived? Dear God, what if she is a witch?

She has to find out. She has to know for sure. She begins to run. Her slippers pad soundlessly on the hard-packed stones of the road.

God has said that no-one, not even He, can be busy that day. But as she runs and runs, he sets his church bells ringing. They erupt from the valley side above her, peeling and peeling, taking over her thoughts, taking over her mind, shutting it off to everything except their urgings for her to go faster, faster, faster.

'Please, Lord Jesus, please let me be there. Please let me be at the witch pool so that the bells can stop, so that I can stop, and so I can know.'

And the Lord Jesus must have heard her, because it seems that in that instant, she is there and she has stopped. She is standing over the abyss with its torrent that will peer into her very soul and judge whether or not she is worthy of death, just as it has for centuries.

She stares into the waters plunging into the black, foaming vortex, and she knows at once that the ancients of Knaresborough had been right: Surely only a true witch could escape from this.

She kicks her feet from her slippers, soaked now with dew and balled with the thick, red clay of the riverbank. The boiling waters seem to be drawing her in as they swirl around and around, down and down into the depths. Their roar fills her senses, shutting out everything except the coffin bell ringing and ringing, and her own voice crying for mercy, and her uncle's rasping words: 'Little girls who beg for mercy, seldom deserve it.'

And then the roar ceases and she is engulfed in an icy, suffocating blackness.

Needles of ice seem to pierce her head, her ears, her eyes, as the waters search her soul. She is pulled down, writhing and struggling against vast, unseen forces; surely the spirits of the river. They turn her, this way and that, squeezing her, mauling her. Something coarse and hard stings her fingertips, and a moment later, smashes against her chest. She gasps and rolls onto her back and her lungs fill with sweet, pure air.

Her eyes open, and Lo, she beholds the Kingdom of Christ. There before her soft, white clouds drift serenely past. Her ears ring with the songs of the birds of Heaven.

'Dear Lord Jesus, thank you.'

She is in Heaven. Now there will be no more death, neither sorrow, nor crying; nor will there be any more pain, because like Grace Darling before her, her courage has been rewarded and she has passed mercifully, mercifully away.

But if this is Heaven, where is her mama? Where are Baby Albert and her papa and where is the Lord Jesus? Why isn't she cocooned on a soft, white cloud? And why, if there is to be no more pain, is she lying bleeding and bruised, sprawled across a wedge of rock with her legs floating in numbing, icy water?

A magpie flutters across the face of the clouds, calling its harsh cry. The discordant sound echoes between the steep walls of the gorge and melts into the roar of the water. And it echoes between the steep walls of her mind — walls that already can barely contain her own anguished cries; cries which grow louder and louder and louder.

She has not gone to Heaven. Oh, Lord Jesus, she has not even died. The spirits of the river have searched her soul with their long, icy fingers and discovered her wickedness. Her own wickedness binds her yet to this world. She can be permitted only to stare up into the next, like Moses before the Promised Land. She can only look to where her dead mama and Baby Albert surely are. It is her own wickedness that means she cannot be with them.

But no! She has saved the life of the boy; she has saved the souls of the girls. She is a true heroine, just as Grace Darling had been, and Mr John Walton had invited her for tea.

The blue of the sky becomes blindingly vivid; the leaves of the trees wonderfully green. She feels as if she can see every branch of every tree in the gorge, and her mind, racing as it has never raced before, tells her exactly what she must do.

The people on the riverbank look at her — stare at her, as if she's some kind of madwoman. An old lady turns, her mouth moving, her lips speaking unheard words, but Lizzie knows instantly that she's no danger and runs on. The certainty of what she must do fills her and consumes her, and almost as if dreaming the dream of Jacob, she reaches the foot of the viaduct once more. She steps forward, towards the beckoning foot of a long, wooden ladder, knowing that this is a causeway, a pilgrim's way, a stairway to Heaven.

And then she is at the top, with the sparkling, blue river far below her and the soft blue sky above. The clouds are sweeping past just over her head, driven hard by a brisk, gusting wind that rattles the tarpaulins, and her mind, and the sheets that cover the workers' tools.

And with the wind comes her rhyme:

'Hush-a-bye baby, on the tree top,
When the wind blows, the cradle will rock.
When the bough breaks, the cradle will fall,
First to the poorhouse, now to the grave.'

The bridge is high – almost eighty feet above the river and the hard, tarmacadamed road that tracks along its gorge. She knows that it is high enough to kill her. Tom has promised that it is high enough to kill her. Tom knows that she is a heroine, and Tom will know why she must do this. Tom knows everything.

Thomas Grainger has embellished his viaduct with battlements in homage to the real castle that stands guard over it. So for a moment, she's back at Budle, leaning through the battlements, gazing down at the whinstone beckoning her from below, and wishing she could fling herself to it. She has wished every night since that she had.

Now she looks down and imagines stepping into the void. She leaves her body and watches herself floating gently down, light as a gossamer thread, into the gorge and onto the hard stones of the tarmacadamed road below. She sees her body slowly being crushed and broken and she smiles as she thinks how not even the gentlemen of the Friday Club will want to touch it now.

Not worth a tramp's farthing.

Her mind is racing as it has never raced before, and she knows now they wanted to touch her. It was no sad duty at all. They wanted to touch her; they enjoyed touching her, because they enjoyed punishing a wicked little girl who was begging them for mercy. And then she smiles again as she sees her soul lifting from her body and ascending serenely into the skies, into the welcoming arms of the Lord Jesus and her dear, dear mama.

She walks forward. The solid stones of the bridge become gently bouncing scaffold boards which themselves abruptly stop and become thin air. Her gut lurches as she plummets down and down and down. No floating, gossamer thread is she. Her scream of terror is just rising, as it becomes a grunt of pain that is cut brutally short. She smashes into the thick timbers of the falseworks and flies back, limp and broken as a little bird, to lie unconscious and bleeding amongst the stone chips and gobs of cement at its very bottom. And there is no serene ascension and no welcoming embrace. There is no causeway to Heaven.

CHAPTER 32

As Detective Inspector Douglas had pointed out so vehemently, re-uniting long lost relatives was a task to which privately commissioned investigators were particularly suited. Even so, it took Atticus and Lucie Fox several long and mentally shattering days of searching the parochial registers to find that Miss Sarah Beatrice Price, spinster, had indeed been married to a Samuel Elswick esquire, a man ten years her junior. What had caused them so much time and effort in their search was the fact that she hadn't actually been married until the Eighth of July of the year Eighteen Eighty-Five, by which time she was fully in her thirty-ninth year. It was also, by coincidence, the day the police were finally called to the offices of the Pall Mall Gazette in London in order to control the morally-outraged crowds baying for copies of Mr William T. Stead's next article in his series: '*The Maiden Tribute of Modern Babylon.*'

Mr Samuel Elswick, the society report in the *Harrogate Advertiser* had noted, was the son of a wealthy industrialist of the City of Newcastle-upon-Tyne.

A tiny voice in her dream was nagging. It was nagging at her to wake up. She dearly wished it would stop, because she was still so very tired. But it persisted; it wouldn't heed the anguished, anguished pleas of her brain begging for it to be silent, to be still, so that she could sleep forever in peace. Again and again, it urged her to wake, goaded her to open her eyes. She tried. Light flooded in — light so very bright that it hurt.

The voice nagged again. She needed to ignore it. It really was just too much effort to keep trying to obey. She drifted back to the womblike safety of sleep. But the voice was still there and it was getting louder and louder and more insistent. Now that she thought about it, she did vaguely recognise it. She thought it might have been the voice of a friend she had had when she was alive. Or it might have been her dear mama!

She forced her eyes to open and the light burned again. This time she could just about make out what might have been a face peering down at her. Was it — could it really be her mama? She blinked, awkwardly and painfully, and the shapes and shadows merged into human form. But it wasn't the face of her mama gazing fondly down at her; it was the face of Mary — dear Mary Lovell. She could hear snippets of her voice as if in the far distance.

"Lizzie — Lizzie, it's me — it's Mary. Please wake up."

She retched and the face dissolved into shapes and shadows once more.

"Lizzie, you're back at Starbeck — in the infirmary; you're back at the workhouse."

So she wasn't dead at all, and Tom had lied to her. The bridge hadn't been high enough to kill her, and she was still here, still bound and imprisoned in her body. In her broken, mortal body.

"They found you on Monday morning, soaking wet and lying inside the bridge works," Mary continued. "What on earth were you doing up there?"

Elizabeth tried to lift her head and the movement filled her eyes with a million dancing stars. She waited for them to fade and settle before she dared to whisper her answer.

"I wanted it to be the End of the World."

"I don't know about the End of the World," Mary said, "But it's the end of your work at the Castle Mill for a while. The foreman — a man called Tom — tried to keep you. He tried to have you treated in the apprentice house there until you were well enough to get back to work. He even tried to have the mill pay for you to be treated in one of the Harrogate hospitals, but the owner, Mr John Walton, said no. He said that it would be commercial folly to do that when there is a perfectly good infirmary here.

You've been hurt in your fall, Lizzie; badly hurt. You could have easily died. I dare say you'll be in this infirmary bed for a time to come yet."

"Where's Rachel, Mary?"

She felt Mary's hands take her own.

"Rachel died, Lizzie. It was a month or so back. She died very peacefully in her sleep."

Lizzie felt a deep stab of grief, and perhaps another of envy. A peaceful death in her sleep: Old Rachel had deserved that. It was a special death, just as Old Rachel herself was special. Grace Darling had not been allowed a peaceful death. Hers was a lingering, tortured death from consumption. But Grace had died when she was twenty-seven, and Rachel had been made to wait until she was old. But now Rachel would be in Heaven, watching over her like she always had, and watching over Baby Sarah.

Sarah! Dear Lord, what if she'd died? What if the witch pool had drowned her with its icy fingers, or Tom had been right after all? What if the viaduct had been high enough to kill her? Mary had said that she could easily have died. What would Baby Sarah have done if she had come back to her and found that her dear mama was dead, just as her own dear mama was dead, and Old Rachel was dead? Dear, sweet Lord, what would have become of her then?

How could she not have thought of little Baby Sarah? How could she have been so selfish?

One and eight and eight and one, was Eighteen Hundred and Eighty-One, when she now knew for sure the world to an end shall come.

She knew also that she was bound, but not only bound; she was chained. She was bound and chained to this world until the day it ended, by her wickedness and by her love for Baby Sarah.

The prosperous town of Gosforth lay just to the north of the great industrial engine of the Empire that was the city of Newcastle-upon-Tyne. It was just far enough from the city for the residents not to be unduly bothered by the noise, or the sight, or the smell, of the myriad mills and manufactories there; nor by the small armies of workers that laboured twelve hours each day in the murk and gloom within them. But it was also close enough for the owners of those same mills and manufactories to watch over them as geese might watch over their golden eggs. Like Harrogate, Gosforth was a town of estates and of villas, of polite conversation and of elegance.

A long train journey up the East Coast Main Line of the North Eastern Railway, and a few polite questions, brought Atticus and Lucie Fox to the imposing front gates of one of the modern, red brick, Gosforth villas. An empty wicker bath chair by the prettily-painted front door confirmed that they were indeed at the house of Mr Samuel Elswick, esquire, and most importantly, of his wife Sarah Beatrice. It also confirmed just how difficult obtaining a private audience with Mrs Elswick was likely to be.

Once again, Atticus took out one of their calling cards and wrote 'Affaires' neatly in one corner. Then he underlined it. The motto embossed onto each card read: *Quo Fata Vocant*. It translated as: 'Whither the Fates call,' and it seemed somehow especially appropriate with this commission, since so many parts of it seemed to lie so firmly in the unknown spinning of the Fates.

"Do we have a plan for this?" he asked.

Lucie glanced at the bath chair and shook her head.

"I think we've no choice but to play this one as it comes, Ad libitum. So it would be better I think, Atticus, if I lead the conversation."

Atticus frowned, but nodded and reached for the latch.

Their knock was answered promptly by a housekeeper, who took their card, and showed them into the drawing room, with the customary promise to enquire as to whether the master was at home. But it was not the housekeeper, but the master of the house himself, who returned a few short minutes later, and he was puce with rage.

"How dare you!" he hissed without introduction. "How dare you come to my home, bringing your abominations with you? Tell me why I shouldn't send for the police this very instant?"

"Because you wouldn't want a society scandal, most probably," Lucie replied evenly, almost insolently.

Elswick glared at her, his face a contortion of hatred and venom.

"Let me tell you exactly what a scandal to society is, woman. It's when people like you take your pieces of silver from monsters like the Roberts and don't give a damn about the consequences or the pain they might cause."

"So you know why we're here?"

Atticus was shocked.

Elswick turned his fury onto Atticus.

"I presume that you've come to take my daughter away with you – or try to, anyway, although I can't see how you could possibly imagine you might succeed. I'm not some derelict who'd sell his daughter for a bottle of gin."

He looked conspicuously at the visiting card.

"'A and L. Fox, Commissioned Investigators.' Commissioned procurers don't you mean? My mother-in-law told me that you'd been creeping around her in Harrogate, and she warned me you might try to bother us here too. Now you listen to me, Fox: I don't care a tinker's cuss what happens to the reputation of Barty

Price. He's dead now anyway, and his widow can live here, with her daughter, well away from any 'society scandal' there might be if she chooses. But I will not give up my daughter to Roberts and his abomination of a Gentlemen's Club. What sort of father do you think I am? Do you think I could just stand by and see another life ruined?"

"Mr Elswick, Mr Elswick!"

Lucie somehow didn't need to raise her voice to break the force of his diatribe.

"I don't know what Mrs Price has told you, but we have no interest whatsoever in taking your daughter, or anyone else for that matter, anywhere."

As he stared, Elswick's expression turned firstly to bewilderment, and then to guarded curiosity.

"You don't? Then why are you here?"

Lucie silenced Atticus with a glance and said: "Roberts' – Alfred Roberts' Gentlemen's Club – closed years ago, and Alfred Roberts is dead. We represent his grandson Michael Roberts, who had nothing to do with the club, and who hated his grandfather and everything he stood for even more perhaps than you do. I presume you knew that your late father-in-law was a close associate of Alfred?"

Elswick nodded.

"I did, and he caused my wife – his own adopted daughter – more misery than you can possibly imagine."

"I can assure you that we have spoken to enough victims of the Friday Club to well imagine exactly what kind of misery your wife must have endured," Lucie said.

"So you know then?"

Lucie nodded.

"Michael Roberts told us. He's an eminent psychiatrist who has devoted his life to helping people who have been forced to suffer exactly as your wife has."

Relief seemed almost to pour out of Elswick, and he turned his face suddenly away from them.

"Did he take her to the Friday Club?" Lucie asked gently.

Elswick turned back. His face was flushed and his eyes were moist and glistening.

"No, Mrs Fox, in the end he never did. He kept her entirely for himself. She was threatened with it though. Yes indeed. He told her precisely what did happen to the young girls who passed through the doors of that Hell-hole: How they were kept locked in a dungeon by a monster of a steward; how they were passed from bed to bed for the gentlemen's pleasure, and how eventually they would be shipped off to God-knows-where to work as whores and slaves for the rest of their lives. He told her that if she ever breathed a word about what he was doing to her, even to her own mother, then she would be taken there and left. He even took her and showed her the sign they had above the door, some Latin expression telling them to abandon all hope. She still sees it in her dreams now. But no, Mrs Fox, in the end she was spared the tender mercies of the Friday Club. She was his own adopted daughter, you see, and he loved her too much to share."

"And what do you know of her mother – of her natural mother?"

"Oh, I know all about her mother too, Mrs Fox. She was a workhouse girl wasn't she? Sarah – my wife – had a blazing row with her father one day and he told her, in the heat of the argument, that she was the illegitimate daughter of a workhouse prostitute."

He shrugged.

"It makes no difference to me who or what her mother was. She had no more control over her mother than this Michael Roberts had over his grandfather."

He managed a weak smile.

"In the weeks leading up to our wedding day, Sarah became very anxious. It made her quite ill in the end. She seemed to me to be looking for a reason to call the whole thing off. Eventually we had sharp words and it all came out; who she really was and how she'd been born in a workhouse; how she had been adopted by her parents and eventually what... what her father used to do to her."

"I understand that one of Alfred Roberts' associates took a young girl up to Roberts' hunting lodge in Northumberland for a time," Lucie said grimly. "A little time later that girl found out that she was with child."

The air in the room froze.

"What did you say?" Elswick asked.

"We've been told that the girl was used wretchedly whilst she was up there," Lucie continued, "And that not long after her return, she ran away to the workhouse to have her baby. It was a baby girl."

"An associate of Alfred Roberts took a girl up to Northumberland and left her with a baby girl? Who was that?"

Atticus and Lucie's brutal silence served as answer enough.

"Price – you mean that Sarah was Price's own daughter, his real daughter?"

The relief in its turn vanished from his face, and he reeled visibly.

"We don't know that for certain," Atticus interrupted hurriedly, "But it appears your father-in-law for one was convinced that she was his own daughter."

"Price used a prostitute?"

Lucie shook her head.

"Elizabeth Wilson, your wife's real mother, was no prostitute, Mr Elswick. She was an innocent young girl who had the misfortune to fall into the hands of the Friday Club. Your wife – her daughter – was the result of her rape, most likely by your father-in-law. I say most likely because it's quite possible it could have been by any one of a number of other men, including her own uncle. Mr Elswick, I'm so sorry."

"So where is this Elizabeth Wilson now?"

"She's presently awaiting trial for the murder of that same uncle, Alfred Roberts."

"Dear God, her mother's a murderess!"

Lucie waited until the dust of the cataclysm had settled. Then she said: "Nothing has been proven yet. Elizabeth Wilson has senile dementia and I, as a nurse, don't believe she is capable of murder. But it's her dearest wish to see her daughter once more before her mind goes completely – or before she is hanged or locked away forever in an asylum."

Elswick bit his lip and said, "I see, Mrs Fox." Then after a moment of pensiveness, "My wife is older than me by quite a margin, do you know?"

"We saw that in the parish register. It's neither here nor there."

"Oh, but it is, Mrs Fox, it is. You see, the reason she married so late in life was because her father left her with a profound mistrust – a fear, even – of men."

He coughed, suddenly nervous.

"Even after we were wed, we had certain, shall we call them, difficulties, in our marriage that we needed to overcome before we could have children."

Atticus coloured deeply and Lucie said, "I perfectly understand what you mean, Mr Elswick. It must have been very difficult for you both. Perhaps Michael Roberts could help her?"

"What I'm saying is that Sarah has reached a level now where she can function perfectly well as a wife and as a mother. You are asking me to jeopardise all of that, all of her pain and struggle, for the sake of someone she hasn't even seen since she was a tiny girl and someone she can only just remember?"

"I suppose we are," Lucie conceded.

Elswick's eyes flickered past her head and widened in guilt. He looked like a boy caught with his hand in the sugar bowl.

"Anne!" he exclaimed.

Lucie turned and Atticus looked up. There, leaning on a walking stick, her face radiating indignation and anger, and perhaps fear, was Mrs Price.

"Not content with bothering me in my own home, you've come to hound my family here too."

Her voice was like the exhalation of a blast furnace.

"These people are relentless, Samuel. I trust that you are going to throw them out before they succeed in destroying both your wife and your marriage?"

"I was just explaining, Mother... and yes, I was about to ask that they leave."

She waved the point of her walking stick somewhere between Atticus and Lucie and the blast furnace ran cold.

"We will not tolerate these intrusions any longer. You will leave my son-in-law's house, and you will leave Northumberland this very instant."

"Mother, I already knew about the Friday Club. Sarah told me everything, long ago."

Elswick's voice sounded suddenly weary.

"So I already knew about her father and I already knew about what he used to do to her."

"Her father was a philanthropist, a great philanthropist like Alfred Roberts," Mrs Price protested indignantly.

"Mother, if Barty Price was such a philanthropist, then why after he died did you have his rooms exorcised?"

Atticus glanced at him, horrified, but Elswick looked away and said: "For my mother-in-law's sake, Mr Fox, please, just do as she asks and go."

CHAPTER 33

"We're all moving to Knaresborough, Lizzie."

Mary's face shone with eager excitement as she made the announcement.

"The parishes have decided to join together into a union, and they're building a brand new workhouse, just behind the High Street."

Elizabeth looked at Mary and tried to comprehend her joyous enthusiasm.

'How,' she thought bleakly, 'Can you be so happy about it? How can you be so happy about anything?'

Knaresborough. In her mind, she pictured again the great viaduct over the River Nidd, and thought of how one and eight and eight and one never did add up to eighteen. She pictured Tom, dear Tom, now gone forever, and felt the heavy timbers of the false-work arch rushing up to shatter her.

"There's to be a new uniform for the inmates," Mary continued, "With pretty blue stripes, and you, Lizzie, are to work in the bake house,"

At last Elizabeth felt the tiniest shiver of interest. There would be knives in the bake house — sharp knives. There would be knives with shining, silver blades, with rainbows at their edge, which could slice deeply into flesh and blood. They could push away the anger and the hatred; they could push away the memories; those awful, awful memories, whenever they fell from that foul, dark, demon-infested place she kept especially for them — whenever they came to hurt her.

The fleeting shadow of a smile flitted across her face and Mary sobbed for her.

"Oh, Lizzie, I'm so glad you're happy about it. There's nothing to be scared of. I'll be going and all the other inmates here will be going. And, Lizzie, you know how you like to watch the railway? You know how you watch out for trains for hours and hours and look in all of the carriage windows as they pass, just as if there might be someone in there you know? Well, the new Union Workhouse is right next to a railway cutting, and the bake house and the bread store are to be just over the yard from it. You'll be able to look out and see the trains all day long if you want to."

And then, in the time it took for a tiny, broken bird to fall from a bridge, she was there; in the brand new bread store of the brand new workhouse, watching through the tiny panes of the window. She was waiting for the train.

She knew it was coming; she had no need for the clock. She knew that for a few minutes each hour, the deep cutting that ran by the workhouse would tremble, and the air would be filled with smoke and steam like the coming of the Apocalypse. And then the monster beneath it would shriek, and plunge into the black tunnel mouth and be gone.

Mary was right. The railway both drew her and utterly repelled her.

'Carriages without horses shall go, And... fill the world with woe.'

And when the monster beneath the smoke shrieked so that the windows of the bread store rattled, and when it plunged headlong into the blackness of the tunnel, so she too would hear the shrieking of her own mind, and it would be louder than any locomotive, and so she too would be plunged into blackness.

One of Old Mother Shipton's prophesies had come true. Whenever the shrieking of the train lashed the walls of the workhouse, lashed the walls of her mind, it would shake loose her memories of the railway, of the carriages, and of what happened when the carriages did go.

They were laughing at her, jeering her. Their hands were prodding her, touching her, grasping at her clothes, pushing her from one to the other, the other to the next, round and round and round the carriage.

From below her she heard the rhythmic clicking of the carriage wheels. It was as if the train had a heart that was beat-beat-beating in anticipation of what was to come. But before it did, she desperately needed it to be a different little girl, being pushed, being pulled, half-naked now between the gentlemen; a different little girl being forever 'it' in this hellish game of kiss-chase where she was always caught, caught, and caught again.

She stumbled to the floor and, as the gentlemen closed in, so she closed her thoughts to everything except her urgings of the train to go faster, for its heart to beat louder, faster, more staccato, to overwhelm her, to crowd out whatever it was they were taking turns to do to her body.

'Please, Lord Jesus, please make the train get to the station, please make it stop, so that finally they will stop.'

But it was when they stopped; when she had to stop being a different little girl and become Elizabeth Beatrice Wilson once again, that she had to stand, as naked and as sinful and as exposed as Eve, to gather together what clothes and dignity she could. It was only then that she could begin once more to hide away the memories.

When the gentlemen of the Friday Club had finished with the waif and stray girls, when Mrs Eire had sewn them up until she could sew them up no longer, and even Mr Otter had had his fill, they would disappear. They would disappear one day in Mrs Eire's wagon with its padded sides and its double windows and its double locked doors. Some, she knew, would be taken away to Brimston to have their babies, or to accommodate the gentlemen there, or to have Mrs Eire 'give 'em the iron.' This she knew was some way to make their babies into cherubs for Jesus without them even having to be born. She had once asked Mrs Eire to give her the iron, to save her baby from being born, but Mrs Eire had just laughed.

If they weren't to have their babies, if they weren't to accommodate the gentlemen visitors or be given the iron, the girls would be taken to York.

Before they joined Starbeck or Knaresborough or even Harrogate to the railway, when she still believed that one and eight and eight and one surely made eighteen, it was necessary to travel to York to take a train. Mr James was a ship owner, and his ships carried passengers and freight from the ports of Yorkshire all around the Empire. Like Mr John Walton, Mr James was a great advocate of the railways. He even had his own railway wagons that carried his freight from the ports of Yorkshire all around the country.

Sometimes Mr James' freight was little waif and stray girls, and whenever this was the case, Mrs Eire would always fetch them to York. There, they would be loaded onto Mr James' railway wagons, taken to a port, and sent on to a new life abroad.

Like Mr Price, and like Alfred Roberts himself, Mr James was a great philanthropist. It was no surprise to anyone, therefore, that whenever he could, he would spread his philanthropy far and wide.

On occasion, Mr James would feel inclined to bring waifs and strays back from other countries in his ships and in his special railway wagons. These would be little girls − and sometimes boys − that he bought from the slave markets and orphanages of the Orient; from Arabia, from India and from Canton, and they would be brought back to be given a 'proper education.'

Mr James would always laugh when he said they were to be given a proper education, as if it were a joke. He would engage Mrs Eire's wagon to fetch them to the Annexe like so many lambs, and Mr Otter would take them downstairs.

Whenever Mr James brought in a consignment of 'native girls,' as he called them, the Friday Club would be every bit as busy as the nights Miss Pearce came down from Budle. The girls looked exotic, otherworldly even, as Mr Otter led them shyly up the iron stairs to the slaughter. They were rarely able to speak English, but that never mattered. A scream was a scream whatever the language.

When Mr James brought in a consignment of native girls, Lizzie would try to relax — just a little. She knew that on that Friday, the shadows on her door would stay still and the only thing that would disturb her would be the sounds of the girls. They would be as shrill and piercing as the railway engines thundering into the blackness.

It was when she still believed that one and eight and eight and one might yet add up to eighteen that the railway had come both to Knaresborough and to Starbeck. But it was when she finally realised it did not, nor ever would, that Old Mother Shipton's prophesy came horribly, horribly true the most.

A carriage without horses had gone forever, and with it, it had taken something precious. But it had been an accident, it truly had. She had been foolish. Perhaps her head had been muddled from the chloral hydrate Mary had given her for her pain, but gone it had, and she had let this fill her world forever with woe.

"So you see no hope of her daughter, of Sarah, coming, Atticus?"

Roberts was rubbing Gladstone's ear gently between his thumb and forefinger, and there was a steady, deep thump as the dog's tail beat against the leather of the chair.

"Very little, I'm afraid. Mr Elswick told us that Price used her, just as we expected that he would have done. It's still too tender a wound to cut open again."

Roberts nodded sadly.

"Mary will be distraught. She had quite set her heart on re-uniting my aunt and her daughter. I suppose the best we can hope for now is that we get our certificate of guardianship; that Aunt Elizabeth is discharged into my care and that in time this Elswick has a change of heart."

Lucie asked, "How is Miss Elizabeth, Doctor?"

Roberts shook his head gravely.

"She seems to be declining quite rapidly now. She keeps asking for her mama all the time. We've quite given up telling her that she's dead. She gets so dreadfully upset, almost as if it's only just happened, and then ten minutes later, she asks for her again. Her memory seems to have fixed itself on her mother's death and on her time at Sessrum. Mary has been hoping for a while that she would regress back further, back to her time at Halcyon − her mother's house − for example. She was happy back then. When she began to ask constantly for her mama, we thought that finally she had. But then she swears it's Eighteen Eighty-One and she's going to Heaven. Then she thinks she's going to Hell. It's awful, truly awful to watch, and very draining on poor Mary."

"May we see her?" Lucie asked.

"Of course, but as I've warned you, she's deteriorating quickly. In my opinion, she's right on the edge now."

"I think she might be on the edge of lunacy."

The Medical Officer's sharp whisper carried across the infirmary ward of the Knaresborough Union Workhouse, empty save for an old pauper woman wrapped tightly in a thin blanket on her narrow, wrought iron bed. She was trembling and gently sobbing as she lay curled on her thin, flock mattress.

"She just keeps saying over and over that she wanted the world to end, that she was promised that the world would end."

"Lizzie has always wanted that to happen, ever since she was apprenticed down at the Castle Mill and someone told her about Mother Shipton's prophesy."

Mary Lovell glanced across the ward at Elizabeth's tiny, shivering form, and there was pain in her eyes.

"What, that the world would end last year − in Eighteen Eighty-One?" the Master exclaimed. "Surely she didn't really believe any of that Old-Mother-Shipton-bunkum, did she?"

Mary nodded.

"She believed it, or hoped and prayed for it anyway. Ever since her little daughter was adopted out from Starbeck, all she has ever wanted to do is to die. She tried to kill herself twice when she was eighteen, and she's been waiting for the world to end ever since. Now that it hasn't, it seems to have utterly crushed her."

"Is she becoming a crawler, do you think?" the Master asked.

The Medical Officer wrinkled his brow in puzzlement.

"A crawler, Mr Liddle? Whatever in this world is a crawler?" Mary answered.

"A crawler, Mr Manders, is a pauper. It's a pauper who has reached such a state of utter wretchedness that they hardly have the will to move. They just sit around and let the world do what it will with them. It is the saddest, the very saddest sight that you could ever possibly imagine."

Manders looked across the long lines of identical iron beds to where Elizabeth lay.

"I don't believe she is becoming a crawler then, no. She is, in my opinion, a depressive, maybe a manic-depressive. It will pass eventually if we rouse her and set her to work."

"It's always passed before," the Master agreed, "And when it does, she works like a demon. It just seems to happen more and more often as she gets older — and for longer each time. I hear she's taken to fetching the bake house knives back to her ward to cut her own arms and breasts with them."

"She's done it for years; it helps her to cope," Mary explained.

"It seems a peculiar way to cope if you ask me. Should we be restraining her then, do you think, for her own safety?"

"No!" Mary's retort echoed between the infirmary walls and Elizabeth started. "No restraints; it would be purgatory for her."

"Very well, very well, no restraints."

Liddle seemed taken aback by her outburst.

"I could never understand why she's still here though, why she was never married. She was supposed to have been quite beautiful when she was younger, and she has high intelligence and very nice, gentle manners. Surely there were offers, I mean other than the unpleasant suggestions she occasionally got from one or two of the vagrants, that is."

"There was one man," Mary said quietly, glancing again at the wretched huddle of blankets. "He was called Tom and he was the foreman at the Castle Mills where Elizabeth was once apprenticed. He was kind and gentle, and desperately in love with her. Poor Lizzie; she could never understand that a man could be kind to her, that he could want her just for who she was. She hated herself, you see. She still does. That's why she mutilates herself, and that's why she wants to die."

Tom, yes, she remembered Tom – dear Tom; Tom, who knew everything and who thought she was a heroine ever as much as Grace Darling was. He had once walked from Knaresborough, all the way from the Castle Mill to the workhouse at Starbeck, and asked to see her after prayers one Sunday. It was not so long after her 'unfortunate mishaps,' as everyone had insisted on calling them.

He had looked odd, all dressed up in his Sunday best, without his usual collarless shirt and ragged waistcoat. He looked just as he had done in Mr John Walton's big parlour on the day he had invited them for tea, standing as if on hot coals. This time he was nervously passing a large bunch of red daisies and carnations from one enormous hand to the other. Mary had told her later that all flowers had meanings, and that the meanings of Tom's flowers were that even though she didn't know it, that she was truly beautiful, and that his heart yearned for her.

In the cramped space between the infirmary beds, Tom had knelt down on one knee and asked her – Elizabeth Beatrice Wilson – to be his wife.

But Tom's words and the words of the flowers had been as a foreign language to her. Why did they speak of marriage, of love and of beauty? Didn't they know, as everyone surely knew, that she was just a wicked, sinful harlot who had to be punished and punished until death's blessed relief?

She couldn't find words of her own for Tom, dear Tom, with his eyes that were filled with kindness. Perhaps that was why he had asked her – because he was kind. But how could she yoke something so good to such badness? So she had wept and sent him away. And he, giant though he was, had wept too, as he gently laid the flowers next to her; had taken her fingers for just a moment in his own, had kissed them, and then had gone.

But as she had lain in her bed through the long days that followed, hugging the flowers as if they might have been her poor, dead mama, they spoke to her still. They asked her if maybe, just maybe, dear Tom could have loved her, wicked and bad though she was. They told her that to Tom at least, she might truly be beautiful. And they reminded her of Old Rachel's words on her very first day in the workhouse; of how one day, she would indeed be beautiful, and of how one day, some kind gentleman would surely come and make her a handsome husband.

And as she hugged them as if they might have been her poor, dead mama, they made her believe it.

Because she was not well enough to leave the infirmary ward, Mary had volunteered, nay, insisted, on going to Knaresborough, to the Castle Mill, to find dear Tom and to tell him that Elizabeth had been foolish, that her head was indeed still muddled from the chloral hydrate Mary had given her for her pain and that of course, she would be honoured to be married to a man such as he.

But hours later, when she returned, Mary had wept too as she told her that, just like her mama, and Baby Albert and Baby Sarah before him, dear Tom had gone. He had returned, utterly distraught to the mill, had resigned his post to Mr John Walton, and had left. He had left on the very next railway train out of Knaresborough. And the worst of it all, the very worst part of it, was that no-one had known where he had gone.

CHAPTER 34

As she always seemed to be these days, Elizabeth was rocking endlessly to-and-fro as she sat perched on the very edge of her seat. And again, as she often seemed to be, she was quietly singing the lullaby under her breath. But it was only after Lucie and Atticus had been seated opposite her for several minutes that they came to realise that she was singing the same line over and over again.

It was, "First to the poor-house, then to the grave," and Mary was regarding her with something akin to miserable anguish.

All at once Elizabeth seemed to notice them as they sat watching her.

"One and eight and eight and one is Eighteen Hundred and Eighty-One," she said to Lucie, and she smiled.

Her smile was like the sun breaking from behind a cloud over the Holy Island, with the blue of her eyes just like the sparkling blue of the sea.

"One and eight and eight and one and one and eight and eight and one... Where's my mama? Where is Tom?"

She looked at Atticus and her smile vanished, leaving only the empty shell that was the old woman she had become.

"I'm not wicked, I'm not wicked, I'm not wicked."

Atticus looked suddenly flustered. He glanced to his wife in alarm and Lucie smiled patiently.

"No, Lizzie, we know that you're not wicked. I'm sure you will see Tom, and I'm certain that you will see your mama, very soon."

"Mama is very poorly," Elizabeth continued, and then stilled for a moment, her face suddenly distraught.

"Please don't let her die. Uncle says she will die, she will die, she will die. I shall have to go to the Annexe."

She began to rock once more and to sing, loud and shrill, as if to smother her own words.

"Lizzie, dearest, your mama did die; she died nearly fifty years ago. Please try to remember."

Mary sounded bone-weary, as if she was at the end of a very long and exhausting day. She reached forward and hugged the old woman, whose shocked and bewildered face peered back over her shoulder.

Elizabeth's eyes, bright and round, caught in a net of wrinkles, seemed to be staring into the Inferno itself.

"Elizabeth, you must prepare yourself, because I have some truly dreadful news for you. I'm so sorry, but your mama – my sister – has died."

Her uncle was standing over her. She could see the deep, full circles of his eyes: eager, ravenous; mocking his words, and boring down into her very soul.

"You are an orphan girl now, and you will have to come and live with me at Sessrum House. We can grieve for your mama, for Beatrice, together. I've had a special new annexe to the house built. You can sleep there, where we won't be disturbed by the noise of the servants, and we can both remember your mama in peace. There will be lots of other children there too, and John, my son, will be there. You like John, don't you? I shall sleep in the Annexe with you all. Your Aunt Agnes is very ill and so I shall look after you myself and make sure that you are being a very good little girl.

You must always take care to be a good little girl for me, and always do everything exactly as I say, whatever I say. That way you can be an angel with Jesus and see your mama again some day, in Heaven."

She remembered the deep, black circles of his eyes creeping down her body, lingering long after his mouth had finished speaking the words. His arm had crept around her and his hand had pulled her tight against the soft flab of his body. Then he had released her with another long, hungry look that, paralysed with grief though she was, froze her very blood to ice.

And then the arm had crept back and she could feel his fingers moving, moving all the time, pressing her and touching her as they stood in the wide, black ring around her mama's open grave.

She needed to force herself to believe that it was really her mama in there, in that coffin; that her warm, soft mama was now inside that hard, wooden shell.

Mary her governess had told her that it was a special safety coffin, with a little bell house that protruded above the grave on a long, bronze tube. If her mama should by some miracle still be alive, then pray God she would move and cause the little bell to ring the alarm across the graveyard.

She stared and stared at the little bronze bell house. Mary had explained that the bell inside was connected to a cord which in turn was carried by the tube to her mama's hands — those hands that were once so warm and soft, so full of a mother's love; those hands that would stroke her hair and gently rock her to sleep while she sang her favourite lullaby.

She stared and stared at the little bell house, ornamented with tiny bronze cherubs, and she prayed for a miracle; for the bell to ring, and for her mama to be alive.

And it did! Just as the straps the bearers were using to lower the coffin into the grave fell slack, the bell-house slipped sharply to the side and the bell inside tinkled. The black ring of mourners began to murmur and whisper and her uncle's hands stopped moving.

The murmur died away and there was utter silence, save for one of the tall funeral horses snickering under its black, ostrich feather plume.

"Pay no heed, pay no heed," the vicar said, smiling, his hands spread in apology. "The coffin is merely settling upon the one beneath it. Rest assured the deceased has not been interred prematurely."

A murmur rose and settled once more, and her uncle's restless fingers began to move again.

She had been given special permission to attend her mama's interment: a time of horror and anguish, when only men could generally be expected to hold their dignity. Her uncle had insisted that because she was his own sister's daughter, she would be made of sterner stuff. He reassured her that if she stuck close by him, and allowed him to comfort her, and perhaps if he were to take her under his own great, black cape, she would indeed be able to cope admirably.

He had, despite his own grief, fulfilled entirely his duties as a loving uncle and renowned philanthropist. He had swept his cape around her to shield her from the prying eyes and carnivorous stares of the undertaker's mutes. He had held her tight as she had wept. He had even taken the precaution of gently massaging her chest under his cape in order to prevent her very heart from breaking in sorrow and grief. And then he had taken her in his own, black carriage, which led the procession back to Sessrum House for the funeral feast.

There, he had explained about her mama.

"Where will your mama be now, do you suppose, Lizzie?" he had asked.

"She'll be in Heaven, Uncle Alfie, with the Lord Jesus and the angels, and – and with my dear papa."

"Will she, now?"

Her uncle's voice had changed and it made her start. It was loud and coarse, and it hinted at bitterness and doubt.

The hooves of the horses counted out the seconds.

"Your mama was a very beautiful woman, Lizzie. Do you realise that?"

Elizabeth nodded.

"Yes, Uncle Alfie."

"She used to have a particular effect on many – very many – of the men around her. Can you imagine what that effect might have been, Lizzie?"

"No, Uncle Alfie."

"She used to arouse them."

He smiled briefly at her look of puzzlement and a flash of ravenous hunger glinted in his eyes.

"She used to arouse them physically as men, Lizzie, and she even, I will admit, on occasion used to arouse me.

Lizzie, there was an Italian writer who lived hundreds of years ago called Dante – Dante Alighieri. Now Dante Alighieri wrote a celebrated poem in which he described what he called the Inferno. Dante's Inferno is what you and I would call Hell. He wrote that it was composed of nine circles, each circle being full of worse sinners than the last. Now the eighth of these nine circles contained, amongst others, seducers and seductresses. And just as seductresses used the passion – the arousal – of others to entrap them, and to draw them into sinfulness too, so they themselves are whipped and driven by demons for all eternity; for eternity or until they have been punished sufficiently to purify their souls and be allowed entrance into Heaven.

I'm very much afraid that your mama is in the Eighth Circle of Hell right now, being whipped by demons to purify her soul. I'm very much afraid that the sound of the bell ringing as she was lowered into her grave might well have been the demons disturbing the cord as they came to claim her soul and drag it away down to Hell."

His smile was sinister as he paused again, delighting in the effect that his words were having.

"You are growing to be a very beautiful young woman yourself, Lizzie. You arouse the men around you. You arouse me on occasion, just as your

mama once did. So as your loving uncle, I am going to help you to avoid your mother's fate. I am going to keep you out of the Eighth Circle of Hell by driving the wickedness out of you whilst you are still a young woman. I am going to undertake nothing less than the purification of your soul.

Tell me, are you familiar with the Beatitudes, Lizzie?"

She shook her head.

"They're verses in the Holy Scriptures, in the fifth chapter of the gospel of Saint Matthew. You may look them up yourself if you wish. Verse ten, for example, says: 'Blessed are they which are persecuted for righteousness' sake, for theirs is the Kingdom of Heaven.'"

He paused again to allow the words time to soak through her grief and her newly born terror.

"So you see, if you want to see your mama again in the Kingdom of Heaven, I must, as St Matthew commanded, persecute you. Do you see that, Lizzie? You're a wicked little girl. You deserved for your mama to die and you deserve, for righteousness' sake, to be punished. Those are St Matthew's words, not my own."

Elizabeth nodded once more, her expression a death mask.

"Then, Deus misereatur; *May God have mercy."*

CHAPTER 35

Atticus Fox is deeply absorbed in a game of chess.

Sometimes, when his mind tends towards chaos and disorder and his thoughts begin to collide and intrude on one another, he seeks the silence and the solitude of night. It is then, when all is quiet and still, when the Ailing sleep and when the bandstands cease to fill the air with noisy distraction, that he can at last properly retreat into the sanctuary of his mind and set about examining the patterns and the paradoxes, the symmetries and the coincidences with which his profession on occasion, torments him.

He finds that it helps these musings and the flights of conjecture they release if he plays himself at chess. It also ensures that his mind remains wholly dispassionate and objective, since each and every move he considers requires that his viewpoint and allegiances must shift in full between the black, ebony and the white, ivory chessmen.

Was Elizabeth Wilson guilty of the brutal and frenzied murder of Alfred Roberts, celebrated philanthropist and benefactor of Harrogate?

The great weight of evidence points to the conclusion that yes, she must certainly have killed him. Whether in her mental state she could be considered guilty, as such, was an entirely different matter. She almost certainly could not.

Atticus particularly values his wife's opinion much more highly than the magistrate's in this. And yet something else is worrying at his mind about the death of Alfred Roberts, and about Elizabeth's part in it... something that will not be stilled. That is why he needs to seek the night of quiet contemplation.

The Assize sessions are only two days away now. Every time he looks in his diary, each time he makes an appointment, each time a date is mentioned no matter how innocent the context, he is reminded sharply of how Elizabeth will soon be forced to endure perhaps the greatest of all her life's many trials.

They have decided already that Elizabeth is unlikely to hang. Much more likely is incarceration in a prison or more probably still, in an insane asylum.

'Asylum': He takes a moment out from his cogitations to consider the word carefully.

Tormented continually in her purgatory of thoughts, any restraint of Elizabeth there could hardly be considered as asylum.

She has failed the McNaughton tests, and the magistrate has declared her sane.

Will her inevitable incomprehension on the witness stand be construed as deliberate obstinacy by his lordship, and therefore as her contempt for his court? And will that presumed contempt possibly then irritate the learned judge sufficiently for him to send her, in spite of everything, to the gallows?

There will be a defence, of course. And as so often also in the game of chess, the best defence will likely be attack. But that attack would inevitably be an attack on the reputations and the good names of some of the stoutest pillars of Harrogate society. It would be an attack on society itself.

He slides the chess board around once again, and opens his mind fully to the cause of the white, ivory chessmen.

So, once again: Had Elizabeth Wilson, guilty or not of malice aforethought, committed the brutal and frenzied killing of Alfred Roberts?

Once again he is forced to conclude that yes, she had. But how can that possibly be? Yes, he had died by her hand, under her knife, but she hadn't the strength of either body or of mind to have carried out the deed herself. Surely it would have needed a different mind and strength far greater than hers to have murdered the man?

Stalemate.

He picks up a white knight from his board and holds it for a moment in his fingers, staring at it as he wrestles with the paradox. The knight is his very favourite chessman: powerful, chivalrous, romantic, the proverbial righter of wrongs.

And then all at once he sees it; he sees it all from the perspective of that little, white knight.

Checkmate.

The riddle is solved; the game is over at last. But for all that, his mind is not eased in the least. His is a brain that works much better in games of black and white, with rules and ordered squares of rank and file. But what he has seen could not be judged comfortably by order or by rules, and it is far from being black or white. He needs someone who understands the shades of grey between. Atticus glances at the little onyx-cased clock to the side of his desk. It will be two, long and agonising hours before Lucie will stir and wake from her bed.

Too long.

CHAPTER 36

"It's good to see you of course, Atticus and Mrs Fox," Dr Roberts exclaimed as he entered the library of Sessrum House.

He was holding one of their calling cards between his fingers with the folded corner marked 'affaires' facing upwards.

"But I wasn't expecting a call today. Is it regarding your account? I'm so sorry that I haven't had an opportunity to settle it yet, what with Aunt Elizabeth's trial beginning tomorrow and all."

"No, Dr Roberts," Atticus replied, "It's nothing whatsoever to do with our account. I'm afraid that it has more to do with your grandfather's death."

"In that case, we'd better go up to the Annexe. You've just missed my lawyer. He's kindly charged me five guineas to tell me that he thinks the case is hopeless and that we need to throw ourselves on the mercy of the judge."

"Perhaps on the mercy of God," Atticus observed, and Roberts bit his lip.

"Mary has been administering chloral hydrate to my aunt," Roberts continued hurriedly. "She's been very distressed and we've needed to increase the dose substantially."

"Is that safe?" Lucie asked. "Perhaps I ought to see her?"

Roberts shrugged.

"Perhaps that might be for the best."

Elizabeth looked serene, sleeping and dressed as she was in a pretty, new silk nightgown. She was propped up on deep white pillows, with a Bible laid across her lap and a tiny silver cross hanging from her fingers on a delicate chain. The Bible was open at her favourite passage of scripture; the twenty-first chapter of Revelation, where they knew that she always found the promise of no more pain, no more tears and no more sorrow, a great comfort.

On one side of her, a large bottle marked 'Chloral Hydrate' stood in an enamelled dish, and on the other, Mary Lovell sat perched on her bedside. Mary's eyes were red, and her lips were pursed resolutely.

"How is she, Mary?" Lucie whispered.

At the sound of Lucie's voice, Elizabeth's eyes, as if in slow motion, seemed to drag themselves open.

"How are you, Elizabeth?" Lucie repeated.

The eyes slid towards her.

"She's at peace, Mrs Fox. I don't believe she's been better since before her mama died," Mary replied.

"That's good."

"She won't be able to cope with a trial, you know," Mary added. "Or with whatever comes after."

Atticus wielded the blow.

"But should she be standing trial at all?" he asked. "Did Elizabeth Wilson actually kill Alfred Roberts?"

Mary Lovell and Dr Roberts stared at each other with identical, stunned expressions.

"Of course she did," Roberts spluttered at last, "You both agreed that she did, and so did the police."

"I have to tell you, Dr Roberts," Atticus said, with a glance to his wife, "That one or two things have perplexed us right from the beginning of this whole sorry business."

"Indeed, Atticus?"

"Indeed, Dr Roberts. For example, throughout the entire ordeal, you have spoken very protectively of a woman – notwithstanding the fact that she is your aunt – whom you had just met, whom you had just had brought here, and who, from the evidence, had just violently murdered your grandfather."

"I..."

Atticus' raised his finger to silence the doctor's protests.

"You didn't – you don't – even want her locked away. You only ever wanted her to live here, in your Annexe, with Miss Lovell taking care of her."

"That would be the only natural justice, Fox, as I've said many times," Roberts replied.

"Secondly," Atticus continued, "When you first told us of the murder and you described your grandfather's injuries, you mentioned in particular the blow that penetrated his brain through his eye socket. You said then that his 'death was instantaneous.'"

"It was, damn it."

"We don't doubt it."

Lucie's softer tone replaced Atticus'.

"But you said, 'death *was* instantaneous,' not, 'would have been instantaneous.' You spoke as if you were actually present at the time that he was killed. And then there is the bloody palm print I noticed on the back of Miss Elizabeth's hand. You said that it was likely your grandfather's, or that it might have been left by Miss Lovell as she brought Miss Elizabeth in from the bedroom. But there is a question there too."

As she spoke, Atticus took a neatly folded pocket handkerchief from his pocket and let it fall open. In the centre was a large, vivid handprint, dark now with the passing of the days.

"I took this impression at the time, you will recall. As you can see, it is a large handprint, much more likely to belong to a man than a lady. Your grandfather had no bloodstains on his hands, so, should we ask you and Miss Lovell to place your hands against the print to compare them? Do we need to do that?"

Roberts licked his lips.

"No, Mrs Fox, you do not. I admit that it is mine. But it proves nothing; it proves nothing whatever. I must have led Aunt Elizabeth at some point, that's all."

"It proves that you've been less than honest with us, Doctor," Atticus retorted.

"There is also the vexing fact that the print was on the outside of her hand and not on her palm, as we might have expected if she had been led anywhere. We also have to question whether or not such a violent assault could have been inflicted by a lady who can barely stand. So please, before she stands trial tomorrow, tell us what really happened."

There was a long, unbearable silence, a silence that seemed to compound with the oppressive air of the Annexe, and grow louder and louder and louder. Then, mercifully, Mary spoke and the tension was broken.

"Elizabeth and I fleeing from Sessrum House didn't mark the end of the Friday Club, Mr and Mrs Fox. Oh no. Long after we had left, any child, female... or male; stranger... or kin, who happened to stray within Mr Alfred's reach, was still in great danger from him and his loathsome friends."

Lucie gasped.

"Long after – any child, female or male, stranger or kin – surely you don't mean that Dr Roberts' father...?"

"Yes, Mrs Fox, even my father, even his own son; even, as it happens, his own grandson."

Roberts' expression crumpled in pain, pain that was resurrected instantly into anger.

"There are three people here in this Annexe whose lives have been destroyed by that man: Mary's, my aunt's, and mine. My father took his own life when I was just a child. Who is to say that it wasn't as a direct result of what my grandfather and his damned Friday Club did to him? I don't know. I never had a chance to ask him.

We all wished Grandpapa dead. Of course we did. We wished him dead with every waking breath. I had never met my Aunt Elizabeth. Her name was hardly mentioned in the household, except of course in whispered conversations among the servants. I knew that she had been condemned to live here, in this Annexe, for over two years, and so I guessed that the rumours had to be true.

I tracked her down. I tracked her down to the Union Workhouse in Knaresborough where the good people of Harrogate send those individuals that the grand visitors to the town might be offended to look upon. I befriended the Medical Officer there and learned about my aunt's condition – about the way in which she had been forced to live her life, and how finally her mind had fallen prey to dementia. But I also learned that Mary Lovell was there too, and that she had devoted her own life to her care.

And so a plan evolved. Mary and I became acquainted and we saw how we could restore Aunt Elizabeth to a modicum of comfort and at the same time ensure that justice was served. Not Her Majesty's justice, perhaps, but true, natural justice nonetheless.

I had already incarcerated my grandfather here, in this Annexe. Not because he was old, or frail, or anything of that you understand.

No, again it was simply in order to serve up plain, natural justice. You see, he had imprisoned countless children in the Annexe over the years, mostly in a big dormitory room below us on the ground floor. For a time, he had me imprisoned in there too, guarded by Mr Otter, the club steward."

He took a handkerchief from his pocket with a trembling hand and wiped it across his mouth.

"I beg your pardons, Mrs Fox and Mary, but my Grandpapa Alfred also used to sodomise me; he and another of his monstrous companions called Mr James. They would bugger me and they would make me do other things to them too vile even to mention."

He shuddered suddenly, violently.

"After my father shot himself, I began to tell people what had really been happening in the Annexe. I no longer cared what they thought, I suppose.

So he had me locked up. Grandpapa had some doctor, a friend of his called Wright I believe, who was up to his neck in league with the Club to say that my papa's suicide had unhinged me and driven me insane. He used it as a reason to keep me imprisoned downstairs, and worse, to discredit my word. Of course, they continued to use me as they wished, and that, together with the loss of my father, almost did drive me to insanity.

Then, one day, my grandmama died."

"Mr Alfred's wife," Lucie exclaimed, "The one who was addicted to absinthe?"

Roberts nodded.

"My poor Grandmama Agnes. Later on, my grandfather would try to blame her for what he'd done. He would say that if she had been a proper wife and if she had paid him his due attention, then he would never have had to resort to buying little girls off the street. Utter nonsense, all of it; she was as she was only because he was as he was. She knew what he did, and absinthe was the only way she had to escape the horrible truth of it. No, Mrs Fox, he enjoyed what they did to those children, to Aunt Lizzie, to Mary, and to me. He enjoyed the power it gave him over us, and he enjoyed the excitement. I hope he is tormented forever in Hell!"

"Did he never regret his actions in the end, Dr Roberts?" Lucie asked.

Roberts was silent and still for a moment, almost as if he hadn't heard her speak at all, but then he shrugged.

"Only God truly knows that, Mrs Fox. He said that he did. The death of his wife and the suicide of my father seemed to change something in him I suppose. But then occasionally one of the old Friday Club members would visit him here, and I would listen to them, revelling in their memories.

There was also a young boy... Peter, I think he was called. They'd taken him up to the Holy Island off the Northumberland coast with some other child victims. They were going to sodomise him I imagine, because Mr James went with them. But it all went terribly wrong. Somehow he managed to escape from them in the dark, and then, as he ran away, he was caught up by the terrible tides they have up there, and he drowned.

The Friday Club was eventually disbanded, and my grandfather began to pretend, even to himself, that it really had just been a philanthropic society. Then he pretended that it had never existed at all. That was when I had the photograph mounted on the wall in the smoking room, out of his reach and protected by the grill. It was to remind him constantly that it had."

Their thoughts turned automatically to the smoking room, and to the portrait of the gentlemen and steward of the Friday Club leering down from high on the wall. Was it their imagination or did there seem to be something more brutal, more bestial, in the rows of unblinking eyes?

"I wanted my grandfather to be continually reminded of them," Roberts went on, "And of his former self, and of what they had done together, every day for the rest of his life."

He smiled weakly.

"It was only natural justice, you see."

The smile withered.

"But it was not enough, it wasn't nearly enough recompense for my father and my grandmother, or for poor little drowned Peter, and for the countless other little children who suffered at their hands."

He lifted his handkerchief once more and held it for a moment against his lips.

"We knew that if we told him that Aunt Elizabeth was coming back, Grandpapa would never be able to resist the opportunity to see her once again after so many years. We also saw to it that when she did come, she'd have had the chance to pick up a knife; one that could be easily traced back to her. The rest of it followed a natural course. My aunt would have wanted to kill him, Mr and Mrs Fox, I'm sure of it. She'd told Mary as much, many times before her mind started to fail. We did too, Mary and I. We wanted him to pay the ultimate penance for what he'd done. We just made certain that Aunt Lizzie had the opportunity, and then perhaps, just perhaps, we might have offered the tiniest bit of... assistance."

His elbow twitched as he spoke.

Atticus and Lucie stared wide eyed at his arm, as if willing it too to take up the confession.

"So you all killed him – all three of you – together?"

Lucie's question wasn't really a question at all.

Roberts nodded.

"I admit nothing of course, Mrs Fox, nor would we in a court of law. I was so sure that my aunt would be allowed to live here afterwards you see. She wouldn't have known the difference, she truly wouldn't. But now you know. Now you know the whole of it."

The relief seemed suddenly to be sweating out of him, forming into tiny beads on his brow.

"But you can't take the law into your own hands, Doctor," Atticus protested.

"You can't administer summary retribution no matter how just you think it to be."

"But I had to, don't you see? My grandfather and his friends were beyond the law of the land. No court would have even tried them, let alone convicted them, of anything. But they aren't above the laws of natural justice, Atticus. No sir. They aren't above the law of the Almighty. Their guilt was beyond dispute. The only question was the manner of their punishment: An eye for an eye, a tooth for a tooth, and a life for a life."

He paused to dab the sweat from his forehead.

"I am your client of course, so you're forbidden to testify against us."

"We're investigators only, Doctor," Atticus replied. "We aren't lawyers, and we aren't bound by any privilege."

"But nor would it be in anyone's interests to pursue what you've just told us," Lucie added, her voice firm. "Atticus and I have been agonising over the morality of all of this for most of the morning. We've agreed that if Miss Elizabeth was just a pawn in Alfred Roberts' killing then, as my husband says, you were both white knights. He isn't usually so poetic to be sure, but I think that he perfectly describes your motives. Call it natural justice if you will, but if ever a man was deserving of death, then I suppose it was Alfred Roberts. So, since Miss Elizabeth would stand trial anyway and since we can prove nothing, we shall let it lie."

"Thank God," said Roberts, and Mary began to sob. "Thank God. We have such plans, you see, for the furtherance of natural justice. Mary and I vowed that after my grandfather's death, we would turn this Annexe into a place for good – into a place of true philanthropy.

Many years ago my grandfather named this house Sessrum House after Sessrúmnir, Freya's own hall in Viking mythology. Sessrúmnir was supposed to have contained many rooms where Freya would bring back those slain in battle to be at peace.

My grandfather offered no peace to those he brought here, but don't you see how we could now? The Annexe does have many rooms. Both on this floor, where those children bound to him in blood, the ones he thought could never run away were accommodated and on the floor below us. That was where my grandfather used to lock the children he procured from the streets. Mr Otter the steward lived down there too. He would guard the children, and take them to Mrs Eire to be certified as Virgo intacta, or to have their maidenheads stitched back up after they had been deflowered. He would drag them up the stairs to be raped. Sometimes he would rape them himself."

He began to soundlessly pace the bedroom, his eyes suddenly alight with passion.

"So wouldn't it be fitting, wouldn't it be perfect, natural justice if this Annexe was turned into a refuge for ill-used children, where they could be brought after their own infernal battles, to find peace? The defloration mania continues; the maidens are still being offered as tribute, and the rooms could be filled many times over. But what was originally designed as a Hell could serve equally well as a Heaven.

As I know only too well, to find true solace, those poor children must feel safe. They must feel secure against those who would torment them. The thick walls, the locked doors, the bars on the windows would provide exactly that. We have a scullery, we have a common room, and we even have a medical room here should we need it. And beyond the walls is Harrogate, the greatest place of healing on earth.

Of course we would need to get rid of the images of Freya and everything else my grandfather thought she stood for. We would need to replace them with something more fitting but that could be easily accomplished.

Mary and I – a psychiatrist and a nurse – both with an intimate knowledge of what it is to be exposed to the most degrading and bestial of treatment, couldn't be better placed to help those poor unfortunates. We..."

There was a sudden mumble of voices in the hallway beyond the door. One of them, the deepest, had the distinct lilt of a Geordie accent, and Atticus was reminded immediately of Liddle, the workhouse Master.

"Damn these double-carpets," muttered Roberts under his breath.

But it wasn't Liddle who appeared along with Mr Petty in the doorway to Elizabeth's bedroom, but Samuel Elswick.

"Mr Elswick," Atticus exclaimed.

"Mr Fox, Mrs Fox."

Elswick greeted them with a polite bow of his head. He padded silently into the room and held out his hand towards Roberts.

"And you, sir, must be Alfred Roberts' grandson."

Roberts grasped the outstretched hand and shook it once.

"I am Dr Michael Roberts, Mr Elswick, and I cannot help my ancestry. May I also introduce my Aunt Elizabeth Wilson, and her nurse and friend, Miss Mary Lovell?"

Elswick turned, nodded his head to Mary, and then stared at the old woman as she lay peacefully sleeping.

"I had an idea that she might look a little like the devil incarnate, you know," he murmured after a time. "But she doesn't. She doesn't at all."

He shook his head sadly and turned to the doorway where Petty still stood, stiff and formal.

"Sarah," he called.

Mr Petty took a dutiful step back, and a woman took his place. Although now past the flush of youth, she was still an exquisitely beautiful woman, with carefully styled blonde hair, and clear, blue eyes. She carried a young baby in the crook of one arm, and in her other hand, she held the tiny fingers of a girl of around three years old, a perfect miniature of her mother.

Elswick seemed to struggle with himself for a moment, and then addressed the room.

"Dr Roberts, Miss Wilson, Mr and Mrs Fox and Miss Lovell, may I present to you all my wife, Mrs Sarah Elswick, and my children, Beatrice and Bartholomew. My wife, as you know, is Miss Wilson's natural daughter, and I understand that after so many years, they are both anxious to meet with each other once again."

Sarah advanced purposefully into the room, her eyes fixed on Elizabeth's.

"She has been heavily sedated, Mrs Elswick," Mary said. "And she has senile dementia. It will be very difficult to converse with her."

"That is a very great pity," Sarah said in a soft, cultured voice. "I understand that she suffered greatly at the hands of my father, and I very much wanted to ask her, I very much wanted to understand, why in God's name she would consent to give me away to such a monster to suffer a similar fate."

"Your mother knew nothing about your adoption until it was too late, until you had already gone," Mary replied. "Your father – Mr Price – was an overseer at the workhouse, and he arranged it all himself. There weren't even any records kept. You just simply disappeared one day. She almost died with grief."

Sarah stood motionless for a while and then she nodded.

"I wanted to know too if Price was my real father."

"She wouldn't have known."

Mary reached instinctively for Elizabeth's fingers.

"She was abused by so many different men at the Friday Club, it could have been any one of them. I'm so sorry, Mrs Elswick."

"That was his excuse too – Price's. That was how he was able to rationalise what he did to me, to his own daughter. He said that there was a possibility he wasn't my natural father after all, so whatever he chose to do to me was fine."

Elizabeth stirred and her eyelids drifted open. She blinked sluggishly. Dr Roberts leant across to her and softly called her name: "Lizzie," as he peered into each of her pupils in turn.

"She's in deep, Mary," he muttered, and the nurse nodded.

Sarah closed her eyes for one, two, three seconds, and then opened them once again. They were precisely the same blue as her mother's. She bent slowly forward and said, "Mama?"

She knew that she was dying at last.

'Oh thank you, Lord Jesus.'

The beastly eyes had gone, and she had finally, finally, been punished enough.

She felt as if she was detaching from her mortal body, spreading and becoming somehow infinite. Everything around her was warm and soft and white, and her mind seemed to be floating in some kind of benign mist.

And then she saw him once more, the beneficent, bearded man, the Lord Jesus before her at last, and he was smiling. Oh, blessed, blessed relief. She was dead. The Lord Jesus himself was speaking to her, calling her name. And then, yes, there she was, just as she always remembered her; it was her dear mama, with her beautiful, golden hair and bright eyes of clearest blue. Her mama had come to welcome her to Paradise, and with her she had brought her darlings. Her mama, weeping with joy, held out Baby Albert for her to see: Dear tiny, perfect Baby Albert, a cherub for Jesus, and yes, Baby Sarah, just as beautiful and as full of joy as she had remembered her, every single day since they parted.

Sarah reached out and touched the cheek of her mama and the years were nothing. Lizzie said, "Mama," and Sarah nodded.

"Yes, I know you're my mama."

She laid her head on her dear mama's breast, and felt again as if she were a girl of two, and not a grown woman at all. She watched her mama's head gently nodding as each tired beat of her heart pushed the chloral hydrate from the big glass bottle further and further through her veins. There had been a lot of chloral hydrate in the big glass bottle by the bed, and now it was empty.

"Shall we leave Mrs Elswick with her mama now?" Roberts whispered. "I fear that she hasn't long left now, and they have so much to say. We can talk in the smoking room."

Without wanting to desecrate the moment with more words, Atticus and Lucie, Dr Roberts and Mr Elswick, all slipped quietly out through the door, closing it gently behind them.

Mary Lovell kissed Elizabeth's forehead and followed them, pausing for a moment only to lift the sash of the window just a fraction. After all these long years, it wouldn't do to keep her shade lingering.

"So this is the Friday Club," Elswick growled.

Atticus could sense him smoulder as his eyes crept around the big room. They took in the walls, with their hateful tapestries and depictions of Freya; they took in the empty chaises longues standing ready, expectant even of reliving past glories, and finally, they came to rest on the photograph set high on the wall. His eyes flared in recognition of his wife's tormentor, and he glared as if almost to deflagrate it with his hatred.

"I'd have torn it down, stone by stone, if it were me."

"Dr Roberts has plans to turn it into a refuge for ill-used children," Atticus told him.

"For just as long as such a thing is needed," Roberts added. "After that, I may well tear it down with my own bare hands and you, Mr Elswick, can depend upon receiving the first invitation to help me to do it."

Elswick grunted, but with the retort came what might have been the merest hint of a smile.

"That time may not be too far away," Roberts continued. "The newspapers are shining the bright light of enquiry into every dark place in our society where the abuse of little children still happens. The cockroach perpetrators are running, and at long, long last, the will of the government is beginning to stamp down on them.

We're just ten short years away from the dawn of a new century, Mr Elswick: the Twentieth Century. I would like to think that, by then, there will be no more defloration mania, and no more maiden tribute; that little girls and boys will be able to walk this earth in safety and enjoy a normal, happy life. I hope that by the end of the Twentieth Century, mankind will look back on our time and say: 'Yes, some truly horrific things were done to the very weakest in society, but, thank God, theirs was the generation that finally ended it."

"I hope so too, Dr Roberts," said Elswick, "But I fear that your faith in society is misplaced. I have real cockroaches by the thousand in my factories, and I find that as fast as I can stamp them out, more come in their stead. That's not to say that we should keep from stamping on them," he added; "We shouldn't, of course. But I believe that your annexe may well be standing for some years to come."

In her bed, Lizzie Wilson smiled. She smiled as if she too were a little girl and not a dying old woman at all. Her heart, full and content now was tired, but there was no pain. Mary, dear Mary, had promised her that, and that no-one would hurt her ever again.

And then, as she lay in her bed, her breaths slowly faded, the heart beneath her breasts stopped beating, and little Lizzie died.

Who sees with equal eye, as God of all,
A hero perish, or a sparrow fall,
Atoms or systems into ruin hurled,
And now a bubble burst, and now a world.

Like her mama so many years before, but nine long years too late, maybe a lifetime too late, maybe a lifetime too early; a hero perished and a world burst, and little Lizzie Wilson, smiling and with her hand in her dear, dear mama's, at long last entered the final and the eternal relief of Paradise.

Lightning Source UK Ltd.
Milton Keynes UK
UKOW03f0342240114

225148UK00001B/9/P